UNDERNEATH THE *Sycamore* TREE

B. CELESTE

Bloom books

Cover design by Stephanie Gafron/Sourcebooks
Internal design by Tara Jaggers/Sourcebooks
Photos by Aroon Phetcharat/Getty Images,
borchee/Getty Images, vnlit/Shutterstock

Published by Bloom Books, an imprint of Sourcebooks
P.O. Box 4410, Naperville, Illinois 60567-4410
(630) 961-3900
sourcebooks.com

Originally self-published in 2019 by B. Celeste.

Cataloging-in-Publication Data is on file with the Library of Congress.

Manufactured in the UK by Clays and distributed by
Dorling Kindersley Limited, London
002-336702-Jan/23
10 9 8 7 6 5 4 3 2

This book is for the chronically ill.
For the people who fight every single day
for relief, belief, and a cure.

This book is about fear.
Fear that drives us to keep fighting whether
we know the outcome or not.

This book is for anybody who feels they aren't heard, seen,
or believed. I hear you, see you, and believe you.

PLAYLIST

"In My Blood"—Shawn Mendes

"Nobody's Home"—Avril Lavigne

"You Are My Sunshine"—Elizabeth Mitchell

"i hate u, i love you"—Gnash ft. Olivia O'Brien

"Late Thoughts"—Hanx

"Team"—Noah Cyrus & Max

"How You Remind Me"—Nickelback

"Goodbyes"—Post Malone ft. Young Thug

"My Immortal"—Evanescence

"Soon You'll Get Better"—Taylor Swift

Prologue

Mama's eyes are golden when she cries. Not like mine, which are a murky shade of dirty pool water—not fully green or brown but a mixture of the two. Though when I was just shy of ten years old and saying goodbye to my sister, Mama told me that my glassy gaze was speckled with emeralds just like Daddy's.

But Daddy wasn't at Lo's funeral. Not when the pastor spoke the eulogy to the half-empty church, or when the slow toll of cars paced the streets to the cemetery, or even when they lowered the kid-sized white coffin into the ground. Mama and I watched every step of the way, her eyes trained on the half of her heart sinking into the dark soil, never to be seen again, while mine stared off into the distance, waiting for Daddy's familiar face to appear.

Looking back now, Lo had suspected the end of our parents' marriage long before Daddy packed his things and left. She always knew it'd end that way.

I wonder what else she knew.

Mama wipes a stray tear from her eye, hoping I won't notice how they glisten in the fluorescent lighting of the drab white room. I want to tell her I'm all right, that everything will be fine. But the weak attempts at comfort would roll off her tense shoulders in disbelief.

When Lo was diagnosed with lupus, it was too late to save her. The disease had eaten away at every piece of her—body, skin, and organs. No matter how hard Mama tried controlling the disease, it couldn't be fought.

Logan died in her sleep.

Everything is different now. Mama is cautious, always keeping a close eye on the things she blamed herself for missing in the past—the sunburns, constant napping, and aches. Despite Grandma telling her not to feel guilty over the unknown, Mama's eyes dull into empty pits every time they swipe over a picture of Logan.

They do the same thing when she looks at me, because Logan Olivia Matterson was my twin. Every feature on our fair faces was identical, down to the button nose and heart-shaped lips. We shared the same silver-blond hair and green eyes that we got from Mama, although I always thought Lo's were prettier.

Mama tries being strong for me, but I see her break apart a little more each day since that sunny August afternoon we laid Lo to rest. There were no clouds or gray skies to match the mood of the moment. No rain or thunder to match the hammering of our broken hearts. It was beautiful. Peaceful. Birds were quiet, the breeze was light, and the sun kissed our skin in comforting caresses. There'd been a bright rainbow in the distance, and I knew it was Lo's last gift to me, because it hadn't rained in days.

Mama's wavering composure next to me makes the too-clean room we sit in much smaller. She holds my hand, squeezing it as the doctor with salt-and-pepper hair explains the results from the labs they ran last week.

Counting the little brown freckles speckled across Mama's hand, I take a deep breath.

The doctor's words fade until silence greets the room. "Do you understand what I'm saying, Emery?" His voice is deep with a mixture of soft sympathy and firm curiosity, trying to pinpoint my level of recognition.

I just wish he'd call me Em. I prefer it over my full name, just like Logan liked Lo. But the doctor keeps calling me Emery and Mama Mrs. Matterson even though she changed her name after Daddy left. She's Ms. Keller now.

Does the doctor see a scared thirteen-year-old girl when he studies me? Or does he see what's behind the mask I wear—the one I wear every day. The very mask I wear when I'm at home wanting Mama to look at me without being sad. The one that covers my features as I take another frame of Logan from the mantel to ease Mama's heartbreak a little more. All the pictures of Lo litter the room I once shared with my twin, stuffed away in my closet, hidden under my bed, covering the bookshelf, anywhere she won't see them.

I doubt the doctor sees that girl at all though. So I lie and tell him I understand. He can interpret my bleak distance any way he wants. I just stare at Mama, watching a second tear slide down her flushed cheek at my reply.

It'll be okay, Mama.

I don't dare breathe the words.

One

THERE'S A DEAD CLUMP of caramel hair resting in the palm of my porcelain hand. I run my chipped yellow nails over the once-silky strands and stare long and hard like I can somehow reattach them.

Two months ago, I tried dyeing it. The evidence of my failed attempt rests in my hand, a mixture of brown and blond undertones. It was a summertime project that Mama told me not to bother with. She insisted my hair was too brittle.

Like always, Mama was right.

Like always, I was too stubborn to listen.

Not only did my tender scalp burn from the dye, but my hair fell out minutes after applying the color. It left my blond strands in patches that Mama helped me rinse out.

Wrapping the evidence of my abnormality tight in my grasp, I stare at my reflection in the large mirror that hangs over the vanity. I see paleness. Baggy, glassy green-brown eyes. Narrowed cheekbones tinted pink but not from the expensive blush like Mama wore once upon a time. Mine is from my body's internal war on itself.

I've filled out since starting new medication last month. The doctor told me it should help regulate my system so I stop losing weight. My cheekbones aren't as prominent anymore, nowhere near as hollow and sickly. Instead of the three pills I was taking before leaving Bakersfield, I take nine. It's worth it, I suppose, to not look so skeletal.

Usually I keep my head down while I go about my morning routine. It's easier than seeing the way my collarbones stick out and my hair thinly frames my face. I hate seeing my reflection because I don't recognize the girl staring back.

Today I force myself to look. Dropping my fallen hair onto the granite countertop, I study what the mirror shows from the waist up. A sliver of my lean stomach peeks out from the blue tank top I sleep in. Travelling my gaze upward, I notice slim arms, narrow shoulders, all the way up to thin, chapped lips. Nothing about me is particularly beautiful, yet I still see Mama in my frailty.

For the longest time, she wouldn't look at me for more than a few seconds. Her eyes would find mine as she told me good morning or wished me a good day at school, but then they would quickly go anywhere else. Grandma would pat my hand and tell me not to let it get to me. It wasn't that easy though.

When Mama looked at me, she saw Logan and the possibility of another early funeral. I was always going to be a reminder that one of her daughters was dead, and for all she knew, I was mere steps behind.

So I called Dad.

Grandma told me I didn't have to move, but I knew it was for the best. I didn't want to know that Mama's eyes turned gold when she cried. They were always a shimmery, golden brown when I was around.

The mirror in front of me is bigger than the one in my old house. Unlike that old stained beige bathroom with chipped tiles, this one is light gray with hardwood floors and all new fixtures. Instead of a walk-in shower, I've got a large bathtub that could fit two sets of twins in it if necessary, and the amount of shelf space would have made Lo jealous.

A knock at my bedroom door pulls me away from my assessment. Brushing the loose hair into the white garbage can by the counter, I walk into the main room and hear Dad's voice on the other side of the door.

"Are you up, Emery?" His voice is gravelly and hesitant, a tone he's held since he helped unpack what little I brought with me from Mama's house to this one across the state.

Truthfully, I'm not sure why either he or Mama agreed. I only ever heard from him on my birthday and Christmas, and the conversation never lasted more than ten minutes if he could help it. He's remarried with a gorgeous wife who's the exact opposite of Mama in both looks and personality and a stepson who's broody and evasive no matter how hard I try getting to know him.

His life here was perfect.

Until me.

I open the door and give him a sleepy smile, which he returns easily. He tries to make me comfortable. His wife, Cam, has been nothing but sweet, and her son, Kaiden, despite his typical avoidance, could be worse. They've been welcoming since I arrived a month and a half ago, giving me anything I needed. A new doctor, a chance to decorate my room how I want, and space. Lots of space.

Dad works at a pharmaceutical company now. I don't remember much of him from when I was little, just the suits he wore and the way he would give Mama a chaste kiss if we were around or a simple nod if he thought we weren't looking. I never realized how unhappy they both were then.

This man doesn't look like the one I remember. His dark-brown hair is peppered with gray, especially around the ears, and his hairline is receding. The natural tan skin I've always been jealous of is slightly wrinkled, and his eyes have a dullness to them that I don't recall seeing in the past. Is that from age or circumstance?

"Cam has breakfast cooking." He rubs his arm, covered by a navy blazer, and gives me a weary look. "If you aren't up to going today..."

Today. The first day at a new school. It's my senior year even though I should have already graduated. After missing too many classes from hospital admissions, I was held back.

"I'll be fine." It's a weak reassurance that neither of us truly believes. It isn't a lie though. I won't be walking into a shark cage bleeding, so there are worse things to experience.

His gaze lingers, his eyes a light shade of brown with the same specks of emerald Mama told me I have. I don't see it when I look in the mirror though.

"Emery..."

I stand there, gripping the doorknob in my hand until my fingers hurt, waiting for him to say something.

He clears his throat. "Happy birthday."

Today. My nineteenth birthday.

The way Dad looks at me is like he's trying to see

someone else. Maybe he wonders if Logan would have looked the same. It's been ten years since she passed, eleven since he left.

What does he remember of her?

Instead of asking, I swallow my inquiry and force a tight-lipped smile. "Thank you."

I told him I didn't want a party or even a special dinner. When I was younger, he and Mama would ask what we wanted for our birthdays—the meal was always our choice. Lo would always ask to go out, while I always asked to stay in. The cake was the same. Red velvet with white buttercream frosting.

Honestly, there was nothing I wanted from Dad now besides temporary shelter.

No home-cooked meal.

No red velvet cake.

Part of me feels like wanting anything from Dad is somehow cheating on Mama. Like forgiving him means I don't care that he left or hurt her or us. No matter what, he abandoned us when we needed him. When Lo needed him.

He tips his head, pauses, and then turns toward the downstairs. Kaiden's room is down the hall from mine, but he doesn't bother him. I wonder if he's already up and ready, an early riser. Sometimes I'll hear him leave his room late at night and watch him sneak out of the house.

I wonder where he goes. Or if Cam knows. Or if Dad does. It isn't my place to ask, so I leave it be.

It takes me fifteen minutes to throw on a pair of blue jeans with one of the knees ripped out and an oversize black sweater that falls off my shoulder. Running a brush through my tangled hair and leaving it loose, I note that it's finally passing my shoulders again. Mama would probably be happy to hear that; she always loved when Lo and I kept our hair long.

Slipping into a beige pair of Toms that have pineapples all over them, I grab my new black-and-white-checkered backpack and head downstairs. Dad is finishing up his breakfast because he has to leave for work, but Cam and Kaiden are both still working on theirs.

Cam greets me with a gentle smile, Kaiden doesn't look at me at all, and Dad gives me a head bob before getting up and rinsing his plate off in the large stainless steel sink.

Their house is huge—two stories, plus a fully finished basement that's mostly used for storage. The outside is painted white, the windowsills on the bottom floor all have flowerpots attached with pink and purple plants, and the backyard stretches far enough to have a fire pit, garden, and grill area.

It isn't anything like the house I grew up in, especially inside. There's so much space to walk around in without tripping over furniture or people. Everything smells floral and fresh, and the modern matching style throughout every room differs from the rustic thrift store finds that litter Mama's house.

But I like Mama's house more.

It may have been small, but it made things more intimate. We could joke about tripping over the coffee table, which all of us had at some point. There was a bright green coat rack by the door that stuck out like a sore thumb against the pale yellow wallpaper that had little white and yellow stripes decorating the bottom half, and an orange bowl that keys, receipts, and other odds and ends always found their way into.

Mama's house is colorful, quaint.

Dad's house is…normal.

I never understood normal.

I'm playing with the scrambled eggs and bacon on my plate when Dad kisses Cam goodbye and tells Kaiden and me to have a good first day of school. We're both seniors.

Since I'm without a car, Kaiden is supposed to drive us and show me where the office is since Dad couldn't get time off to bring me to the school early and show me himself.

Cam tried getting Kaiden to take me last week to familiarize myself with the campus layout, but I didn't want him to feel obligated, so I lied and told her it was fine. Truth is, my heart is pounding so hard in my chest from nerves that I worry I'll die from a heart attack long before my disease does me in. If the room gets any quieter, they'd probably hear it drum an uneven tune.

I'm halfway done with my breakfast before I glance at the clock and then at Cam. She knows my worries and gives me a small smile before passing me a granola bar, money for lunch, and a signed piece of paper with Dad's name on the bottom.

For school records, she tells me.

Slipping everything into my bag, I ask Kaiden if he's ready. His response is nothing more than a grunt before he pushes away from the table, grabs his bag and car keys, and then gestures toward the front door.

He doesn't tell Cam goodbye.

She doesn't wish us a good day.

She just smiles sadly as we leave.

I want to ask Kaiden why he's so angry and won't talk. Cam seems like a nice woman, so I don't get why he acts so dismissive around her. I know better than to pry in other people's business. Then they'd have a right to pry in mine.

When we get to the school, I follow Kaiden inside from the student parking lot already packed with cars. He simply points in the direction of the office and shoots me a sarcastic "Good luck" over his shoulder before disappearing into a crowd of people who slap his back and greet him with big smiles while completely ignoring my existence.

Happy birthday to me.

There's a decorative brick wall behind the principal's desk that matches the exterior of the building. It doesn't necessarily match the white walls or the rest of the classy decor, though I haven't had time to explore yet.

The dark-haired man sitting in front of me is young and burly, probably late thirties, and doesn't seem to be particularly organized based on the way he searches through papers for my file. He seems flustered. I'm sure if I look hard enough, I'd see sweat dot his brow.

He gives me an apologetic smile before rifling through a different stack. "The guidance counselor usually handles this."

I'm not sure why he tells me that, so I just nod. I could ask him the counselor's whereabouts, but I'm not sure I care. If Mama were here, she'd keep conversation going easily by asking about the school's history or why Exeter High is home of the Wildcats and not something more fitting of the purple and gold colors.

She's not here though.

Neither is the counselor.

Neither is Logan.

Principal Richman, according to the nasally secretary who guided me to his chaotic work space, finally lifts a manila folder off his desk and looks at me triumphantly.

"Emery Matterson."

At this rate, I won't make it to class until third period. Participation in government, or PIG as my last school referred to the civics course, isn't exactly what I want to start my day with, but it's better than math. I'll miss first period geometry and second period phys ed. Nothing to cry over, that's for sure.

His dark eyes scan the contents of my file before tugging on the collar of his white button-down. Clearing his throat, he reads over the paper I gave him with my father's signature.

"Right." He nods, setting down the papers and giving me a quick once-over. "Well, Ms. Matterson, it looks like you were mailed the schedule and school policies already, and you'll receive textbooks in your classes today. Your schedule should list your locker number, which you'll get the lock and combination to from the phys ed teacher. Your father mentioned setting you up with weekly check-ins with our guidance counselor and nurse. Our counselor won't be back until next week, but I can take you to Ms. Gilly in the nurse's office before I have someone show you to your locker."

Wait a minute. "Why would I do weekly check-ins with the counselor and nurse?"

He hesitates, brow furrowing for a moment before locking his hands together on his desk. "Typically, we have transfers meet the counselor about the transition to ensure they're comfortable during the first few weeks. Most students have been in the district their entire lives, so they know the whereabouts. We understand new schools, especially for later-admitted students, can be difficult to adjust to."

My jaw ticks. "And the nurse?"

He shifts uncomfortably in his chair until it creaks under his weight. "I assumed your father would have spoken to you about it. Students with extensive medical problems tend to build relationships with nursing staff early on. It's our understanding that you've had some issues in the past..."

Issues. What exactly has my father told the school? I'm sure the file transferred from my old one says plenty about me without his influence. My twin died, I missed too many days because of the same disease that killed her, and now I'm here. But did Dad emphasize that I'm better than I was in their apparent conversation about me?

My spine straightens. "My father must have forgotten to mention it to me. But it's not something I need to do, so—"

"All due respect, Ms. Matterson—"

"It's Emery or Em."

He nods once. "Emery," he corrects. "I agree with your father that it's of the utmost importance you get comfortable with the nurse here. Things happen despite medication and self-care. If there's an emergency, it's best Ms. Gilly knows what to do."

Like call 911?

Biting back the retort, I force myself to nod, because arguing with the principal doesn't seem like a smart thing to do. I've never gotten in trouble before and don't plan to start now.

"If you don't mind me saying, the guidance counselor also does sessions for those who grieve the loss of loved ones. Perhaps you'll find a friend in her."

I'm sure he means well by the suggestion, but it doesn't sit well with me. "Principal Richman, my sister died ten years ago. I may never move on from that, but I have learned to cope all on my own by now."

He flattens his already pristine shirt. "I won't force you into anything, then. Come on. I'll show you to the nurse's office."

Before we make it to his door, the nasally secretary with box-dyed blond hair and thick glasses calls out his name. "The new high school English teacher is here for your meeting." The way she eyes me has me narrowing mine before glancing at the half-empty hallway.

Principal Richman sighs and gives me an indecisive stare. Shifting from one foot to the other, I grip the strap hanging on my shoulder. "I can find my way. I brought the map that came with the schedule."

There's still time to make it before second period, so I'm thankful when his expression turns from reluctance to relief over my suggestion. I'm sure he doesn't want to give the new student a tour anyway.

"The high school classrooms are all on the eastern wing of the second floor, separated from the new middle school wing, just up the spiral staircase down the hall. I'm sure if need be, we can get your stepbrother to show you around." He clears his throat for what seems to be the thirtieth time. "Kaiden Monroe, if memory serves, correct?"

I nod.

He purses his lips. "Well then, you best be off. Welcome to Exeter High, Ms. Matterson. We're happy to have you."

I don't bother correcting him on my name.

Logan would have.

Two

THERE'S A FRECKLE ON my wrist that keeps my full attention during last period. It's been a quiet, uneventful day, and I'm glad. Minimal staring, no trouble getting a table at lunch, and nobody to ask me to recite fun facts about myself.

I've made mental notes to myself throughout the day. There's no time to stop by my locker in between the morning periods, so I'll just carry my bag. The lunchroom is like a mosh pit scattered with rectangular and circular tables, with no particular cliques like the high schools in movies. UGG boots are making a comeback.

Personally, I'm not sure how I feel about any of those things. My shoulder aches from carrying my backpack on it all morning, the lunchroom was too loud from the chatter, and UGG boots have always been hideous. Then again, my pineapple Toms get just as many judgmental glances.

What strikes the most interest in me is watching Kaiden interact with his peers—boys in letterman jackets and girls who twirl their hair and bat their lashes at them. He's popular here, an entirely new person. He talks and jokes and argues. People seem to love him despite equally seeming to envy him.

I wonder why he isn't that way at home. Does his mother know how he acts at school? I heard a pink-haired girl tell her friend at lunch that he's going to take the lacrosse team to the national championship this year. She said it'll be his farewell, his send-off before graduation. Apparently, he's so good, he's been offered a full sports scholarship at a handful of colleges. Does Cam go to his games? Cheer him on from the stands? Dad mentioned he played but never said if they attended any events. He never mentions anything about Kaiden, like talking about somebody else's kid is somehow cheating on me and Logan.

Maybe he does feel guilty.

Brushing the thoughts off, I focus back on my surroundings. Ninth period. Two twenty-five. There are twenty-three minutes left until my first day at Exeter is complete. Only two hundred and sixty-nine more to go until senior year is over.

Advanced English drags. The exhaustion seeping into my bones from first day jitters and the noise level of the packed classroom put me on edge and keep me glancing up at the black clock on the wall. I swear barely five seconds pass each time. I can feel a flare forming under my skin and nestling into my joints, which hopefully a nap before dinner will ease before it gets worse.

Instead of focusing on the mindless conversations Mr. Nichols, a young twentysomething fresh out of grad school, lets us have after he explains class expectations at the beginning of the period, I look at the artwork littering the colorful walls. They're scenes from books, I realize. By the looks of it, each wall is a different novel, ranging from *To Kill a Mockingbird* to *The Hunger Games*.

Someone drops into the seat beside me, scraping the metal legs against the tile floor. I peel my gaze off the walls to see Kaiden staring at me with indifference. The redheaded boy who occupied the chair before is now across the room, staring wide-eyed in our direction.

"What are you doing here?" A few onlookers are invested in the exchange between us, peering back and forth between me and him.

"I'm in this class."

AP Literature allows for college credits. My schedule says I can apply them at community college for gen ed credits in my major. Is that why Kaiden is here too?

I'm not sure how I didn't notice him when I came in. When I saw how swamped it was, my main focus was on finding an empty seat, not examining who was occupying the others. When Mr. Nichols did roll call, I obviously didn't pay attention to names until I heard mine.

My eyes go back to the wall and focus on the mixture of greens and blues. I wish I could paint. Mama used to spend a lot of time in the spare room painting pretty pictures of still lifes and landscapes. Sometimes, she would paint Lo and me.

After Lo, she stopped painting altogether.

"They did a vote on what books to put on the walls a few years back," he explains, catching me off guard. "People were miffed that the majority choice didn't make it because of some bullshit that happened in the book."

My nose scrunches. "What book?"

"Hell if I remember."

The brunette girl sitting in front of me turns around after dutifully ignoring me the entire period. "It was the Jodi Picoult book about the sick girl who needed a transplant to survive."

Wetting my bottom lip, I nod. *My Sister's Keeper* was one of Lo's favorite movies to watch because the ending didn't match the book. It was sad because the sick girl didn't survive but happy because her pain no longer made her suffer.

"Anyway, the student counsel nixed it because there was a girl who was going through the same thing and they wanted to be considerate of her feelings," the girl explains, flipping her brown hair over her shoulder.

I blink in disbelief. "That's why they didn't go through with it?"

She shrugs. "Plus, it's sad."

One of my brows twitches. "*The Hunger Games* is literally about kids killing other kids for sport. How is that not sad?"

Kaiden snorts as the girl rolls her eyes at me like I'm the one being ridiculous. "That isn't real. Duh."

Not sure what to say, I shake my head and stare back at the wall. People hate realistic stories like Picoult's because they could happen to anyone. People die—of cancer, accidents. There's no discrimination in death. I guess wearing rose-colored glasses is easier than dark shades.

The girl goes to speak, but Kaiden cuts her off. "You might want to stop talking, Rach. You're not coming off very intelligent. Plus, you know what I told everyone."

I gape at his blunt statement.

Rach, presumably Rachel, glares. Giving me a quick once-over, she rolls her eyes before glancing back at him.

"You don't have to be a dick, Kaid. I'm just telling her what happened."

He leans forward. "Funny, you didn't seem to mind me being a dick earlier when you begged me to screw you in the locker room."

Her cheeks turn pink.

...and so do mine.

Clearing my throat, I sink into my seat and pull out a notebook to doodle in until the bell rings. Kaiden and Rachel leave me alone, though their staring contest doesn't go unnoticed by me because Rachel looks like she wants to stab him with the pen she's holding.

When the bell chimes, I stuff my belongings in my backpack and stand up. Everyone files out of the room in fifteen seconds flat, ready to leave for the day until they're forced back tomorrow. Kaiden hangs behind, which seems suspicious to me. Reluctantly, I walk over to where he stands by the door with crossed arms.

"Your shoes are hideous," he states.

Glancing down at my Toms, I click my heels together. After a few seconds, I lock eyes with him again. "So is your attitude."

He grins. "Ready?"

His lack of denial is semi-endearing. At least he knows it, accepts it, and doesn't pretend he has manners. Although, it may be nice not to be on the receiving end of his insults.

He nudges my shoulder as we walk down the hall. "Don't look so sad. I'm like this with everyone. Can't play favorites just because your dad is boning my mom."

I stop and stare at him.

"What?"

"You're…blunt."

"What's the point of bullshitting?"

I'm not sure.

"Way I see it, we're stuck together. I'm not going to hold back what I think to save you from getting your feelings hurt." He starts walking, causing me to follow close behind. "If it makes you feel better, I told your dad the same thing. He's not my biggest fan."

"Seems mutual," I murmur.

Those lips twitch higher. "Doesn't seem like you're his biggest fan either from what I've seen."

I don't answer.

"Daddy issues can be hot."

My eyes narrow. "Stop talking."

He chuckles and shoves the front doors open, not bothering to hold them for me as I quicken my pace to catch up to his long strides.

The students who hang around talking and joking in the lot don't spare us a glance. It's like outside the high school doors Kaiden is a different person, and everyone knows it. And me? I'm no one.

Our ride home is in blissful silence.

When we get there, he ignores everyone.

The week goes by in welcome monotony. Most people wouldn't like living the same routine, but I find it peaceful. There were too many days in my past that I couldn't predict.

Would I be able to get out of bed?

Could I go to school?

Would I be able to make it throughout an entire day without tearing up because my body aches so brutally?

Chronic illness gives little wiggle room for peace of

mind. Having "good" days doesn't mean the pain isn't there; it just means that it's not as noticeable—like a limb that's sort of falling asleep but still functioning. Days where I have energy can end abruptly for no reason other than fate playing games with me.

Like oncoming hip pain that feels like you continuously slammed your hipbone into a wall. Or finger pain that feels like you've shut your fingers into a door until they're so swollen you can't straighten them. I've nodded off in the middle of a class more times than I can count, not because the material is dry but because my body is tired of fighting its own cells. Inside the sad shell of my agonizing existence is a battlefield, and I'm on both sides holding trigger-ready guns waiting for the bullets to leave the barrels.

Yet I feel lucky. I'm still breathing.

There are a few girls who sit by me at lunch and also share classes with me throughout the day. Sometimes they'll ask me questions, but usually they leave me alone and talk about the teachers and classmates, like Mr. Nichols and Kaiden. Thankfully, I don't think they know who I am to Kaiden. I'm sure they've seen me get out of his car, even sure I've seen a few guys stare and make jokes when Kaiden leaves me behind as soon as the ignition is off.

Nobody says a thing about it.

Knowing that people view him as Exeter High royalty, thanks to one of the lunch table inhabitants, makes it better that they don't associate us. Then again, it's a smaller school. Dad told me it only has a little over eight hundred students total, which means that it's not much bigger than my old district in Bakersfield. We may live in an urban area, but it's not big enough to keep secrets for long. Not when Kaiden is involved.

Like when one of the girls gives me the briefest look before leaning into her friends and mentioning some person named Riley. I don't know who he is, but apparently he no longer attends Exeter. Why they look at me in relation to him, I have no interest in asking. If they wanted me to know, they would have included me in their conversation.

On Friday afternoon, Mr. Nichols asks me to stay behind while everyone else leaves the room. Mentally, I go through a list of possible reasons. I turned in homework, did the readings, and even participated twice in class. I've done nothing warranting trouble.

Unlike Monday, Kaiden doesn't wait up for me at the door. He's been hanging out in the parking lot with his buddies, who I learned are on the lacrosse team with him. They'll joke around and shove each other and hit on the girls who linger until I make it out the front doors. Kaiden always shoos them away, and like loyal followers, they obey without complaint.

Mr. Nichols smiles from where he sits behind his desk. I can see why girls always giggle and gossip about him. His face still screams youth, which isn't a surprise. He told us on the first day that he only just graduated with his master's, putting him somewhere in his midtwenties. His eyes are a chocolate brown, his hair a dirty blond and chopped short, and his body is in physically good shape highlighted by the button-up shirts he wears with sleeves rolled up to his elbows and pressed dress pants that seem to emphasize long legs. It's hard *not* to notice a cute teacher like him.

"I won't keep you long. I'm sure you're eager to start the weekend like everyone else," he promises lightly.

Shrugging, I readjust my bag strap over my shoulder.

"It isn't like I have any exciting plans. Did I do something wrong?"

He straightens. "Not at all. I'm sorry if I worried you. I actually wanted to talk to you about the paper you turned in."

On the second day of class, he assigned a short paper for us to write about our favorite novels. It made most people groan to have an assignment so soon in the semester, but I didn't mind. During my worst days, I'd stay in bed with a book by my side. There are always two on my nightstand waiting to be loved.

When he told us that we had to explain why we chose the specific book, it seemed like an easy assignment. It was informal and we got to talk about literature in a way that's personal to us. Yet I learned based on the muttered complaints and protests that reading isn't a common hobby among my peers. Another reason why I have yet to make any friends here.

He rests his hands on his desk. "I noticed that you didn't just choose one book. You like reading, don't you? The ones you talked about said as much."

Wetting my lips, I manage a nervous head nod. Maybe I should have just chosen one, but he never said we couldn't write on more than that.

"The ones you chose," he says, "they all seem to have a common theme. I'm curious as to why you selected them."

He knows about my condition. School policy states that teachers must be made aware of all students with chronic illnesses that can impact their attendance and performance in school. Personally, I think it's an invasion of privacy. Dad and Cam think it's a good idea though.

You'll have people in your corner, Dad told me in comfort.

I wanted to say, *Like you?*

Hostility gets us nowhere though.

"You told us to pick our favorite" is my reply. It's quiet and unsure, like I'm not sure what he wants me to say.

"And those are?"

Another nod.

He studies me for a long moment. "They all seem to question mortality. I wonder if it's a reflection on personal matters. We tend to hold on to stories when we relate to them."

I shift on my aching feet. "If you're going to suggest I see a counselor, I already turned down the idea when Principal Richman insisted."

Despite Dad telling me I had no choice, I never made an appointment with either the counselor or nurse. When I told him that setting aside a free period just to tell the counselor that school is fine is a waste of time, he saw my point. The nurse…not so much. He's insistent that Ms. Gilly will be a handy ally here.

I told him I didn't need an ally.

I haven't needed one in years.

Nichols's smile widens, making him look even more boyish. "I was actually going to suggest joining the book club."

Taken by surprise, my lips part. I didn't even know there was a book club here. It's not on the school's list of activities students can join. Cam convinced Dad I should consider looking into different options to make friends faster. I only looked to get them off my back.

He takes my silence as consideration of his suggestion.

"We meet every Thursday after school, usually around three thirty. It's held in the library, although sometimes it's moved to the classroom."

"We?"

"I'm the faculty supervisor."

Oh.

He feels the need to explain when I make no move to say I'll come. "The last English teacher was responsible for it, so I agreed to take over for her when I met with her before the year started. It seemed like a passion project of hers that she wanted to see remain. It's small. The list is only about ten people long. You should consider joining if you love to discuss books. They're seeing if it'll last past this semester, and if it does"—he shrugs—"then great."

Pressing my lips together, I glance down at my shoes. Another pair of Toms, except these are light-purple cloth with a big brown button off to the side. They look handmade according to Cam. Maybe that's why I like them so much; they're unique like me.

Mr. Nichols brings my attention back to him. "Just think about it, okay? Your paper was very well written, and I think you'd make a great addition to the club."

I give him a timid smile and start to turn to the door. He calls my name before I make it, causing me to glance at him once more.

His head tilts. "Which of the ones you spoke of is your favorite? I couldn't tell."

"*My Sister's Keeper.*" He doesn't ask why, yet I find myself explaining anyway. "I find that the books with the saddest endings are the best because they make us feel. We don't always get a happily ever after no matter how hard we work for it."

I think Lo always knew that.

His smile is genuine. "Have a great weekend, Emery."

I murmur a "you too" before grabbing my jacket from my locker. It's been raining on and off throughout the week, nothing unusual for upstate New York's early fall season. With summer fading into the distance, the transition from sunshine and warmth to clouds and cold hasn't been a fun one. Especially not with my sensitivity to abrupt weather shifts that has me hunkering down in layers.

Dad put a small electric space heater in my room when the sixtysomething temperature turned into fiftysomething with the nonstop rain showers. My fingertips turned blue until I'd have to walk around with winter gloves on. Cam would frown and ask if I want the heat turned up, but nobody else has the same problem as me, so I always tell her no.

The heater is a peace offering, a way to tell me that it's okay to ask for help. I think it was Cam's idea, though Dad must have thought it was a good one since I watched him set it up and show me the different controls on the tiny remote. When Kaiden saw it in the corner of my room, he stared with furrowed brow before leaving without a word.

When I walk outside, jacket zipped up all the way and shoes hitting the tiny puddles, I see Kaiden all alone leaning against his car. It's new, probably made in the past few years, and a polished black. Dad mentioned he'd look into getting me my own if I wanted since Kaiden will start going to practices soon. Lacrosse doesn't start until the spring, but he trains for the season with his friends. Dad tells me it'll be easier if I don't have to depend on Kaiden for rides.

Kaiden pushes off the car as I approach him. I note the

empty parking lot before walking toward the passenger side of his Audi A6. Until a few days ago, I didn't know what it was, just that it had to cost a pretty penny. One of his jock friends, the one with moppy brown hair like Kaiden's, was begging to take it out for a spin with his leggy girlfriend. Kaiden's response was the usual bluntness, something about not wanting to get it back with a stained back seat. I stopped listening to the conversation after that.

Just as I'm opening the door, he taps on the roof of the car. "You can't screw Nichols, you know."

Halting with the door half-open, I stare wide-eyed at him. His expression gives nothing away, as if stating something like that is no big deal, much less offensive.

"Excuse me?"

I think he shrugs, but the car hides his body from my view because of the height difference between us. He's at least six foot to my five four.

"All the girls at school seem to think they can stay after class and flirt their way into his attention," he replies casually. "The guy seems smart enough to not fall for their tricks. I'm just saying, he won't sleep with you."

I'm gaping, trying to gather a reply. There's a lot I could say, could call him, but nothing gets past my lips besides a squeaky noise that he laughs at.

"I think I'll call you Mouse."

"M-Mouse?"

He grins. "You're quiet like one."

Stunned speechless is more like it.

"Mouse," he repeats, nodding. He taps the roof of the car again and gestures toward the interior. "Get in. I want to go home. Got shit to do, people to see."

Climbing in after he does, I drop my bag on the floor by my feet and buckle up. "Doesn't seem like you like it there."

"Doesn't seem like that's your business."

I glance out the window as he pulls out of the parking space and toward the exit. "Your mom seems nice. I like her."

No response.

"You should talk more at home."

"Mouse isn't a fitting nickname if you insist on talking," he informs me, turning onto the road heading home.

My jaw ticks.

He sighs. "Cam and I have an understanding that you wouldn't get."

I shift toward him. "You call your mom Cam?"

He grunts.

"But she's your mom."

He looks at me. "You call Henry Dad, yet I can tell you don't want to. It bothers you to label him for what he is. That's where you and I are different. I don't have to call Cam anything that I don't want to."

Why is on the tip of my tongue, but I swallow the question. He won't answer it. And if he does, it'll lead to some snarky remark that I don't have the energy to dissect, so what's the point?

The ride home is quiet like always. I watch the scenery pass, the patches of evergreens and sycamores changing into developments that look identical to each other. Lo and I used to want to live in houses just like these right next to each other. Mama would tell us that it'd change when we got older because we'd be two different people, but neither of us believed it.

Mama probably wishes she could see us live out that

old dream. Identical twins living in identical houses, raising families together and being happy. Coffee dates on Sundays. Our children on swings in a park somewhere. Lots of smiling and laughter.

She hasn't called since I moved. Sometimes she'll text me and ask how I am but when I respond, I'll only ever get a one-word reply back. Even through the screen, I can feel her sadness. It seeps into the words that I picture her typing with glassy, golden eyes.

I don't realize we're home until Kaiden asks if I'm getting out. He doesn't say it in a rude way, but I grab my bag and slip out of the car without so much as looking at his expression, which I only assume is as unreadable as ever. Sometimes it would be nice to have someone close by who gets me like Lo used to.

That's asking too much now.

Nobody could get me like Lo did.

Three

SATURDAY IS QUIET. DAD and Cam went to a farmers market in the morning. I pretended to be asleep so they wouldn't ask me to go and then listened to them leave before pulling out a book and curling under my warm blankets.

Kaiden left a little before noon, not saying a word when he saw me making a sandwich in the kitchen. He grabbed an apple and stared at the pajama shorts I wore before grabbing his keys and leaving. I went back to making lunch before closing myself in my bedroom and cranking up the heater.

Glancing at all the furniture in the room has me comparing everything to my old one. Here everything is white and gray. The bedding is white and fluffy and warm, the sheets a deep gray, the pillows a mixture of the two that match the patterned curtains. In the corner is a full-length mirror trimmed with white with dangling lights in the shape of stars. I keep them on at night in case I need to get up. That way, I don't trip on the shoes I kick off in the middle of the floor.

When I saw the stars, I immediately thought of when Lo and I begged Dad to take us out to watch the night sky. He told us once that he and Mama went stargazing on their first date. Did he put them there to remind me that he thinks about it too? How we all laughed and pointed and made up names for the constellations because none of us knew what they were called?

The room is huge, and almost everything is new. It's the exact opposite of the one I shared with my sister. Cam said she had a lot of fun decorating it by adding canvas art on the walls with quotes and images—flowers, animals, people. Dad said she always wanted a daughter.

By midday, my body starts aching. It begins in my wrists, a telltale sign for more to come. I struggle holding my book, so I decide to rest after taking some Motrin. An hour nap only settles the pain in my elbows and shoulders, and when I try getting up for some water, I cringe at the dull pang in my hips.

Pushing past the feeling, I force myself to walk out to the living room. Both Dad's and Cam's cars are in the driveway, and I hear them talking from the backyard. When I glance out the window, I notice them in the garden together.

Since when does Dad garden?

Cam laughs and brushes dirt off Dad's face, only smearing it worse. He smiles and says something before looking up and noticing me. Cam glances too, waving at me with a bulky beige glove covering her hand.

I open the glass door and stand at the doorway. My feet are bare, my legs exposed by my sleep shorts, and my body still sore from the oncoming flare. Instead of showing them, I give a tiny wave back.

Dad helps Cam up and brushes dirt off her pants. He gives my attire a once-over, clearly wanting to say something. They walk to me, Cam ditching her glove and putting it on the picnic table. When they stop in front of me, Dad lets go of her hand.

He looks disapprovingly at my pajamas. "Don't you want to change into actual clothes? It's a bit late to be wearing those."

Instead of frowning like I want to, I tug on the hem of my tee. "I've just been lounging. Why bother dirtying regular clothes if I'm going to stay in all day?"

Cam pats my arm and I try not to wince at the ache radiating from my joints and muscles as she does it. "Your father and I were thinking about taking the family out to dinner tonight. How about we all get cleaned up and get ready?"

Shifting my weight, I debate on telling them I'd rather stay in. If I do that, they'll ask questions. Dad will shove pain relievers in my hand, Cam will ask if I need to go to the hospital, and Kaiden will glower like I'm an inconvenience—like his mother's attention toward me is pathetic.

I wonder what Cam's eyes look like when she cries.

"Kaiden isn't here" is my weak attempt to back out of the dinner. Going out when I don't feel well is too much of a hassle. Pretending to be okay for the sake of others is a draining act to an already underpaid show.

Cam waves her hand in dismissal. "He'll meet us there. Let's go inside. The Cantina isn't a formal restaurant, so jeans and a blouse will be fine to wear."

The Cantina sounds an awful lot like it serves Mexican food. Considering Dad said he did some research on my disease, something tells me dietary habits isn't something he googled.

I don't say anything. Cam seems excited and Dad seems happy because Cam is, so I walk into my room and slip into a pair of black leggings and slide on a loose long-sleeve shirt. Sliding into the pineapple Toms that Kaiden called ugly, I make my way back out to the living area.

Dad is cleaned up and wearing a new pair of jeans and a black button-down, like his version of casual only half exists. Cam is in a sundress with her dirty-blond hair pulled back, and she looks a lot like Kaiden. Same tan complexion, same round eyes, and same plump lips. Their hair and eye color are different though, and where her features are soft and inviting, his are hard and repellent. It makes me wonder if he got his brown hair and eyes and rough personality from his father. Where is he?

Cam grabs her purse from the counter. "I know you'll love the food, Emery. They have the best nachos. In fact, they make everything from scratch! How many places can say they do that?"

Not many, I admit. Still, the idea of fried, spicy food has my stomach churning already. It doesn't sound appealing, and I doubt this place has many salad options that aren't coated in the type of stuff that'll make me feel worse.

Internally sighing, I get into the back of their car and pull out my cell from where it's tucked under my leg. No text messages. No calls. Nothing from Mama.

I stare out my window in silence.

Grandma put a lot of money into getting me seen by dieticians to formulate a special diet that would limit any food inflammations. Honestly, it's not a plan I follow as closely as I should. I limit the amount of dairy and gluten I eat, but cheese pizza is my weakness just like any other person, and carbs are my one true soul mate.

Mama used to make me bland meals with no taste and high iron and protein because that's what the dietician told her to do. But I know Mama hated the food as much as me, and her on-again, off-again employment made it hard to keep buying the type of foods that were better for me. She lost her full-time job as a pediatric nurse because she was taking too much time off bringing me to appointments and tending to my every need.

It's why I told her I didn't need special organic brands or gluten-free snacks or lactose-free alternatives. I think she believed me because she was desperate to see the truth in it. She didn't want to let her unemployment impact me any more than it had, but she didn't understand my guilt over her situation.

She struggled because of me.

She hurt because of me.

Pain comes in countless forms. The worst is seeing what your suffering does to everyone around you. Mama is my biggest victim.

But I'm also hers.

When we arrive at the restaurant, I paint a bright smile on my face like I'm excited. Maybe I'm an artist after all. The Picasso of the modern era.

The restaurant is dimly lit and playing soft instrumental music from the speakers. It's a cute little eat-in that's small and intimate. People talk among themselves, some louder than others, and the servers come over donning big smiles and warm welcomes.

Everything is dark wood, like the color of espresso—the chairs, the tables, the booths. There's no cloth or cushions to soften the seats, which makes my tailbone hurt. Every time I shift, the seat creaks and Dad and Cam stare at me like I'm weird for fidgeting so much.

Kaiden hasn't shown up yet. Cam insists she knows what he'll want, so Dad waves over our waitress and they start ordering. I've been staring at the menu for fifteen minutes, stalling by ordering water and sending them away to decide between the lightest options. At this point, a taco salad is the best I can do.

Dad and Cam talk about work and school. They ask me how I like my classes, if I made any friends, and if I've heard from Mama.

Dad cringes when Cam brings Mama up. I don't see why. It's been a decade since he had to deal with her. Maybe he feels bad for me, like digging up my departure will hurt my feelings. I don't think that's it though.

Thankfully, Kaiden arrives just before I'm forced to answer. I don't want to talk about Mama with any of them, especially Dad. He left us and couldn't even bother to care when Lo got sick. He never checked in when I told him how Mama acted or how bad Lo was getting.

Dad doesn't deserve to know anything.

Cam's eyes bulge when she sees Kaiden drop into the only seat available next to me. At first, I don't know why she looks so freaked. Then I turn and notice Kaiden's eye is all red and puffy, and his cheek is colored an off blue. It makes the usual tan tone even darker, and his eyes hold a type of smoke in them from a fire he clearly extinguished. Except he did so with his fists, based on their puffy nature.

His signature don't-give-a-shit smirk returns despite his mother's reaction to the shiner he's sporting. "What'd I miss?"

Dad clears his throat. "Emery was just about to fill us in on how things are going. How *is* your mother doing?"

My lips part. Are they really going to ignore his face like they don't see anything wrong?

I won't. "What happened to you?"

Cam makes an audible noise.

Kaiden's smirk vanishes and his jaw ticks like he can't believe I asked. If our parents won't, someone should. I'm not exactly used to this commonality as if it's nothing out of the ordinary. Unlike them, I need answers.

Apparently, so does he. "I wouldn't want to keep Daddy Dearest waiting on that answer. Tell us, Emery, how *is* your mother doing?"

My nostrils flare.

His lips twitch upward as if he enjoys my reaction, so I push my emotions away. "I don't think that matters when you show up bruised after being gone all day."

He leans forward, crowding my space with his confidence. "Aw, what's wrong, Mouse? Did you miss me?"

Dad murmurs a questioning "*Mouse?*" before glancing between Kaiden and me. Neither of us offers an explanation on the nickname.

"Your eye," I emphasize.

"Had an accident," he says plainly.

Something tells me it was no accident at all. Fists must have been involved based on the mark left behind. Part of me wonders what the other guy looks like.

Cam tries drawing us back together, but the smile she offers is distant. "I ordered your favorite, Kaiden. I even asked them to put hot sauce on the side for the fajitas."

Kaiden peels his gaze from me to his mother, lips pinched. "I wish you'd stop assuming I like the food here. Did you even ask Emery if she likes Mexican?"

While I appreciate his point, I don't like being used as a means to verbally attack his mother. She's trying. "It's really—"

His eyes cut to mine. "Do you?"

Dad intervenes. "Emery loves Mexican food. She used to demand it all the time when she was little."

My heart cracks when I realize he's talking about Logan. *She* used to demand we order Mexican food. It was *she* who always wanted tacos for dinner and nachos for dessert. Every birthday, she'd choose some new Mexican restaurant to try.

"That was Logan," I say quietly.

Kaiden snorts. "Who the hell is Logan?"

The crack in my heart expands a little wider. "Who's…?" My eyes slowly lift to Dad's in question, like I misheard Kaiden's rude question regarding the existence of my other half.

Cam gasps. "Kaiden!"

"Dad?" I whisper brokenly.

His shoulders tense. "Emery…"

"Don't you talk about her?"

"Em—"

"Why doesn't it surprise me that you wouldn't say anything about her?" Pushing back against the table, I go to stand just as Kaiden opens his big mouth again.

"What's crawled up your ass?"

Cam covers her mouth with her palm, and tears prick

my eyes. Jerking the chair so it scrapes loudly against the floor and causes people to stare, I stand up.

Dad mimics me. "Sit down, Emery."

"Don't bother to start telling me what to do now just because your image looks bad. I mean, that's probably why you left. Right? You were afraid what having a sick kid would do to the squeaky-clean family-man reputation you have going on."

"Emery," Dad warns under his breath.

Cam reaches out. "Henry—"

I grab my phone from the table. "It must really suck that you weren't happy stuck in an imperfect family. I wonder what your old coworkers thought when they found out Lo died. Did they know she was sick? You never took time off when the doctor appointments started. Mama told you something was wrong, and you always said you had to work, like having a career meant more than having a daughter."

Kaiden swears.

Anger bubbles through me. "You want to know how Mama is doing, Dad? She's terrible. She hasn't verbally spoken one word to me since I moved, which isn't much different from how it was when I lived with her and Grandma. She wasn't the same after we buried Logan. Whenever she sees me..."

She sees a dead girl.

Tears threaten to spill, so I shake my head and walk around my chair.

"Where are you going?" Dad calls out.

Yet he doesn't move to stop me.

I laugh sardonically but don't answer.

I'm halfway down the street when I hear tires slowing

down behind me. Part of me is shocked Dad would chase me down. I remember all the times I was younger and he never made an effort. He'd miss dance recitals and family dinners and everything in between because of work. His coworkers never met us, especially not when Lo started acting funny, and Mama never went out with him to work functions. He was ashamed of us. Maybe still is.

When a car stops beside me, it isn't Dad's. My steps falter when I see Kaiden leaning down to see me from the open passenger window. He pushes on the door.

"Get in."

I blink. A car honks from behind him before passing, visibly irritated as they give us the finger like Kaiden isn't pulled off to the side of the road.

"Emery, get in the fucking car."

Glancing back at the faded restaurant behind us, I wonder if Dad and Cam are cancelling our food or waiting for it to-go. Are they even going to come out? To go home? To search? It's doubtful.

Not knowing what else to do, I slip into his car and close the door. Walking home would cause me twice as much pain. There's no way I'd be able to get out of bed tomorrow.

He tells me to buckle up before pulling away, not even sparing me one look. It's fine by me, because I'd prefer staring out the window so he can't see the tears dampening my cheeks. Wiping them away is no use because the more I replay what just happened, the more that fall.

Dad never told them about Lo.

About his *dead daughter*.

Maybe I should give him the benefit of the doubt like Grandma told me to give Mama. I know that everyone grieves differently, but Dad acts like nothing even happened. How could he pretend as though Lo never existed?

When we get closer to the house, Kaiden doesn't take the turn. Instead, he goes straight and stays on the main road. There's no music, only the sound of the wind against the car and the distant sound of traffic filling the silence.

"Where are we going?"

"Not home." He pauses. "Yet."

I want to tell him that's a bad idea, but maybe it isn't. Maybe it's exactly what we need. At least me. I'm still not sure what Kaiden needs, and I think he likes staying mysterious.

I watch as the buildings and houses fade into the tree lines the farther we drive away. Dad came this way when he brought me into Exeter. On the outskirts is a large cemetery on a hill and not much else other than various trees and fields.

It's a strange mixture of urban and rural here. We're not near the big city, but not too far away. It's almost like the area can't decide if it's trying to evolve or stay the way it's been for decades.

In a way, it's comforting. Seeing fields, hills, and trees reminds me of home. Lo and I would go exploring in the woods behind our childhood house, the one Grandma had to move into after Dad left before we lost it to the bank. We'd spend hours climbing trees and playing hide-and-seek. Lo always won.

To my surprise, Kaiden turns onto a narrow road leading into the cemetery. It should probably scare me, make me nervous, something, but it doesn't. After all, he saved me from walking back to a home that doesn't feel like home at all.

We get to a large fenced-off clearing, and he puts the car in Park and shuts it off. Shoving open his door, he gestures for me to follow him out. Hesitantly, I obey, unbuckling and stepping out onto the paved path we're pulled off to the side of. He starts walking past the fence, jumping over it like it's nothing but waiting expectedly for me to do the same.

Blinking, I stare between him and the chain fence separating us, noting the rust on the top and the odd holes throughout the rest of it. There isn't an opening big enough for me to crawl through.

"Well?" He crosses his arms.

I blush. "I can't jump that high."

He sighs like I'm a burden, despite bringing me here of his own free will. "Can you climb and get at least one leg over?"

Swallowing, I study the fence. I used to be part of the cheer squad at my old school. Flexibility and strength never used to be a problem for me until the past couple of years. But I'm curious about where he wants to take me.

Nodding, I pull myself up on the fence. It hurts my tender palms and arms, and my hip pops loudly when I swing my leg over, but I pretend it doesn't bother me when I balance on top.

I yelp when I feel two strong hands on my waist, lifting me up and setting me down on the ground like I'm a toddler.

"You really should have eaten dinner," he notes, giving my body a thorough once-over with narrow eyes before shrugging and walking away.

I catch up with him and tug my shirt closer to my body when the wind starts picking up. Without any buildings, there's nothing to block the assault of cool air against us. I refuse to use Kaiden as a wall because I think he'd snark if I even tried getting closer.

We walk for what feels like forever until I see a large sycamore tree in the middle of a field of purple flowers. It seems out of place yet perfectly set at the same time.

Kaiden walks over to it and sits down, leaning his back against the thick trunk. He seems at peace, which is a new look for him. His body is eased as he stretches his long legs out without a care in the world.

I stare. Not just at him but at the tree. It's huge with its long branches and bright green leaves transitioning into yellow and orange and red that give the space a beautiful kind of life. Lo would have loved this spot. She would have dragged me out and stayed here until Mama called our names in frantic worry. Lo always wanted to be free, out in the open, surrounded by trees and plants and animals.

Suddenly, the tears that had finally stopped falling on the way over begin building again until everything blurs. Bottom lip trembling, I hear Kaiden's heavy sigh.

"What's wrong now?"

I answer silently what my emotions won't let me speak aloud.

Lo was buried under a sycamore tree.

Four

KAIDEN'S EYES BURN INTO my face as I feebly attempt to contain my tears. Closing my eyes and palming my lids with the heels of my hands, I suck in a deep breath and think positive things to distract my mind from Lo's image. No matter how hard I try thinking of sunshine, good weather, and how pretty the purple flowers beneath my feet are, all I see is Lo's headstone.

The last time I went to visit her, there'd been bird droppings and grass shavings all over the polished granite. I cried and worked hard under the punishing sun until it was spotless and shiny again. Then I'd fallen asleep in the shade beneath the sycamore, pretending Lo was right beside me.

It was Grandma who'd found me, not Mama. When she got me back inside, I asked where Mama was. Grandma told me she was resting. Part of me was glad I hadn't worried her. Another part of me hated her for not noticing I'd left to begin with.

"You need to breathe, Mouse."

His gruff words pull me out of my memories. Cracking my eyes open, I see his blurry image where it still rests against the tree. Despite the buildup of tears, I see his frown perfectly clearly. Even seemingly angry, he looks gorgeous.

"Why do you look mad?" Blinking rapidly to dry my eyes, I force myself forward until I'm next to him. He doesn't invite me to sit or make any move, just stares up at me with pursed lips.

"Don't do well with crying."

Most men don't. Like when Mr. Wilson, the man who acted like a father figure to us after Dad left, looked uncomfortable at Lo's funeral. His face was pale as he stared at her coffin, and he left before the service was over.

I sit beside Kaiden, drawing my knees to my chest. Resting my chin against the top of them, I blow out a long breath until the ache in my chest lightens. Suddenly, breathing doesn't seem so hard, so I close my eyes and let the wind and shade caress me into calmness.

"Your father is an asshole," he says.

I don't argue with him.

"Sorry about…shit, you know."

My lips twitch upward. I guess he doesn't do well with apologies either. "She was my best friend," I tell him.

I'm not sure he cares, but I need to tell someone about her. If not today, someday. Not talking about Lo would do her memory injustice.

I lean against the tree trunk and exhale a slow breath when I feel the scratchiness against my back. The discomfort eases me into a familiarity of summer afternoons with Logan in the woods. "Did my Dad really not say anything?"

He clears his throat. "No."

Pressing my lips together, I nod.

What I said back in the restaurant is probably true. I've thought about all the reasons he left, theorized what made him stay away, and hated him a little more each day for it. Normally I wouldn't say a thing, but it's been years of bottling up every thought and feeling toward the man who couldn't even support us when Lo died.

"I'm not sure why he took me in."

The doubt is making sure its presence is known and it's justified. Dad couldn't waste more than mere minutes on me before now, so I have no clue why he bothered picking up the phone when I reached out for a very last-minute unexpected third call of the year. I never thought he'd say yes to me moving in with him.

Finally, I glance over at Kaiden. He watches me with something sparking in his eyes. I'm not sure if it's good or bad because he gives nothing away.

Swallowing, I shake my head. "I found out he was remarried through a friend of the family. This older woman was gossiping at the grocery store when I went to pick up paper plates." I surprise myself by laughing. "Weird that I remember what I was getting, huh? I was in the aisle trying to choose between the off brand or name brand with little blue flowers on the edges of both. Then I heard Mrs. Wallaby tell someone in the next aisle that she heard about Dad getting married to a 'pretty young woman with a son of her own.' She said it must be nice to get a fresh start and a new chance at a family."

My lips pull down at the corners. Mrs. Wallaby turned the corner and saw me staring with tears flooding my cheeks. She didn't try to apologize, just stood frozen and guilty when she realized I must have heard.

Kaiden shifts next to me, visibly uncomfortable by my story. "I don't usually come here to talk."

What does he do, then?

Thinking of the possibilities, my cheeks tint at the probable answers. "Oh."

He chuckles unknowingly at where my thoughts went. "I come here to think."

Double oh.

I can see why he'd come here for that. It's quiet, isolated. The perfect spot for someone to sort through their thoughts if they needed to.

The conversation isn't the best one to have with him anyway. I'm not angry at him. I'm angry at Dad. Plus, Kaiden didn't ask for me to invade his space. I bulldozed my way into their home—the home they've been building, just the three of them.

"What really happened to your eye?" I ask in a soft voice.

His tongue clicks. "Got into a fight with someone over some shit-talking. No big deal."

Knowing it's all I'll get from him for now, I nod. "Who's Riley?"

His entire body freezes at my random question. "Where did you hear that name?"

His voice is rough, like it's a subject I shouldn't have changed to. Cursing myself, I nibble my bottom lip. "Some girls were talking about him at lunch. It just seemed like something had happened because I've heard his name a lot lately."

In the halls on the way to class.

In the cafeteria.

Riley is a hot topic.

"Riley is a girl," he murmurs after a stretch of time that

I figured he'd use to talk his way out of answering. "She doesn't go here anymore. Left after some rumors spread."

I frown. "What rumors?"

His jaw ticks. "People kept giving her shit about her body type. Had an eating disorder or something and got caught throwing up in the bathrooms. Rumors got pretty bad. She... It doesn't matter. She doesn't go here anymore."

"So she transferred out?"

He hums.

I think about all the times people glance at me before saying her name, like we're connected somehow. But I don't ask Kaiden any more about it because he's clearly shutting down. I'm shocked I got as much as I did.

Kaiden draws one leg up so it's bent at the knee. He drapes his arm over it and looks at me with distant eyes. "I am curious about something."

I hold my breath.

He grins, any tension vanishing with that dangerous smile. "Which paper plates did you buy?"

A relieved laugh bubbles from my lips.

"I didn't buy either."

We fall back into silence.

At some point, I fall asleep. I only know this because I'm pressed against a warm wall of hard muscle that smells faintly like cedar and cinnamon. Christmas trees and cookies. Kaiden grumbles as we near his car, but I can't make out the words. I'm tired—too tired to tell him to put me down. I close my eyes and nuzzle into the warmth, feeling him tense.

The next time I come to, we're passing streetlights. The yellow color casts shadows on Kaiden's tight expression, which I get a perfect view of from where he put me in the back seat. His jaw is hard, but the way it moves is like he's grinding his teeth.

My head feels too weak to pick up, so I lie there and watch him. The radio is playing a rap song I'm unfamiliar with, but I listen to the lyrics and try to stop staring at Kaiden like a weirdo.

He glances back when the car slows for a stop sign, seeing my tired eyes on his. "Would have been nice if you'd woken up before I had to carry you."

How did he get over the fence at the cemetery? I ask him as much and he grumbles and starts driving again.

"Had to walk the long way around."

"Oh." My voice is tiny.

He doesn't say anything for a long moment. We just sit there until the song ends and a new one begins. "We're almost home."

I force myself to sit up, yearning to cry over how my body reacts to the movement. Dizziness sweeps over my vision and everything around me blurs until I almost collapse.

Kaiden, unfortunately, notices. "Have you eaten anything today?"

Thinking back, I realize the last thing I ate was a sandwich late this morning. It's going on nine o'clock now. "Not since you saw me making something earlier."

He curses and pulls into the driveway. I frown when he turns to me with an irritated expression on his face. "You have to eat, Mouse. You're too skinny as it is."

Skinny. I hate that word.

People use it as an insult, whipping it with concerned voices because they have no clue what they're talking about.

My jaw ticks at the comment. "What has my father told you about me?"

Silence.

I scoff. "Let's just go inside."

He sighs and gets out, surprising me by opening the back door. "What? Do you have an eating disorder or some shit? You could be prettier if you just gained some fucking weight."

Not wanting him to see me cry, I slide out of the car and storm to the front door. Maybe the Riley conversation triggered something beyond my knowledge, but it's no reason for him to treat me like trash.

There aren't any lights on, but the front door is unlocked. As soon as we're inside, Kaiden stops me from going anywhere.

Biting my lip to contain the yelp of his grip on my wrist, I glare at him. "Let go of me, Kaiden."

He does. "Go to the kitchen."

"Don't tell me—"

"Christ, Emery. I'll make you dinner."

I'm speechless at his words. This is only the second time he's used my name. And the sound of it rolling off his tongue...

I swallow. "I'm sure they brought back the food they ordered. I'll eat that."

He crosses his arms on his chest, causing his shirt sleeves to hug the biceps I shouldn't be staring at. "You don't even like Mexican food."

"I ordered a salad."

"You need protein."

"I'm sure there are beans on it."

He scoffs. "Just get your ass into the kitchen. I'll make you eggs or something."

My brows rise.

"Don't let it go to your head," he informs me coolly. "I want an omelet, so I'll make you something too. I won't be your bitch boy again."

For some reason, I follow him into the kitchen and sit at the island. The stools are cushioned, so I'm not uncomfortable as I watch him pull things out of the fridge.

"What do you want?"

"Scrambled is fine."

He gapes. "You need more than scrambled eggs. Will you eat bacon if I make it? Toast? Cheese, for the little Mouse?"

"Stop calling me that."

He waits for an answer.

"Fine. Yes, I'll eat those too."

He smiles victoriously.

While he gets to work, I peer around the empty kitchen. The fridge is littered with pictures and random magnets, there's a calendar with dates circled and bill payments in Sharpie on it, and the dish towels are all the same shade of blue as the place mats on the table.

There's no noise, but I know Dad and Cam are here. Their cars are in the driveway, indicating as much.

"Where are our parents?"

"They know to leave me alone when I leave for a while" is his terse reply.

I play with an orange from the fruit bowl placed strategically in the center of the counter. Everything about how

Cam decorated the home is with a plan—the exact opposite of Mama's house. There, nothing matched. It was organized chaos.

"They don't know that about me."

He shrugs. "You were with me."

"How could they know that?"

"Because I told them I'd get you."

Nothing but the butter sizzling in the pan fills the silence. He cooks effortlessly, like he cooks his own meals all the time. He's rarely at dinner but almost always eats breakfast with us.

By the time he's finished, he sets a steaming plate full of eggs sprinkled with cheese, bacon, and a slice of buttered toast down in front of me. My mouth waters at the sight and smell as he passes me silverware.

He cleans up his mess, hands me a bottle of water from the fridge, and leaves the room.

He never made himself an omelet.

Five

I'M OUT OF SCHOOL Monday after waking up Sunday in my worst flare yet. When Cam found me in bed with swollen arms and a tear-stained face, she made Dad call my rheumatologist. Since I refused to go to the emergency room, the doctor suggested staying in bed and resting.

I nearly laughed when he also advised me to try avoiding stress. Life is stressful. While I attempt to minimize putting myself in situations that can cause flare-ups, they happen. Since moving in with Dad, new stresses have presented themselves—his actions toward me, Mama's silence…

Early Tuesday morning, I'm sporting fuzzy yellow pajama bottoms and a sunflower tee when Kaiden shows up in my room. He doesn't knock before opening up, so I'm thankful that I'm just curled up with a book beside me.

He takes one look at me and frowns. "I take it you're not going to school again?"

I shake my head. The exhaustion is still bone-deep, but the pain is nowhere near as bad. Besides a migraine I've been battling since yesterday afternoon, everything else has been tolerable to deal with. Yet the judgment in his tone doesn't make me want to continue the conversation.

He gestures toward my pajamas. "Aren't you hot in those? It's, like, eighty outside and probably just as warm in here." Walking over to the space heater, he shakes his head at the setting I have it on.

I heard him ask Cam yesterday why I've been in bed. It's one of the few conversations I've heard him have with her. The others usually end in a fight with him storming out and her clamming up. I want to feel bad for Cam, but I'm still not over how dinner went down that weekend.

From what I overheard, Cam never told Kaiden what's wrong with me. In a way, I'm grateful for that. When people hear you're sick, they have three reactions—they either pity you, refuse to come near you, or don't believe you at all. None of those situations are worth my time, not the fake sympathy of people who pretend they understand what I go through, not the people who think I'm contagious and stay ten feet away, and certainly not the people who refuse to accept invisible diseases are a thing.

I'll always remember the doctor appointment that led to me breaking down in the passenger seat of Mama's car. As soon as the doctor walked in and realized I was the patient, his mind was set. I was "too young" to be sick. I was like any other young girl who liked to "exaggerate" for attention.

My tears had streamed silently down my cheeks, but Mama was no fool. She pulled over and coaxed me into looking at her. What she saw, I'm not sure. Probably someone flawed and broken—someone utterly defeated.

It didn't matter that there was a family history of medical

problems. If doctors can't find one single element that stands out the most physically, they think you're overreacting because that's what young people are known for.

As if children don't die from cancer.

As if Logan didn't die from lupus.

He must have seen the note in my file.

Sister: deceased
Cause: systemic lupus, kidney failure

He didn't care. None of them did. I wasn't showing any physical symptoms. I was in pain. I was tired. I was…young. Just young.

Nowadays, there's no denying I'm sick. Just like Lo, you wouldn't have thought anything was wrong at first. I wasn't rail-thin, my hair wasn't falling out, and I looked healthy. Inside, my immune system was waging war against itself until every part of me was drained from the fight.

I'm glad Kaiden doesn't look at me any differently than before. Cam never mentioned that what I have is lifelong or that I could suffer the same fate as Logan. Since I barely said anything about her the day he took me to the sycamore, I haven't divulged any further information about my best friend.

It hurts too much, and he knows it.

Sometimes I'll find little Post-its of pictures in different places though. Pictures of paper plates with blue flowers, sunflowers, and trees with endless green leaves. I save every single one I find in places only I would be.

The way he watches me with eyes full of irritation doesn't put me at ease. While I don't want his pity, I also don't want his unwarranted hatred either. Sometimes, I wonder if coming here was a mistake. Like moving in was an act against him for space and attention. Although he doesn't seem like he wants any attention when he's here.

He gets his fill at school.

"Are you going tomorrow?"

I sit up so my back is against the frame of my bed—white metal bent into an intricate design that I don't get. But it's pretty, prettier than the boring wood frames that Lo and I had in our old bedroom.

"I plan to," I answer quietly.

He nods once but doesn't move. I'm not sure what he's thinking, but he acts like he wants to say something. Instead, he shakes his head and leaves, almost angry. I'm reeling as to what I said or did to make his lips pinch that way before he slams my door closed behind him.

Realizing it isn't worth my time, I curl up on my side and open my newest book. Dad checked on me before leaving for work. He's been going earlier the past few days, probably so he doesn't have to deal with me. I can tell my illness makes him uncomfortable, like he doesn't know how to treat me.

I don't either, but I can't tell him that because then we'll have common ground. I'm not sure I want to have any with him. I don't hate him, but in many ways, I don't love him either. We're stuck at an impasse—a merry-go-round of unspoken feelings and questions.

Why did you leave?

Why did you barely call?

Why didn't you love us?

Forcing the thoughts out of my head, I lose myself in

my novel. It's better than thinking about reality. Reality is ugly and painful and full of the kind of heartache that some books help you forget exist for a short period. I get to fall in love thousands of times over, a feat I'm afraid I'll never accomplish if my illness brings me to Lo instead of my future husband.

I fall asleep wondering if Lo is watching over me.

When Lo and I were young, Mama always sang "You Are My Sunshine" to us when she was in a good mood. I remember days in the kitchen when she'd sing and make chocolate chip cookies, our favorite, splitting up some dough for us to share while she baked the rest.

To this day, I love the song. It reminds me of Mama when she was happy. When I saw the rainbow at Lo's funeral, it made me think of the tune. I even started humming it until Mama walked away from us. Grandma told me it was okay, but I still feel guilty.

The song is one that I play on my bad days. It gets me thinking about all the good times I had growing up. My childhood wasn't sad, not until Lo passed. Mama and Dad would take us on long rides every Sunday where we'd stop for snacks and sodas. They'd take us to water parks where we'd ride every single ride until we were sunburnt and sore. Dad leaving was only step one into the roller coaster of hell, but up until that point, we were fine.

When I get out of bed to an empty house, I'm reminded that it's no longer like that for us. The family outings I used to look forward to are nothing but distant memories. When

Dad and Cam leave, they don't always ask if Kaiden or I want to go. They assume we won't want to, and it makes me want to ask if he remembers the Sunday rides and little vacations like I do.

School tomorrow will be a nice distraction from here. I can bury myself in homework instead of thinking about what once was. Staying in the past means halting the future. I may not get one, so I want to at least try making the most of the present.

After pouring myself a bowl of cereal, I sit on the couch in the living room and turn on the television. It isn't often I watch anything because Dad and Cam like to watch the news at night after work, so I leave them to the depressing reports on twenty-first-century racism, sexism, and shootings. The few times I do watch TV, I indulge in my two guilty pleasures—soap operas thanks to Grandma and reality shows thanks to Mama.

It's ironic, really. Mama would always tell Grandma how ridiculous soap operas are because they're not real, yet any reality show I've watched is the same. It's all fake drama focused on one-upping people in extravagant ways, highlighting the type of lives that people like us fantasize about having. Mama likes getting lost in a life she doesn't live, just like Grandma loves losing herself in drama that isn't her own.

They just have different motives. Mama doesn't want to think about Lo. Grandma doesn't want to think about Mama's denial.

And me? I just like the posed fights.

I'm surprised when three o'clock rolls around and the front door opens. I'm still bingeing episodes of *The Bachelor* with my bare feet perched on the couch when Kaiden strolls in. A few feet behind him is Rachel.

Her high-pitched giggle makes me cringe as Kaiden closes the door behind her. She's got a huge pink purse dangling from her elbow as she brushes against Kaiden's arm. I feel awkward staring, but it doesn't seem to faze her.

Kaiden notices what I'm watching and makes a face. "You actually watch this shit?"

I blush. "I used to watch it with my mom."

Rachel glances at the screen. "Oh! I love this show. This season has been amazing."

Kaiden snickers. "See, *you* I'm not surprised over."

The insult seemingly goes right over her head because she smiles at him like he just complimented her. I stifle a giggle and cover it with a cough. Kaiden catches on, grinning at me from beside her.

"Aren't we going to your room, Kaid?" Rachel practically purrs the words at him. Suddenly, I feel awkward for being here and blush over what I may hear if they do disappear behind closed doors.

I didn't know he was dating anybody.

My eyes widen when he grabs her bag and pulls something out. "We brought you some homework. Figured you'd want to catch up on some shit before tomorrow."

Hesitantly, I accept the papers.

Rachel whines. "Kaiden—"

"Head up. You know where it is."

When she turns, he smacks her butt. My cheeks burn. Trying to play it off, I glance over the homework to see what I've missed.

"Thanks for getting this."

He doesn't answer.

I look up at him. He's watching me with a tilted head and curved lips. "You might want to put some music on. Rach gets loud."

My jaw drops as he winks and heads for the stairs. Not knowing what to do with that, I grab my phone, earbuds, and backpack before heading outside. It's nice out, not too hot or too cold, which makes it perfect to settle at the picnic table with my schoolwork.

When "You Are My Sunshine" pops up on the screen at random shuffle, I get the answer to my question earlier.

"I love you, Lo," I whisper to the wind.

Six

During lunch on Wednesday, I choose the farthest empty table from the others and pick through my salad. A dull headache still resides in my temples, which does nothing for my appetite. I force myself to nibble on some lettuce since I skipped breakfast this morning despite Cam's insistence on me eating my eggs.

The morning flew by. I handed in my late assignments and caught up on class notes. Teachers told me I could see them during free period if I need help, but I have no intention of doing that. Once I get home, I'll close myself in my room and go through what I missed. Thankfully, nobody bothers me there, so there's no excuse as to why I can't study.

I'm playing with a crouton when a chair across from me is pulled back, the legs scraping noisily against the tile floor. Wincing at the noise, I glance up to find Kaiden there. Brows arched, I sit in silence, waiting for him to tell me why he's graced me with his presence.

As weird as I find our lack of communication during school hours, I've gone along with it. If he doesn't want to engage with me in the halls or before class, fine. It isn't like we have much to say anyway.

I learned that three days a week, he isn't even here in the morning, which is why I rarely see him. He goes to Exeter Community College to take classes before coming back during lunch.

Was it his idea to earn credits? Or Cam's?

He eyes my salad. "You should really eat something more than that. They've got other stuff to choose from."

They have a buffet of inedible-looking food choices, none of which looked half as appetizing as the limp lettuce mix. At least I knew what the contents were, because the chicken they offered looked more like meatloaf.

"I like salad."

"Doesn't look like it."

I've barely eaten more than a few leaves of lettuce. Most of it rests untouched in the plastic container I bought it in. When I get headaches, the nausea makes my stomach churn. The smell of whatever they're overcharging for doesn't help.

"I'm just saying, you need to eat more."

My teeth grind. "Stop telling me what to do. Just because everyone else at this school blindly follows you doesn't mean I will."

The tables around us get quiet. Biting the inside of my lip and glancing at the stares I warrant from the simple statement, I realize I just made a big mistake. People don't say anything about what Kaiden does to people who talk back, because nobody is dumb enough to do it.

Shrinking down, I stare at my lunch.

"You know," he replies casually, "the reason why people do what I say around here isn't some power play. It's all about tactics."

My eyes lift to meet his. He reaches over and plucks a crouton from my salad, rolling it in his fingers before popping it in his mouth with a crunch to fill the short-lived silence.

Wiping his hands, he crosses his arms on his chest. "They know I don't come from a powerful family. My mother is just some lovestruck fool who married a man who, as far as I'm concerned, is more pathetic than any other human I know, and my father is a deadbeat who isn't worth my time. The people here know who to follow because it benefits them. They want popularity? They make me happy. They want to be left alone? They stay out of my way. And you know something, Mouse?"

I'm silent.

"They do what I tell them to." The threat is there, but my gut tells me it's an empty one. I don't believe he'd make them do anything to me. After all, it's been a week since I arrived and not one person has bothered me.

Though if they didn't know about my involvement in their leader's life, they probably do now. The possibility of their fake interest after this leaves me a little uneasy.

He grabs my salad and tosses it behind him, letting the contents scatter across the floor. My lips part in shock when I see my lunch lying wasted in between the tables of peers surrounding us.

I will not cry.

Locking my jaw to keep me from saying a word, I watch him reach into his pocket and throw five dollars down on the center of the table. He stands up and gives me a displeased once-over before shaking his head.

Ignoring the mess he made, he turns around and calls out, "Go buy some fucking pizza," before leaving the room.

Refusing to meet people's stares, I stand up and leave the five-dollar bill behind before exiting through the glass side door. Maybe someone else could use it to buy lunch.

When the sun hits my face, I wish I had my sunglasses to protect my sensitive eyes. They're in my backpack, which is stuffed in my locker. Sitting in the shade beneath a sad-looking oak tree in the courtyard, I listen to the distant chatter of students who are probably talking about the little cafeteria showdown that just occurred.

Frowning, all I can think is *Screw you, Kaiden Monroe.*

Shortly before my diagnosis, I'd dropped twenty-five pounds without meaning to. Besides cheer, I didn't do much else for exercise. Sometimes the squad ran the track at school or used the weight room, but I ate more than any of them. They always envied how tiny I stayed.

Weight has been a sore subject since. One of the doctors I went to made Mama step out of the room before telling me it was a safe space to admit what I was doing. He thought I wouldn't say I had an eating disorder if she were around. He didn't believe me, just like the string of other doctors who didn't.

Mama wrapped me in her arms as soon as we had gotten home. She was worried and sad for me and angry at the doctor. That was before she shut down, grieving for Lo too much to care about anyone else.

After being diagnosed with lupus, it was like Mama gave up on me because she thought there was nothing left to do.

I suppose I gave up on her just as much, pushing her away on the rare occasion she did reach out. When Grandma calls and asks how I'm doing, I'll always divert the conversation back to Mama.

Tell her I'm not dead yet is how I ended our last conversation when she told me Mama would come around in her own time.

Someone sits beside me on the ground and drops a five-dollar bill in my lap. Looking up expecting to see Kaiden glaring, I'm surprised by the long locks of chestnut-brown hair instead.

Rachel isn't looking at me. "I think we both know it isn't a good idea to ignore him. At least pretend you bought something with it."

I stare down at the crisp bill. "Why are you talking to me?"

"Because Kaiden's an idiot."

My eyes widen.

She sighs. "He only did that because Danny Walsh from the lacrosse team commented on how tiny you are and then got the guys talking about what they'd do to your body. One guy said he could wrap one hand around your waist while he screws you from behind."

My cheeks prickle with heat as I look to the ground. "I don't see why he felt the need to cause a scene like that all because boys were talking about me. That's just…"

"It's what Kaiden does." She says it in an exasperated tone. "He threatened the guys in the locker room and then made a point in the cafeteria that he's the only one allowed to mess with you."

Am I supposed to be thankful?

She shakes her head. "He just gave you his protection. You should be glad."

High schoolers shouldn't need protection from each other. Then again, look at Riley. Nobody has said anything more about her since Kaiden told me what happened, so I wonder if their silence was another royal decree.

I extend my legs out in front of me. "I'm not sure why you're telling me any of this. What's in it for you?"

Her laugh is airy. "I know everyone thinks I'm a total moron, but you know what? It's easier to be a fly on the wall when people don't think you're capable of listening in."

I blink in surprise.

She grins at me. "I like Kaiden. He and I have been on and off for a long time. The more popular he gets, the more girls want him. But he keeps me around."

"He insults you."

"He's Kaiden."

If that's supposed to justify how he talks to her, I'm not sure what to say. I don't know Rachel, but anyone deserves better than that. Even if he has his own methods of keeping control of people, it isn't right.

"Anyway," she says with disregard, "I don't have to worry about those girls. He isn't interested in them. And frankly, I'd like to think he isn't into you, but I can't be too sure."

I gape at her. "Our parents are married."

She rolls her eyes. "Don't you get it? If anyone gets what they want no matter the situation, it's Kaiden. He could feed you to the sharks if he wants to, but he hasn't yet."

Yet. Wonderful.

"So I'll play nice. For now." She shrugs casually, like there's no threat behind her words. I'm not sure what she'd do if she thought I was somehow in her way.

"I don't like Kaiden," I state firmly.

She stands up and glances down at me with a smile painted on her face. "I believe you, Emery. However, Kaiden has a way of getting under people's skin one way or another. And unfortunately, he's willing to take on an entire sports team for you."

"So?"

She flips her hair over her shoulder. "I guess we'll just see how long it takes before things change. He wouldn't even sleep with me when I came over the other day. I was bored out of my mind." Pointing toward the money next to me, she adds, "You might want to go to the vending machine or something. He won't care if it's not pizza you get as long as you eat."

When she starts walking away, I call out her name. "You never really said why you're talking to me. I get that you like Kaiden, but if he wants everyone to leave me alone, then why warn me about him?"

She adjusts her purse on her arm. "If Kaiden likes you, that means you're competition."

It won't matter what I say to her about what I am to him. She already thinks I'm someone to look out for because of him standing up for me. If it means having enemies over, I'll be sure to tell him to throw me to the sharks. I'd rather go down on my own terms anyway.

Rachel leaves without another word, and from the hallway window, I see Kaiden staring. He doesn't look angry. He looks…amused. I'm afraid to find out what's so funny.

When I meet him at his car at the end of the day, I get in, buckle up, and drop the five-dollar bill onto his lap.

He stares at me.

"I wanted my salad."

Seven

THURSDAY BOOK CLUB IS small and intimate, a circle of upholstered armchairs set up in the quiet section of the library. Most of the seats are occupied by girls, and when I see them ogling an oblivious Mr. Nichols, I shake my head and take one of the last chairs.

At three thirty, Mr. Nichols welcomes all of us and explains the general idea behind the after-school club. It seems obvious that reading and discussing books is the reason we're here, but then I'm reminded by the Little Mermaid wannabe next to me that's not true when she asks silly questions to get Nichols's attention.

For the duration of the meeting, we talk about selecting different novels for the year. I'm interested when he pulls out a glass bowl, small pieces of paper, and a handful of pens from his bag. He tells us we'll each write a book down on the paper, fold it, and put it in the bowl. He'll write down the order of books we'll read and discuss throughout the term as they're pulled out by us.

I'm eager to write down mine but can tell the others aren't as interested. A brown-haired girl with pretty caramel highlights raises her hand and calls Nichols over, asking him questions about how to choose a book. He's nice in his reply, as any teacher should be, but I can tell even he is exasperated by their lack of understanding of something simple.

I stifle a wavering smile when I see him shake his head on the way back to his own seat. My eyes widen when he looks up knowingly at me, giving me a soft smile as if he gets my humor.

Maybe he's not oblivious after all.

It takes the girls fifteen minutes to write a title down, and I wouldn't be surprised if *Twilight* pops up more than once. I saw the blond with huge eyes glancing at the shelf next to her like she was just going to write down the first title she saw. Then again, half the books are ones I haven't read yet, so I wouldn't mind.

They occupy my time when I'm at home avoiding reality.

Mr. Nichols mixes up the folded papers before passing me the bowl. "Choose one, Emery."

I reach in and pluck one out, reading it off so he can jot down the title and author into his notebook. Admittedly, I've never heard of the book before.

As we go around the room, I struggle to keep quiet when *Twilight* pops up twice. Mr. Nichols suggests us choosing a different book to replace one of them, but nobody speaks up.

Until Nichols calls on me. "Emery, why don't you think of something? I know you've got an arsenal of ideas."

Little Mermaid glances at me with a scrunched nose before turning to Nichols. "How come she gets to choose?"

"Nobody else spoke up, Aria."

Aria. Ariel. Same difference.

Clearing my throat, I shift until I'm angled toward the girls. "If you want something similar to *Twilight*, we can read a John Green book. He writes young adult literature."

The blond tilts her head. "Isn't he the one who wrote about the dying chick? I think I saw the movie with my ex-boyfriend."

I wonder if she threw in the *ex* for Mr. Nichols as if he's supposed to care. "He has other books that aren't as well known as that one."

"Who wants to read about dying kids?" The brunette scoffs. "That sounds depressing."

"She finds love," the blond says in defense.

Nichols intervenes. "It can be a group decision for next time. Until then, we've got the title of our first book, which we'll discuss starting next week. Be sure to have a copy before then."

After he dismisses us, I gather my things and get ready to go before Nichols calls my name. A few girls glance back at us, whispering among themselves before turning around and heading out of the library.

"You were quiet," he notes, packing up his own belongings. "Those girls aren't exactly here to have deep conversations about literature. I have a feeling you'll pull the bulk of the load."

My lips twitch. "You don't say?"

He chuckles, zipping his messenger bag and draping it over his shoulder. "This club has the potential if we have the right people in it."

"And you think that's me?"

"And Annabel."

Annabel…

"She was the other quiet one," he muses.

Oh. There was a black-haired girl he called Anna. I vaguely remember her from one of my classes—global studies, not English. I think she suggested we read Margaret Atwood's *The Handmaid's Tale.* Someone mentioned how morbid that was, and Anna didn't say a word. I should have told her I was excited to read it.

He gestures toward the doors, so I follow him out of the library. "I've always been interested in literature. I love reading it, talking about it, everything. You remind me of me."

My brows raise as we walk side by side toward the spiral staircase that leads toward the front doors of the school. "Because we like books?"

He lets me go down the staircase first because of the narrow structure. "Because we like them more than reality. It's easier to lose yourself in fiction, right?"

We stop at the end of the stairs. There's noise coming from the high school gym down the hall—practice for some sport maybe. It helps lessen the awkwardness of standing here next to my English teacher while he waits for my response.

He smiles at me. "We all have something we want to escape from. That doesn't mean some of us aren't still in tune with reality even when it's…"

"Shitty," I murmur. My eyes widen over what I said, shooting up at his amused features. I've never sworn in front of a teacher. "I'm sorry, Mr. Nichols—"

He laughs. "School is over, Emery. I can't hold you accountable for what you say. I also can't say I agree with you." Readjusting the strap of his bag, he tips his head and begins walking away. "Can't say I disagree with you either."

He tells me he'll see me tomorrow and then leaves. I stand there for a minute before genuinely smiling. Gripping my bag and slipping it on my back, I turn to head to the side exit.

Kaiden told me he wouldn't wait for me. I didn't want to complain, so I just nodded. There's a late bus that boards by the loading dock off the middle school wing at five. I can wait another thirty minutes.

After fifteen, I go outside and sit on the brick half wall. My legs dangle over the side and the sun hits my face mixed with a gentle breeze. There's a book in my backpack I want to read, and I'm about to pull it out when a car pulls up.

Not just any car.

"Want to go to the sycamore?"

Kaiden.

I wet my lips. I should tell him no…

"Sure."

I tell Kaiden about the song—our song. Mama's, Logan's, and mine. He stares at me blankly as I admit how many times I listen to it every day. It plays in my head on repeat, a tune that never gets old.

He tells me it's stupid. But his eyes tell an entirely different story. In the depths of their jaded tone, there's an understanding.

What's your song, Kaiden?

"She wasn't just my sister." My voice is quiet as I pick

blades of grass out of the ground and examine them in my hand. "She was my twin, my other half."

My better half, I don't add.

Where she was outgoing and confident, I was an introvert and self-conscious. She loved to be part of everything while I watched from the sidelines. The only things we did together since we were little were cheer and dance, and that was only because she begged me to. I liked it...until I couldn't do it anymore. Not just because I wasn't physically able to but because everything I did reminded me of her.

It's why I don't hate Mama.

Because I understand.

"Lo was better than me in every way."

"Doubt that," he murmurs.

I look over at him. He's watching me, his gaze intent on studying my distant features. I want to believe that opening up to him will somehow make him reciprocate. He's angry. I just don't know at who.

Who am *I* angry at?

"You didn't know Lo," I argue. "You would have liked her way more than me. Everybody did. Mama always said she loved us equally, and I think she meant it. But there was this...I don't know, glow about Logan."

I used to think there was two of us because one wasn't made right. Never once did I think the faulty edition was Lo but me.

He's quiet for a minute. "Technically, I wouldn't have ever met either of you if she hadn't gotten sick."

Sucking in a breath, I let his blunt statement soak into my chest. He either doesn't know how to use his filter or doesn't care. I think it's the latter.

It's sort of…comforting.

Sighing, he shifts slightly. "That was fucked up, even for me."

I shrug. "Not untrue though."

"Tell me about your mom," he prods.

My brows shoot up. "What?"

He remains quiet.

"Uh…" I shake off my surprise and hug my knees to my chest. "She was a great person, a loving mother to Lo and me. When we were little, she used to let us help her cook dinner almost every night even though we were in her way more times than not. She'd find reasons to laugh when we messed up simple recipes, but it was fun."

Smiling, I remember how Mama taught Lo and I fractions through baking. Whenever she would make brownies or cupcakes for school bake sales, she would make sure we understood measurements and how to add and subtract the right amount of ingredients. It was the same for spelling. When everything was in the oven, she'd have us play with the magnet letters on the refrigerator, making silly sentences that didn't make much sense but used new words we'd learned.

Mama cared about us. I never doubted that for a second when we were younger. She would sing to us and play with us in the backyard. Even after a long day of work, she would read stories that we'd heard hundreds of times. She never hesitated.

Until she did.

"She still is," I correct, though I'm not as confident in saying so. It's hard when I live so far away from her and Grandma now.

"You sure about that?"

"What about you?"

One of his brows lifts.

"What's your dad like?"

"An asshole."

"Must be where you get it from."

He glares. It feels good to get a reaction from him instead of the other way around. Still, the joy doesn't last.

"So?"

"So what?"

"Your dad."

His jaw ticks. "The guy ditched. I'm not sure there's anything to say. Not everything can be clean-cut or rainbows and fucking unicorns."

Is he implying that's what my life is? "I don't think anybody lives with that perception. Not even the people who haven't experienced loss."

He snorts. "Think again, Mouse. People want to believe the world is this beautiful place. Some of us just aren't as stupid."

I know he's only making his point to divert my attention away from his lack of an answer. He doesn't think I'll notice—maybe he doesn't believe I'll push. After all, mice are known for being quiet.

They're also known for being sneaky.

"Maybe you're right," I murmur. "Not all of us are capable of talking about our feelings. My dad is like that. I'm not sure if you've noticed, but he avoids tough topics at all costs. You know, like the one at the restaurant."

Nothing.

I shrug, sighing lightly. "Mama used to tell Logan and

me that men find it hard to express themselves because society told them it wasn't okay to feel. Even before Dad left, I had this preconceived notion that men had it worse than women because they weren't allowed to grieve or cry or do anything women could so freely. When I pictured Dad in that situation, I felt bad for him. Then he left and I wasn't sure what to think, and then Lo died and..." I wet my bottom lip. "And I stopped feeling bad for him and started blaming him instead. Mama never talked about how hard it was for men to express themselves after that, but I could tell she still believed it. Maybe you're upset with your father too, but you're afraid to tell anyone." He doesn't make a single sound, so I turn slightly to him and see his sharp jaw tick. "I know we don't really know each other, but I know how hard it is to feel like you have nobody to express yourself to. If you want, I can be that person for you. You don't have to bottle everything up, Kaiden."

His shoulders go back when I say his name, and he slowly turns his head to meet my eyes. When his dark gaze locks on my face, I pipe down when I see how skeptical his expression is.

Reaching out, he gently tugs my face closer to his, leaning in ever so slightly until I can feel his breath on my cheek. My heart is going into overdrive as he brushes the pad of his thumb over my soft skin, leaving a trail of fire scorching the surface.

Suddenly, his caress stops. The darkness in his tight lips melds into morbid humor as they tug upward at the corners. "That's just the thing, Mouse. I never wanted a sister. Least of all someone as damaged as you."

My lips part as he drops his hand and leans back, eyes

distant like he didn't just insult me. Resting back against the tree trunk, he looks out at the field.

Shaking my head, I stand up. "I don't want a new sibling. That feels like I'm cheating on Logan. All I want is a friend while I'm here, because like it or not, you're stuck with me."

He scoffs in disbelief. "You can run back to your mom anytime you want. From what I hear, you *chose* to leave her. Not the other way around."

He sounds bitter about it. Is that what his problem is? "Not everything is so black and white. My choice to leave wasn't an easy one to make."

"You still left."

My eye twitches. "It was for the best."

"For who?" He finally looks at me, challenge flaring in his eyes. "You spew bullshit about men struggling with grief and their feelings, but what about your mom? You left her behind when she's at her weakest. You have a place to live, someone who needs you, and you fucking left her."

My fists clench at my sides. "I want to go home, Kaiden."

Nothing.

"Kaiden—"

He bolts up and gets in my face, causing me to flinch back. A headache builds, radiating in my skull and making its presence known. "I could leave you here if I wanted. You know that, right? You have no friends. You have nobody to rescue you."

Because you told everyone at school not to associate with me! I want to scream at him.

If there was even one person who would give me the time of day while we're trapped in desks with the smell of dry-erase markers permeating the air, it would make things easier. Even him, the very asshole who cemented my isolation. I would appreciate a simple smile from where others could see.

"Your point?" I whisper.

"I'm sure you had someone before."

Before Exeter.

"I did."

I had Lo.

"Then go back to them."

If only it were that easy...

"I can't."

Hesitation. "Sucks to be you."

At first, I think he's going to leave me. He pulls his keys from his pocket and starts walking back up toward the car parked in the distance without a word.

Then he slows, and without another glance back at me, he says, "Are you coming or not? I don't have all day."

Kaiden can pretend he doesn't care.

That he doesn't want anyone.

But I'll change his mind.

Nobody deserves to be alone.

Eight

I DREAM OF LOGAN. I can't see her, but I can sense her presence and hear her laughter. At one point, I think I can feel her. Like when she'd grab my hand and lead us into the woods.

Then it all changes. My sister is nowhere to be seen, but Mama is. Her eyes are golden as she reaches out to me, but she doesn't call me Emery. She tries holding my hand, but there's nothing to latch on to. It makes her cry harder when she realizes Logan is untouchable.

I wake up with tears streaming down my cheeks. Furiously, I wipe them away and feel the heaviness settle in my chest. Glancing at the clock, I frown and realize I have time before I need to be up for school.

I think about what Kaiden said to me regarding Mama. I know how sad she is over Lo, so I thought leaving was for the best. Seeing me made her worse, and I wanted her to feel better and figure out her life without me burdening it more. Maybe I should have stayed, endured the torture that seeing me brought her, like Grandma suggested.

Then again, Kaiden is no expert. He can't deal with his own problems, so what makes him entitled to judge me and mine? He deflected his own issues with his father on me, and like always, I let him.

I let everybody use me.

I'll always feel bad for seeing Mama cry, but I shouldn't have to carry the weight of burdening her with my absence or I'm damned either way. Plus, Kaiden doesn't know the whole story. He never asked how Logan died and I never offered the information. He doesn't know I'm sick or how Mama reacted when I got the official diagnosis.

Kaiden Monroe can pretend he knows everything about people, but he's the biggest fool of us all. Unlike his blind followers at school, I won't be so easily convinced he's who I want influencing my choices. Too many other things already do, so I need what little control I do have to stay in my own hands.

Slipping out of bed, I stretch my stiff muscles and go to the bay window that I have yet to make into a reading nook. I used to tell Mama that I always wanted one, so I could put pillows and blankets on it and read while enjoying the view. Unfortunately, the view is nothing more than a paved driveway, stone pathway, and a few perfectly trimmed flower bushes between the street and sidewalk. The only time sitting here is worthwhile is when I see Kaiden sneaking in and out.

Sometimes he'll come back looking angry, sometimes looking happier than when he stormed away. Does he go to the tree? Or does he go somewhere else? Does he meet up with Rachel or another girl? He hasn't come back with any more shiners, and the one on his face is nothing more than a faded yellow bruise. Soon it'll be like it never existed.

Pushing off the wall, I crack open my bedroom door. It's quiet since it's not even five in the morning. There's no light except for the tiny one illuminating over the sink in the kitchen. I gravitate toward it, wanting a glass of water to quench my dry throat.

When I turn around, I'm startled by Dad standing in the doorway in a pair of dark pajamas bottoms and a T-shirt. He looks tired but more surprised than anything.

"I thought I heard someone up."

I just nod.

He clears his throat. "Figured it'd be Kaiden, to be honest." Walking over to the cupboard, he grabs a glass and fills it with water just like I did. "Can't sleep?"

It feels weird to be having a conversation with him like the restaurant never happened. I can avoid bringing it up, pretend it doesn't matter, but it does.

"I had a dream about Logan and Mama."

He's quiet for a moment. Then, "Do you want to talk about it?"

It's a painful question, like he's silently begging me to say no. I take pity on him. "It isn't anything I can't handle. I've been doing that for a while—dealing with things on my own."

I feel no guilt when he winces slightly. "I deserve that. We should probably talk about what happened."

I want to ask him when. When I was little? At the restaurant? All of it? Instead, I stay quiet and follow him toward the table.

He pulls out a seat and sits, so I do the same at my usual spot. We're surrounded by silence for a moment, nothing but the soft hum of the refrigerator filling the open space.

"Cam knows" is what he begins with. "I have always been up front about you girls and your mother with her."

How relieving. *Not.* "Did you leave us for her? Or were you too afraid of us falling apart and ruining your reputation?"

I never knew what happened. I'm not sure I want to know now after spending years coming up with my own theories...accepting that it doesn't really matter in the grand scheme of things. Maybe it does, though, because time feeds the bitterness festering under my skin.

He unwraps his fingers from the glass and slowly nods. "I know it seemed like I loved my work more than you girls, but—"

"Don't lie," I say, cutting him off. "I deserve answers after all these years, don't you agree? I don't want you to bullshit me like you did Mama."

"Emery," he warns firmly. "If there is one person who I've always been honest with, it's your mother."

I'm silent, unsure of what to say in return. She never told me that Dad lied, but she never told me why he left. He was just gone one morning and never returned. Lo and I thought of plenty of reasons why he went away, but Mama never confirmed or denied any of them.

"Why?" I whisper.

"We fell out of love."

No response.

He leans forward, resting his elbows on the edge of the table. Mama used to scold all of us for doing that when we lived together. "I know it's hard to understand, but people don't always stay in love like in the books you read. The fairy-tale ending is just fiction. It's not real life. Your mother and I weren't good together, and we didn't want to subject you girls to it."

Life isn't a fairy tale? I scoff. "Do you think I'm a total idiot or just naive?"

His lips part.

Crossing my arms on my chest, I glare at him. "Don't you think I know what life is really like? I had to watch my twin sister die, Dad. I watched her deteriorate right in front of me. I had to see Mama break down and never fully recover, and then I had to go to a funeral and accept that my own dad wasn't going to be there when I needed him." He tries to answer, but I hold up my hand. "If you fell out of love with Mama, then fine. But somewhere along the way, you fell out of love with your surviving daughter, and I won't ever understand that no matter how you spin it. *I'm* still alive, Dad."

His body tenses as his gaze goes to the table. Like Mama, he can't look at me. I realize in that moment that Kaiden is the only one who's looked at me since leaving Bakersfield. *Really* looked at me. He doesn't see Logan, Mama, or my past. He sees me in all my flawed frailty.

"Does Kaiden know?"

It's a loaded question. Obviously Kaiden knows Lo died. I'm pretty sure there isn't anyone who was at the Cantina that night that doesn't. There's always more to a story though, and I wonder how much Kaiden's invested.

"No," Dad says quietly, "he doesn't."

"About anything?"

He shakes his head.

Kaiden doesn't know I'm sick. I don't take him for an idiot, so he won't be in the dark for long. I've already had one flare, and there are always more to come. Worse ones. Tolerable ones. As long as the new medication cocktail I'm on keeps working, hopefully he won't catch on until later.

Much later.

Despite being hyperaware of Lo's symptoms, no two cases are identical. Not even for twins. Her demise may not be mine, but the endless possibilities of fatality with lupus keep me on edge.

Kaiden probably wouldn't care anyway. After all, he said he never wanted a sibling.

"Lo and I would pretend you were on an extended business trip for work," I admit with no emotion lingering in my tone. He finally looks up at me, his eyes pained and distant. "I would think about all the cool things you were doing on your trip and act like you'd bring us back presents. Lo would sometimes say that you were probably on one of those cruises where they take you to the Bahamas. She always wanted to go on one, you know. When she got sick..."

I force myself to breathe past the sudden nausea taking over me. It's not the typical kind my system is graced with when the pain becomes intense but a bone-deep nausea of acknowledgment when it sinks in that Lo is nowhere on this planet as a breathing entity.

When she got sicker, she would tell me that everything would be okay. She promised Dad would come home and Mama would stop obsessing and we'd be a happy family again. No matter what the circumstance, she remained optimistic.

Then she got worse.

Dad never came home.

Mama became manic.

The night before Lo passed away in her sleep, I held her hand as we curled up in her little bed. She told me I should pretend she was going away for an extended vacation.

I'm finally going to the tropics, Em.

That was when I knew what she'd known all along. Dad wasn't coming home, Mama probably wouldn't be all right, and she wasn't going to make it through the night.

I wonder if Lo is finally able to enjoy the sun without it hurting her skin.

"Emery..."

Maybe for the first time since arriving, I see how much Dad has truly aged. His eyes are wrinkled at the corners and his forehead is creased with lines I don't remember from before. He's not even fifty yet, but he looks older.

I push up from the chair. "When Logan got sick, she was so strong. She's always going to be the strongest person I know. Unlike you, who's always been a coward. We had to pretend you were coming back to make sense of what you and Mama couldn't explain to us. And what makes it worse is that you couldn't just own up to your own mistakes long enough to say a final goodbye to your *dead daughter.*"

"Emery—"

I walk away from the table. "Did you enjoy it, Dad?"

A pause. "Enjoy what?"

"The trip."

Nothing.

My teeth grind. "I bet Lo is loving hers."

I can see the words hit the target as his throat bobs with who knows what emotion.

Bull's-eye.

At least I know he's willing to feel.

I pass Kaiden in the hall, who's still dressed in yesterday's clothes, which means he probably just got in. He stares at me with arched brows, and I wonder how much he heard.

We don't say a word to each other as I pass him, but my shoulder smacks into his without any pain radiating from the petty contact. I'm angry at a lot of things—Logan leaving me, Mama checking out, Dad's idiocy. Kaiden sees me but doesn't *see* me. At least that's what he pretends.

When I wake up the next morning, there's a torn piece of notebook paper on my door with Dad's messy handwriting on it.

Sorry, Emery.

I don't want Dad's apology.

I don't know what I want from him.

Nine

I've only cried once since my diagnosis. It wasn't when the doctor told me my immune system was compromised or when I saw Mama break down. It wasn't when I decided to leave and had Grandma try convincing me to stay, or even when I called Dad and asked to move in with him.

It was when I couldn't wrap my fingers around the doorknob to leave for school. My arms ached, my legs ached, my heart ached, and my swollen fingers wouldn't straighten as I backed away from the door in defeat. I remember staring at the white wood until it blurred in front of me, then dropped onto the couch and realized I couldn't do such a simple task.

My body failed me in such a mundane way, I knew everything was about to change.

Grandma came into the room and saw my tear-filled eyes, and when she asked if I was okay, I broke. I soaked the knit pillow she made until she pulled me in her arms so I could soak her shirt instead. I cried and she held me and told me it was okay, then she called the school and said I wouldn't be in.

That was the start of the end.

The swelling in my fingers shifted upward to my arms, and I was bedridden for three days with Mama or Grandma bringing food to me or helping me in and out of the bathroom. I felt like nothing—incompetent and useless.

I cried a lot during that period, wondering if Lo ever felt so helpless. She never cried. Mama would dote on her the best she could, but Logan hated it. She would tell Mama she was fine, and we always believed her.

Because she could still climb trees.

Because she could run around the yard.

Because she could open doors.

Lo was always the stronger one of us.

No matter how bad I want to cry now, I won't. The stress of Dad not understanding how much his words hurt or how little he seems to care about my disease can't deter me from being strong. Lo would tell me to smile and then force me to do something fun to distract myself from Mama or anything that upset me.

Now's no different.

I busy myself with school, homework, and books. A few times a week, I even leave and explore the different stores within walking distance. Most of them are café corporations instead of the homey, retro kind that I'm used to going to with Mama and Grandma. It took me walking into Starbucks once to realize I prefer the isolation of rural nowhere.

Sometimes I miss Mama, but the old version of her. The one who loved smiling with her non-golden eyes. She was the person I looked up to, but I can't find myself doing the same now. Not because I don't love her but because I can't hate her like I wish I did. It would make the guilt go away faster.

Being here makes it easier to forget about how she reacted. Dad acts like he doesn't care, Kaiden doesn't know, and Cam plays dumb. At first, I hated them for pretending everything is okay when I know it isn't. The more I think about it, the more I realize it's a blessing in disguise. I don't have to be that girl—the sick one.

I can be Emery.

Book nerd.

Teacher's pet.

Weird shoe lover.

Realistically, though, I know it can't last.

It didn't for Logan.

Rachel joins me for lunch on Thursday. We spend most of the time not saying anything, just eating while people stare. Since Kaiden's show of dominance, nobody dares even sit at the same table as me. Much to Rachel's dismay, Kaiden pays us no attention from where he sits with his teammates, which I'm sure is why she disobeyed his wishes to leave me alone.

I want to ask her about herself, pretend to care. For some reason, I can't muster the energy to. Usually, I can put on an act. Smile and play nice like Mama taught me. I don't have to be that person here, so I don't waste my time.

Rachel doesn't seem to mind.

She rambles on about some fight between a few basketball

players. I think it had to do with one of them getting caught with pot in their locker, which ended in a game suspension, but I don't know. I only half listen because I don't want anyone to think I'm feeding into her game.

She can use me to make Kaiden jealous, but it won't work. At school, he and I have nothing to do with each other. At home, we only exchange a few small conversations here and there. There's nothing she can gain from hanging around me.

After lunch, Kaiden falls into step with me as I head to my next class. People catch notice and watch us, making me uncomfortable.

"Have a good time with Rach?"

"Jealous?"

He laughs. "Definitely not."

Figured.

I stop at my locker. "She has it in her mind that getting close to me will somehow cement your relationship."

He leans his shoulder against the neighboring locker. It makes the black T-shirt he's wearing stretch across his taut muscles that some girls ogle in passing. "We're not in a relationship. Never have been."

Grabbing my afternoon books, I turn to him with a raised brow. "You might want to let her know that."

"She knows."

I say nothing.

Pushing himself off the locker, he shoves his hands in his pockets. "Things at home have been weird. We should go to the cemetery after school."

Weird how? We go home and go our separate ways. Sometimes he'll comment on English class or complain about the homework. Occasionally he'll show up at my bedroom door and ask if I want to go to the tree. Nothing seems out of the ordinary or strange, save our parents' façade of normalcy.

I'm used to parents acting though. My parents could win an Oscar for most believable roles in the movie called life.

"I can't."

He waits for me to explain why.

I sigh. "I've got book club."

"Skip it."

"Why?"

"Let's be honest," he says. "The only reason people go to that is because of Nichols."

Refraining from rolling my eyes, I shake my head in disagreement. "Some of us like to read, Kaiden."

He knows my love for books because on the rare occasions he's in a teasing mood, he'll mention the book stack next to my bed. And if Dad can take notice of the so-called fairy tales I escape into, there's no doubt Kaiden acknowledges I'm in book club because it's my only happy place.

It's my freedom here.

When his lips tip into a crooked, devious grin, I know something bad is about to happen. "I know for a fact that isn't true. I've seen the girls in that group, Mouse. Let me tell you a little secret—a reminder of an old conversation we've had. You can't fuck Mr. Nichols."

A few giggles sound from around us, followed by a deep clearing throat. When I look off to the side, I see Mr. Nichols looking uncomfortable and shifting his weight from one foot to the other by the water fountain across the hall.

Kaiden winks at me before strolling away to wherever Satan likes to hang out. Probably the boiler room downstairs.

Not able to meet Mr. Nichols's eyes when he calls my name, I quickly walk to my next class and try thinking about how I can get out of English. I could pretend I'm sick. It shouldn't be hard to pull off.

Then again, the chance of me needing actual sick days means I need to reserve my absences.

Maybe I should have built a friendship with Ms. Gilly in the nurse's office. She could have given me free passes out of pity. Too late now.

Silently cursing Kaiden's name, I force myself to pretend it never happened. In two periods, I'll go to English and just play it off.

But when last period comes around, sweat dots my brow. Keeping my head down as I walk into the room, I can feel a pair of eyes on me that I know belong to the teacher. I don't look up. Instead, I focus on preparing for class.

Notebook.

Pen.

Book.

He doesn't call on me throughout the class, and I don't offer any answers. It isn't unusual for me to stay quiet but never silent. Anyone could chalk it up to not having anything to say. Maybe they think I didn't do the reading.

Kaiden smirks when he catches my eye.

I glare.

After class, Mr. Nichols does what I should have known he would. He asks me to stay behind. What does surprise me is him asking Kaiden the same thing.

We remain in our seats, Kaiden looking bored and me looking nervous. Mr. Nichols waits until the hallway is cleared enough before turning his attention on us.

"I don't like when students say things that could cause problems for me," he says directly to Kaiden. I've never heard him sound stern before, but it seems like the perfect moment to be. "I am aware that my age puts me in a difficult spot with teenagers, but that doesn't mean anybody should speak to their teachers, or peers for that matter, in the way you did earlier to Emery."

Kaiden doesn't look the least bit guilty over being scolded. In fact, he smirks like he couldn't care less. Me on the other hand? I gape. I've never heard a teacher talk to Kaiden like that, and I'm sure plenty have witnessed how he treats the other students. I assumed it had to do with his spot on the lacrosse team, because every school seems to give free passes to the boys who fill the trophy cases. And I've seen the trophies sitting behind the thick glass in the halls. Kaiden's name is on a lot of them.

Mr. Nichols leans back in his seat. "I want you to apologize to Emery."

Kaiden laughs abruptly. "I don't apologize to anyone."

"Now's a good time to start, then."

I squirm. "Um, Mr. Nichols, I don't—"

Mr. Nichols puts his hand up. "Let me put it to you this way, Mr. Monroe. I was warned about you on my first day. While other teachers may be hesitant to say anything because of whatever circumstance, I'm not. I want to see my students treat each other with respect. Given your situation with Ms. Matterson, one would think you'd want to treat her with more respect than anybody here."

Sinking into my chair, I let my hair shield my face. The headache I was glad to be rid of is coming back, taunting me. It's the slightest drum of pain, a dull pound of a bass beat where my spine meets my skull. Stress-induced, for sure.

Part of me wants to cut in and tell them to forget about it. I don't need this right now. I don't think either would listen. Mr. Nichols seems intent on making a point, and Kaiden seems intent on ignoring it.

"Emery doesn't mean anything to me just because we live under the same roof," Kaiden states dryly, sparing me no look.

His words sting. I wish they didn't, because it isn't a surprise to me. He's shown me indifference ninety percent of the time. It isn't like he's put in an effort that proves otherwise.

Except the sycamore.

Except the eggs.

Mr. Nichols reaches for something. "I suppose you'll have time to consider how you treat people in detention tomorrow after school. If you miss that, you'll go to in-school suspension on Monday."

My lips part in shock.

Kaiden's jaw ticks. "Fine."

Mr. Nichols jots something down on a pad of paper before ripping a piece off and setting it on the edge of the desk. "You may be excused, Mr. Monroe."

Kaiden gets up and grabs the paper before heading out of the room. I toy with my notebook before finally meeting Mr. Nichols's eyes.

"Like I said, Emery, you and I are similar. However, as I get older, I realize how important it is to stand up for myself. You can't let people walk over you like that."

How sad. My only true friend at Exeter High is my English teacher.

The headache starts to worsen, burning my eyes, and I don't have any Motrin in my backpack.

"I'm not feeling well," I tell him quietly. Standing up, I slip my belongings in my backpack before sliding the strap over my shoulder. "I think I'm going home."

"Emery—"

"Thank you, Mr. Nichols."

Noticing Kaiden's car missing in the lot, I start the walk home. By the time I make it to the front door, everything hurts.

At least I can turn the knob this time.

Ten

On Saturday morning, I wake up to see a missed call from Mama. It jump-starts my heart until I realize there's no voicemail. She called at three in the morning.

She found Lo at three in the morning.

Today marks the official ten-year anniversary of Logan's death. When realization hits, my heart plummets into the pit of my stomach like it's made of cement. Mama reached out to me because of Lo.

And I didn't pick up.

Why didn't I hear it ring?

It's on silent.

Feeling tears build in my eyes, I blink them away and rub the back of my wrists against my closed eyelids. I won't cry. Mama could have left a message and told me to call her back. She could have texted me saying she loved me or that she missed Logan.

She never once told me she missed her with words.

Throwing the blankets off my overheated body, I head to the bathroom and splash cold water on my face. My eyes are puffy and bloodshot, and my lips are chapped and bleeding. The girl in the glass looks pathetic, and I'm sick of looking at her.

Sometimes I wish I could break the glass—put my fist right through it without risking cuts and infections. Maybe I'll tack a sheet over it so I don't have to see the reminder of who I'm forced to be.

Jaw ticking, I turn away from the mirror and grab my hairbrush from where it sits on the counter. When I run it through my brittle hair, I don't expect to see the mass of strands fall onto the countertop in front of me.

My hairbrush stills.

My hands shake.

My breath stops.

Slowly, I reach out and pick up the large chunk. Blowing out a rough breath, I force my gaze upward to see a section of hair that's thinner than ever.

When I turn my head, I see my scalp. Burning-hot tears well in my eyes as I stare. "Oh my God."

The brush drops onto the floor with a loud crash, the plastic clattering against the hard floor. I don't care. Instead, I focus on my head and how thin my hair has gotten. I've noticed more and more meet my shower drain, but usually I ignore it. Women lose around fifty to one hundred strands per day. I looked it up.

I've had to unclog my drain once a week, to clean off my pillow with the countless strands that greet me in an unwelcome way every morning. I tell myself it's no big deal.

It's just hair. But hair is everything. It's a way to express myself, to hide, to feel pretty. Without it, who am I?

Stepping away, I drop the hair onto the counter and carefully play with what remains on my head. My scalp hurts today. Usually, it's a dull pain that I can tolerate as long as I don't play too much with it. Today is different, like I've slept with my hair in a tight ponytail all night. Eyes watering all over again, I try hiding the bald spot, but nothing I do seems to work.

Cam calls my name from outside my bedroom. Did I lock my door? I never do. Will she come in? She never has.

The knob turns.

"Emery?" Cam says again.

Do I pretend I'm not here? I swallow my pain and brush away my tears and take a deep breath. "B-bathroom."

I'm not sure why I say it. Maybe if I said nothing, she would have walked out. Part of me needs her though.

Needs a maternal figure.

Because mine didn't leave a message on the anniversary of my sister's death.

Cam's knuckles rap against the open door before she peeks her head in. Her eyes note the hairbrush on the floor, which she bends down and picks up before seeing the hair on the counter.

"Emery?" Her voice is quiet.

I meet her gaze with tear-filled eyes.

"Oh, sweetie." She reaches out and takes my hand, brushing her thumb against my skin. I don't pull away or wince, because I need her warmth and comfort right now.

"I don't know how to fix it..." My voice cracks when I turn and show her what I mean. She gently brushes hair over the spot before realizing what I've already concluded.

She gives me a soft smile. "How about you and I go to my favorite salon? The girls there can try giving us advice on how to cover it. Maybe you could do a new style."

Us, not me.

Cam wants to do this together.

It causes a tear to slip through the blockade I try trapping it behind. She wipes it away with her thumb and pulls me in for a gentle hug, rubbing my back in circular motions.

When I was little, Mama used to run her fingers through my hair. It soothed me anytime I had a fever or cold and needed her touch. My body would ease into hers as she sang to me. She wouldn't stop playing with my hair until I fell asleep, and she wouldn't move an inch even when I was sure her arms had gone numb.

I want *that* Mama back.

I want someone to play with my hair without it hurting or falling out.

But for now, I've got Cam.

At least I have that.

"Okay," I whisper, sniffing back tears and pulling away.

She squeezes my upper arm. "I know things have been tough for you, especially since moving here, but I want you to know that I'll be there for you in any way I can. There are reasons your father hasn't told Kaiden about his past, and it's not because he's ashamed."

"Then why?"

"How about we talk about it later?"

Her eyes go to the door, as if she's afraid of who might hear. So I nod and silently hold her to it. I know better than to pry into people's pasts, but if she's offering answers that Kaiden won't, I won't turn down the information.

She lets me finish getting ready while she makes a call to the salon. I slide into a pair of boot-cut jeans and a plain white tee, then shrug on a yellow zip-up hoodie and slide into my favorite pair of pineapple Toms. I used to get teased at my old school for my weird style. Whereas most people preferred tighter, shorter outfits, I liked baggier ones. When your skin is so sensitive and it's practically paper thin, any piece of clothing that hugs it feels like sandpaper in comparison. Nobody understands that a single touch can hurt, that cashmere is brutal, or that my so-called weird style is more necessity than personal choice. My shoes were always out of the ordinary but the only things I can really choose for myself for their style, and I owned way more yellow than most other humans, but it always reminds me of sunshine and Logan and how happy she was.

Heading out to the kitchen, I'm surprised when I see Kaiden and Dad eating breakfast.

"The girls can see you in an hour," Cam tells me happily. "I think we should make a day of it. We can get breakfast on the way if you'd like, and maybe do some shopping at the mall afterward. It'll be fun."

I haven't had a girls' day in a long time. Grandma took me with her shortly before I moved to pick out some new clothes, but I only left with a new pair of shoes and some books. It was more about spending time with her than getting anything, and I know she didn't have a lot of money to spare since starting to help Mama pay the bills.

I smile and tell Cam I'd like that. It's not a lie either. Knowing that Dad talked to Cam about his past, about us, makes me like her a little more than after the blowout. She's done nothing but show me kindness, so there's no reason not to like her.

Kaiden eyes me and then his mom, his lips twitching like he wants to say something. To my surprise, he doesn't. Instead, he stuffs more food into his mouth and ignores me completely. I don't miss the way his jaw ticks like he's pissed.

We leave shortly after. Dad gives me money for the mall

that I have no intention of spending. I never like taking handouts, especially from him. It already feels like I'm doing that daily by living in his home. Taking his money for anything I want seems like pushing things too far.

After we grab some breakfast from the McDonald's drive-through, I turn to Cam and pick at my hash brown. "What did you mean earlier when you said Dad didn't tell Kaiden about the past for a specific reason?"

Cam lets out a soft sigh. "Kaiden is a tough boy to understand because he puts up walls to protect himself. He gets that from his father, I suppose."

I'm quiet as I wait for her to continue.

Her grip on the wheel tightens. "My ex-husband's name was Adam. He was the type of man who bottled everything inside until it destroyed him. No matter how much I tried helping him or understanding what he was going through, he wouldn't let me. Adam had multiple health conditions. He struggled with pain and depression, which made him irritable. Inevitably, that's what broke us up. He hated people helping him like he was..."

"Useless?"

She glances at me. "Yes. In his mind, he wasn't the picture-perfect man. He struggled keeping up with work because of his chronic pain, he had brain fog that made remembering things difficult, and during depressive episodes, he'd lash out. He got fired from multiple jobs, which left us financially disadvantaged. We had to file for bankruptcy when he couldn't find new work because my job could only pay so much.

"Through all this, he put being a husband and father behind everything else. He stewed in his misery. He neglected Kaiden no matter how hard Kaiden tried getting his attention, and it was heartbreaking to watch. Eventually, Adam became emotionally and at times physically abusive because he couldn't deal with how things had turned out. He'd always prided himself on being the breadwinner, on being strong. His illness took that away from him until he lost everything he thought he should be.

"Kaiden had trouble understanding why his father did the things he did," she explains, slowing for a stoplight. "He was young when his father started turning into a different man. He always looked up to Adam, and it was heartbreaking to see the way Adam would treat him as though he couldn't stand the attention Kaiden gave him. When I filed for divorce, Adam didn't fight me on it. He didn't even want Kaiden around, even though Kaiden begged to stay with his dad when I started packing our things. I couldn't let him do that. Adam wasn't taking care of himself. He refused to see a doctor or seek any type of treatment for his pain. No matter how much research I did, he wouldn't accept that he could get better.

"About three months after I moved into a new place with Kaiden, I got a call from a local hospital that Adam had gotten into an accident. I was still his emergency contact, so I had my mother watch Kaiden so I could drive to see him. The doctor said they found a tumor that was putting pressure on his brain stem. It was causing an array of symptoms, mostly neurological but also misfiring the pain receptors throughout his body. His original fibromyalgia diagnosis wasn't technically wrong. It just wasn't the reason he was truly sick. By the time they found it, it was inoperable. The only solace we got was a final explanation over why the man I fell in love with changed so drastically. He couldn't control how he felt because his brain wasn't working the way it needed to. He refused to see Kaiden because he didn't want Kaiden seeing him like that. Withering away in a hospital room.

"Sometimes, I wish I had brought Kaiden anyway. I know he's angry with me for keeping him from his father. He knew he was sick, but he never..." She lets out a shaky breath. "I never told him about the tumor. I should have, but he was still young, and I didn't think he'd understand. But the boy I raised who loved life and looked up to his father became so much like his dad before Adam's death. I worry that I messed up having a relationship with him all because I kept the truth from him. Now he won't look at me. He'll barely speak to me..."

My chest aches for Cam. She fights off a frown but loses the battle. Her lips weigh downward as she watches the road.

"You could always tell him now," I say.

She nods slowly. "I could. I *want* to. Adam was always the type of man who worried about his appearance. Not just physically but people's perception of him. He didn't want anyone to know how sick he was, especially Kaiden."

I cringe, knowing what I said to Dad at the restaurant must have hurt Cam in ways I never intended.

"Even after all these years without Adam, I feel like telling Kaiden will break the promise I made to him. I want Kaiden to remember his father in a good way, but I just don't want to lose him. When I told your father about this, he felt like telling Kaiden about your illness, about your sister's, may bring up too many memories."

My lips twitch. "Don't you think he'll figure it out eventually? I'm not going to get better, Cam. I may be out of the house by the time things progress, but there's still a lot that doctors don't know about lupus. I'm not guaranteed to be this functional months from now."

She presses her lips together and stays quiet, absorbing the truth in my words. "You're right. Your father is just protective of me. He knows how much I want Kaiden to heal from what happened."

"Does..." I hesitate. "Kaiden knows that his father is dead, right?"

She turns to me in surprise. "Of course. Why do you ask?"

I shake my head, not wanting her to know that Kaiden acts like his dad lives somewhere else. The way he talked about him made it seem like he up and left them to be with another family or something. Maybe it's his way of coping, but it won't get him anywhere.

"He'll be angrier if he finds out we've kept it from him," I say instead. "The thing about chronic illness is that you never know what you're going to feel like when you wake up every day. It's a new battle, because the good days don't mean that you don't hurt. They just mean that you can tolerate the pain better. I could wake up tomorrow and struggle to get out of bed. I could miss more days of school. He's not stupid, Cam."

"I know he's not."

"You need to tell him, then."

She pauses. "I know."

I wet my lips. "Cam?"

"Hmm?"

"I'm sorry about Adam."

She reaches out and squeezes my hand.

Eleven

I ASK CAM HOW she dealt with Adam's death. She told me it was about realizing he was at peace now. It's how I accept Lo's death too, so I nod along in genuine understanding.

"We never truly get over losses," Cam tells me, walking us to the salon's glass entrance. The windows stretch from floor to ceiling, with two wide doors centered in the middle that have white print on them with store hours. "We just absorb them until they mold us into someone new. Like any creation, it takes time."

"What does?"

"Creating a masterpiece." She holds the door open for me. "It isn't the same for parents who lose their children. You have to understand, Emery. We're not supposed to outlive you. If I ever lost Kaiden…"

"Even though he doesn't talk to you?" I wince at the blunt statement, but Cam doesn't seem to mind.

She gives me a small smile and nods as she walks me into the overly white reception area. It smells like expensive shampoo, and the music playing softly in the background is on a pop station. Everything is white, black, and silver—modern and sleek. It's not like any place Mama ever took Lo or me to get our haircuts.

"Especially then," she whispers, writing my name on the sign-in sheet.

"Why?"

She turns to me. "Kaiden is my son. He's still here, even if Adam isn't. That means I have time. Hope. I'll never stop loving him even if he finds a way to stop loving me. The truth is, we never stop loving our children even if we lose them. I know things with your mother are difficult now, but she needs time."

"To mend?"

A single nod.

What if Mama doesn't become a masterpiece? There are pieces of art far less desired that take just as much time to create. If she becomes a canvas wasting away to dust...

A woman with platinum-blond hair walks over with a big smile on her face. She's probably around Cam's age but looks closer to mine with flawless skin and shining eyes and perfect teeth. I never used to envy people as much as I do now, simply for looking healthy.

She hugs Cam and turns to me. "You must be Emery."

"Em," I murmur.

"Ready?"

For some reason, I look to Cam for guidance. It's something I used to do with Mama when I was unsure. Like when I was little and the doctor asked me simple questions that I couldn't find the words for.

I've had no choice but to be better at communicating with them these days.

When Cam nods in encouragement, my throat thickens. Mama did the same thing. Maybe it's maternal, like a switch that's flipped after having a baby. Maybe Cam's just a good person.

What would I be like as a mom?

Suddenly, I'm angry at Kaiden for being such a hypocrite. He can pretend like I'm horrible for leaving Mama, but he's doing the same thing. Just because he lives under the same roof as her doesn't mean he's emotionally here. If anything, he's worse than me.

Mama shut down because she struggled with Lo's death and my diagnosis. Cam is the opposite—she wants to embrace him, and he pushes her away.

Everyone grieves differently, Grandma would tell me.

I don't think Kaiden is grieving though.

Pushing the thought away, I let the hairstylist, Jess, guide me to the sinks. I used to love getting my hair done—feeling the stylist massage the shampoo into my scalp. It relaxed me. Sometimes it even put me to sleep. Now all I can feel are the pinpricks of pain radiating across my skull as gentle fingers work my frail strands. It's why I don't get my hair cut often, because the small gasps as chunks come out into the sink despite me telling them it could happen never stop my face from heating.

But Jess just reassures me. She doesn't make a sound, even when I'm sure the drain is becoming well acquainted with my hair. She hums along to a song and then asks me how school is.

What year are you?

What's your favorite subject?

What are your future plans?

Senior.

English.

Not to die.

I don't tell her the last one. Instead, I say that I haven't decided yet and get the generic *you have time* response. But do I?

There are lots of quotes about time.

Time is fleeting.

Time is valuable.

Time shouldn't be wasted.

The trouble with time is that we only think we have it. It's an illusion—an excuse to linger in existence. Some people use it to be reckless; others use it to hold themselves back.

The kids stamping *YOLO* on their foreheads have no idea what they're bartering with when they tempt death. They think they're invincible. And me? I have to watch healthy people with thousands of chances live like they're not afraid of death at all.

Time is a luxury we can't all afford.

Twelve

THE TIPS OF MY blond hair kiss the tops of my shoulders. I'm not used to the style—side bangs and choppy layers—but it's cute. Different. It also manages to hide my thinner sections without much hassle.

Looking in the mirror now, I see Mama. I see her round green eyes and her tiny nose and how her top lip is a little thinner than her bottom. I was always told I looked like a perfect mixture of both my parents, but in the moment, I don't see Dad at all.

Carefully, I run my fingers through my hair. To my surprise, barely any falls out. Jess told me everything she used, including some special shampoo for people with brittle hair. Cam insists on buying some before we leave, and I feel bad knowing it costs a pretty penny.

She says she doesn't mind.

She says she wants to help.

It's been a long time since anyone has really wanted to help me.

Following her out the door, we enter her vehicle in silence. The wind catching the back of my neck is foreign and makes goose bumps appear on my arms, but I don't mind it. It's warm today, so the breeze feels nice even if it's a reminder of the necessary new style.

Cam looks at me and smiles. "You look beautiful, Em."

Em. Not Emery. My heart warms to this woman even more. The woman who's not my mother but the very one who's given me more chances than my own back in Bakersfield. I want to feel guilty for liking her, for even considering her better, but I can't. I see why Dad loves her so much.

We spend two hours at the mall going through each store. I want to tell her after an hour that I need to sit down, my hips hurt, and I feel my knees start to buckle. They nearly do when we get to the Shoe Depot. I sit down on a black leather cushion right as my legs give out, weakness settling into the joints in brutal bluntness, but Cam is too busy looking at the wall of purses to notice.

I smile faintly when she glances over at me and tell her the purple one she's looking at is my favorite. It's not. It's the yellow one to the right with the gold chain and zipper.

Thankfully, she doesn't mind me sitting while she looks around. It gives me time to relax and glance around the shoe displays. They have a section for Toms right in front of me, but I know I don't need any more.

Still…

"Those are cute," Cam says from behind me. I startle and pull away from the black-and-white-checkered pair.

Lo would have loved them. It reminds me of the matching dresses Mama bought us for kindergarten. The teachers couldn't tell us apart despite the bow in my hair being yellow and hers being pink. After that, we weren't allowed to be in the same class.

Sitting back, I say, "They are."

"Aren't you going to try them on?"

Wetting my bottom lip, I shake my head and clear my throat. "No, I have plenty of shoes. I'm actually pretty tired. Do you think we could go home?"

I could use at least an hour nap, which will probably lead to sleeping away the rest of my Saturday. My body tires on days I'm always on my feet. Tomorrow I'll probably be worse, which means I need to double my normal medication to make sure I can move. I also know that means risking being twice as tired since one of my meds knocked me out during the first week and a half of being on it. Doubling it, though recommended by my doctor, could mean sleeping for thirteen hours straight and still waking up groggy.

Goodbye, weekend.

Internally sighing, I stand up.

After paying and leaving the store, my eye catches a yellow beaded bracelet from a small kiosk by the mall entrance. There are scarves, hats, and sunglasses all hanging colorfully from the sides. It's not those I focus on but the bracelet in all its simplicity.

Walking over, I examine the little sunflower charms mixed into the plain beads. My fingertip runs over the words.

You are my sunshine.

Trying to swallow past the swell of emotion in my throat, I blink back sudden tears and shake my head. I never believed in signs until Lo passed away, and now they're everywhere—in the sunshine, my music playlist, and in the sky after a rainstorm.

Cam notices what I'm looking at and gently rubs my back. "How much?" she asks the older woman manning the booth.

"Five dollars."

Cam pulls out her wallet and I don't stop her. I used some of the money Dad gave me on new sweaters and a movie I've wanted to see because Cam kept insisting I treat myself.

I take the bracelet from its hook and grasp it in my palm like I'm afraid it'll disappear. I've broken beaded bracelets like this so easily in the past. I don't want to harm it.

Cam helps me put it on, clicking the clasp in place and smiling at me. "It's perfect."

Yeah, I want to say. *Perfect*.

Dad asks if I had fun. Cam insists I show him my purchases, and he tries to act interested as I hold everything up. I can tell he isn't, even though he nods along.

When Cam points to my bracelet, his lips flatten just long enough for me to notice. I don't need to tell him the importance. He must know it was Mama's song for Lo and me.

Kaiden comes into the kitchen with an empty glass and notices what Dad is looking at. His eyes train on the little letters, his body language stilling in the middle of the room before he goes about his business. From the corner of my eye, I see his lips twitch before going neutral again.

I want to be angry with him, especially when he glances at Cam without a word. Part of me wants to yell, to throw something at him. He needs to stop being an ass and accept that his father is gone and not coming back and that his mother is here and living and willing to love him unconditionally. Doesn't he get that unconditional love is hard to come by?

Instead, I watch him walk out of the room with a single head nod toward Cam. That's all she gets. A nod.

My teeth grind.

"I'll go put these in the washer," she tells me, collecting my clothes. I want to stop her and say I'll worry about it later. Dad just shakes his head at me like he knows what I'm thinking.

Cam needs space.

Cam leaves.

Dad tips his chin toward my bracelet. "I like it. It's… fitting."

I want to ask him how. Would he answer if I did? He could just be making polite conversation. It's foreign for us, but he's trying. At least he's doing what Kaiden can't.

I swallow. "I love it."

I love her.

"I know you do," he whispers.

I shift on my feet.

"Your hair looks good." His compliment surprises me. "It makes you look older."

Does he think I look like Mama too?

"Thank you."

My voice is quiet as I toy with my shirtsleeve, unsure of what to say. We haven't talked, *really* talked, at all. We would exchange tiny conversations and basic pleasantries like I'm his coworker rather than his daughter.

I never minded it.

Maybe I should.

"Do you do stuff with Kaiden?"

His brows arch wide on his forehead.

Clearing my throat, I rub my wrist. "I think it might be good for him. Cam and I had fun and it didn't take much. Maybe you and he…"

I have no suggestions. I don't know what Dad likes or what Kaiden does. In fact, I'm sure they share no common interests. But maybe what Kaiden needs is somebody to fill a void. Dad is by no means a model of the perfect father figure, but he could be.

He could…change.

Maybe.

"I haven't considered it."

"Why?"

He's at a loss for words.

Not surprising.

"I think he needs…" *Someone.* I blow out a tiny breath and shrug. "Never mind. I'm not sure what he needs."

Dad sits back and looks like he's considering what I'm saying. "You two could be good for each other. I know he's not your sister…" My heart stops. "…but he's the same age. I'm sure you share more common interests than he and I do."

Is he suggesting *I* hang out with him? I'm not sure he understands where I'm coming from. Either that, or he doesn't want to play the father figure to anyone.

Jaw ticking with irritation, I avoid eye contact. "Everyone needs a parent to be in their corner. I'm not saying Cam isn't, but maybe he'll be more apt if someone else is until he gets over whatever it is he's—"

A door slamming startles me from finishing.

Kaiden.

My shoulders tense. "Forget about it."

He stands when I begin turning. "I'm not dismissing what you're saying, Emery. I just think it's important to know that you two get along. You're not actually siblings, but you both could find comfort from the past."

The past.

In order for Kaiden to seek comfort, he has to accept he lost someone. I know Lo is dead and not coming back, no matter what I need to tell myself to cement that she's better off than she was. Kaiden isn't that strong. He's latching on to a *could have been* situation that doesn't even exist.

He's delusional.

"He gave up his room, you know."

His words stop me again from storming away. I want to go to my room, change into my pajamas, and go to sleep.

"What do you mean?" I ask instead.

Dad walks over to me. "When Cam and I told him you were moving here, he moved into the spare bedroom. It's smaller than the one you have and doesn't come with its own bathroom."

My lips part in shock. The room's colors are mild enough to fit Kaiden. All dark tones. I've seen his bedroom before to know he's got all black bedding and sheets, posters of people I don't know on his walls, and dark furniture. I wouldn't have guessed my room ever housed him, much less that he'd be willing to give it up for someone he dislikes so much.

"Kaiden is troubled," he tells me when I make no move to answer. "But there is far more to him than any of us gives him credit for. We try giving him space, thinking it'll help, but I know we might be giving him too much. I don't think he'd accept me trying to build a bond with him at this point. But you..."

He gave up his room for me?

"I can't offer him anything."

"That isn't true." His tone is firm, confident in the statement I'm sure is false. "If there is anyone in this world who can break past his shell, it's you. You're strong, Em. Stronger than me and your mother combined."

I don't say anything.

I go to my room.

Or...not my room.

Kaiden's room.

But before I can enter, I'm pulled back and pushed against the wall. I'm too startled to make a noise and freeze in the grip Kaiden has on my upper arm. My elbow aches despite his palm barely squeezing me, but my joints are tender, and he isn't exactly being gentle.

"You don't know shit about me," he hisses so low I almost miss it. His hot breath hits my face and makes me wince further into the wall behind me. "Don't talk to your father about me, and don't assume you know what's best. You don't and you never will."

Holding my breath when he lets go of my arm, I count to five before letting it out. The area he grabbed me stings, but I push it away. "I know you gave up your room for me."

Nothing.

"And I know your father passed away."

Still nothing.

"I'm—"

"Don't," he warns.

"—sorry."

His nostrils flare as he steps back. "I don't want your fucking sympathy."

"Then what do you want?"

"For you to go home."

I frown.

"Your mother needs you," he states.

My eyes narrow. "Funny," I retort. "So does yours."

He looks like he wants to say something but chooses to smack the wall before turning back to his room. His door slams, leaving me standing abandoned in the hallway.

I look at my arm.

It's already starting to bruise.

I need more iron pills.

Thirteen

ANNABEL FROM BOOK CLUB tells me about what I missed, which was a whole lot of nothing. It's nice though, even if Mr. Nichols told her to catch me up. She didn't have to.

I tell her I like her shirt. It has the Superman emblem on the pocket. Lo and I would sometimes catch Mama watching *Smallville*, but neither of us followed what was happening. We'd go outside and play instead.

Annabel and I don't talk much after that. It isn't like I expect her to keep the conversation flowing. I've never really had friends before. I used to think it was because nobody knew how to deal with the sick girl or the girl who lost her twin, but no one here knows any of that.

Maybe it's me. Maybe it's better. Kaiden is doing me a favor by making sure everyone leaves me alone.

When I'm changing in gym, one of the girls whispers when she sees the light purple bruise on my arm. Nobody can tell it's a palm print, but it wraps around the skin like one.

I never bruised so easily before. Once, I fell out of a tree Lo and I were climbing and only got a little scratch. Now it takes someone accidently bumping into me in the halls for little ones to pop up on my body. The first time I noticed them was a few weeks before moving in with Dad. I bumped my hip into the wall and noticed a large blue and purple mark that night. Grandma playfully swatted me with her crossword puzzle one time. An ugly brown bruise formed.

Frowning, I tug on my sleeve until it's hidden. The last thing I need is rumors spreading about some sort of abuse at home. There was a boy at my old school who lied about his mother hitting him. When Child Protective Services got involved, a lot of bad things happened.

I may not be happy where I am, but I'm content. Sometimes that's better than nothing.

The gym teacher has us do four laps around the room. I'm out of breath by the first one, while everyone speeds past me. Girls laugh in their groups over unknown gossip, boys joke about the girls. They mostly ignore me other than to move around my turtle-pace form.

I walk the last two despite everyone else moving on to the lesson. My last gym teacher wouldn't have allowed that, but I'm grateful they pay my red face and heaving body no attention. I could get a note and excuse myself from even bothering with this class, but I don't want to.

I want to be normal.

Even if normal is being laughed at for being slow, or missing the basketball hoop, or only doing one sit-up, I'm okay with that. Most of the time, people do their own things and talk with their friends, so it isn't like I have to worry about being the butt of everyone's jokes.

But that's probably not because they don't want me to be. It's because of—

"Mr. Monroe," Mr. Jefferson says.

My head snaps up to see Kaiden standing at the side entrance of the gymnasium. He's watching me, facial expression seemingly angrier than usual.

"I need to speak with Emery."

Mr. Jefferson glances at me before turning back to Kaiden. "Regarding?"

"Family emergency."

My heart races as I quickly walk over to him. The teacher waves us off as we head toward a side hallway rather than the main office across the hall.

Is Cam okay? Dad? The last time this happened, Mama showed up tear-stricken with Grandma. They signed me out and took me to the hospital where the school had sent Logan after an episode she had during class. I didn't feel anything—no twin telepathy or tugging. I felt like I failed her that day.

I can taste my anxiety. It's choking me as Kaiden guides us down the corridor leading to empty classrooms and janitor closets. He stops when we get to a little alcove beneath the back stairwell leading to the second-story high school wing.

"Kaiden—"

He lifts my arm with surprising gentleness and raises the sleeve. Sucking in a small breath, he examines the bruise, careful not to touch it or bend my elbow a certain way.

I swallow. "Is everything okay at home?"

His eyes meet mine. They're hollow. "I lied. There's no family emergency."

I'm crossed with a mixture of relief and anger. Just

because he doesn't know my circumstances doesn't mean lying about a family emergency is any less awful. I don't bother bringing that up though, because his jaw moves like he's grinding his teeth as he stares at the bruise. It has faded considerably since he gave it to me, but that doesn't seem to ease the tension built in his shoulders.

"I didn't mean to hurt you." His voice is uncharacteristically soft. Clearing his throat, he lets go of my arm and watches as I adjust the sleeve.

"I know you didn't." I cross my arms over my chest. "It happens. I bruise easily."

He watches me, then his gaze dips to my bracelet. "Seems like a good thing that you went with my mother, huh?" His fingertips graze the beads, causing goose bumps to pebble my arms.

"Yeah." I know he doesn't want to talk about her, but that doesn't mean I'm going to remain silent. "About what you overheard—"

"No." He turns to leave.

Instead of letting him, I grab his wrist. "I know you're hurting, Kaiden. But you need to understand that Cam loves you. There's no reason why you should blame her for losing your father. It's not her fault. He was sick."

His eye twitches.

"Sickness isn't pretty," I whisper. "It turns the person you love more than anything in the world into somebody different. It isn't just a physical transformation but a mental and emotional one. When it takes over, there's very little in their control they can do. Whether you want to give Cam the time of day or not, you need to know that your father didn't want you seeing him like that. And you know what?"

I take a deep breath and shake my head. "It's ugly. Watching someone you love die from illness is hideous and heartbreaking and so many other things.

"Think what you want of your mother, but she was just doing what your father asked. The people who have to witness watching the people they look up to die so brutally are never the same. Cam saved you from that. So did your father. Be glad your parents love you enough to protect you from that sort of sight."

He's quiet. His gaze isn't hard or soft but somewhere in between. I like to think he's considering what I've said, like maybe he's accepting that I know what I'm talking about.

And I do.

Disease is the monster in the dark. It lingers, waiting for the perfect moment to strike. It rears its ugly head and takes what it wants, when it wants.

Yet there's one disease that is worse than any kind of invisible illness in existence, and it is something the world is plagued with.

Indifference.

When Kaiden drives us home, he doesn't leave the house right away like he usually does. Instead, he gives Cam a barely there smile before disappearing into his room.

Fourteen

THE NEXT FEW WEEKS are peacefully mundane. I go to all my classes and don't miss another book club. My headaches come and go, and so do the aches and pains. For the most part, everything is tolerable.

Tolerable is contentment.

Kaiden doesn't actively seek out Cam, but he hasn't completely ignored her either. Sometimes he'll answer her about school or thank her for breakfast. It's strange how so little could mean so much to a person, but I can tell Cam is over the moon whenever he tells her goodbye before school or good night before bed.

He won't talk about his father.

He won't even talk about himself.

It's a step in the right direction though.

One night when Cam and Dad announce they have to go to a work function for Dad's company, Kaiden asks if I want to go to the cemetery. It's cooler out, but going to the tree sounds like the perfect way to end the night.

When we get there, I'm surprised when he pulls out a

thick blanket from the back. He gives me a small shrug before guiding us to the spot and resting the blanket on the cold grass.

The sun is setting, the crickets are singing, and everything around us is tranquil. It helps me ease into the blanket and close my eyes, not caring what Cam or Dad are doing or what's going through Kaiden's mind beside me.

"Do you miss her?"

One of my lids pops open. "Who?"

"Your sister."

"Every single day."

He's quiet for a moment. "Does it get any easier?"

I could lie to him. "No," I answer honestly. "No matter what, she's still gone. That part doesn't really get any better. It's just about figuring out how to move on from it."

My attention turns to his fidgeting, like he wants to ask how but refuses to. I sigh, knowing he's too stubborn for his own good.

Drawing my knees up, I tug on the oversize sweatshirt I brought. "You need to find something to take your mind off it. I like to read. I'm sure sports will help."

"He loved lacrosse."

"Your dad?"

A head nod.

Surprise flickers across my features, but I try masking it. "Did you guys practice together?"

I swear his lips tilt upward, but when I blink, there's no evidence of a smile. "Yeah. He used to play when he was my age, so that's how I got into it. We used to talk about me playing in college someday. He always knew I'd be good enough to get scholarships to play. Sometimes he would take me to the batting cages too because he was a big baseball person."

"Are you?"

"Nah." He clears his throat. "I just went because it made him happy."

We fall to silence.

The wind picks up and shuffles my hair in my face. It's easier to do now that it's shorter. It hasn't grown any but also hasn't fallen out since taking extra vitamins and using the fancy shampoo Cam got me. It's a win, I guess.

"I wish I could visit Lo." It's probably random, but I can tell he isn't interested in offering up any more information about his dad.

"You could."

"It's a long drive."

"I could..." He trails off.

I stare at him.

He grumbles. "I could take you."

A smile cracks across my lips. "I appreciate that, but it's okay. Maybe I'll see if Dad could drop me off during school break. I think it'll be good if I see my mom and Grandma."

He stretches his long legs out. "Don't you regret coming here? Your family is hours away from here, you don't have any friends, and you don't really do anything but read when you're at home."

I consider my answer. "No, I don't regret it. You wouldn't understand, Kaiden. Mama was really struggling to cope, and me being there wasn't what was best. I don't fault her for it..." *Anymore.* "Because I know it must be hard."

"It'd be hard for anyone."

"Like Cam?"

He sighs. "Yeah, like my mom."

At least he accepts that.

"Break is coming up," he notes.

"Yep."

"So...are you going to leave?" His hesitation is thickened by something.

I laugh when I realize what. "You sound sad."

"You sound surprised," he counters.

"You don't exactly like me, Kaiden."

His eyes pierce mine. "I don't dislike you either, Mouse."

The nickname has become oddly endearing, and I'm not sure what that means. It's a sign though—a good one. Like maybe Dad could be right about Kaiden and me being there for one another.

"Are you saying I'm tolerable?"

He grunts. "Not if you keep fishing for compliments. You sound like Rachel."

I fake gasp. Rachel hasn't bothered me in a while, and I wonder if it's because Kaiden has ignored me. Sometimes she'll glance at me in English or if we pass by each other in the hall.

"I think you like me, Kaiden Monroe."

He doesn't say anything.

He doesn't deny it either.

"You know it's your fault," I say. "Me not having friends, I mean."

His eyebrow quirks.

I run my hands across the rough material of the blanket. "People are probably scared to talk to me because they think King Kaiden will do something to them."

"It's for—"

"You don't want me being bullied," I say to cut him off. "Fine, I appreciate the concern you won't admit to having for me. But you can't keep reminding me that I have nobody here because you're the reason for it."

Crickets chirp in the distance.

"You have someone," he murmurs.

My brows pinch.

He glances at my face. "You have me."

When we get home later that night to find our parents already in bed, Kaiden and I go to our rooms, but before I can even change into my pajamas, Kaiden is at my door.

He looks around the room, his hands tucked away in the pockets of his jeans.

"What's up?"

I want to ask him why he gave me his room, but I don't. It seems like there are limits as to how much he's willing to reveal. Baby steps.

"Want to watch a movie?"

A movie?

Glancing at the time on my alarm clock, I give him a curious look. "Usually you're…"

A small smirk quirks his lips. "Gone?"

Blushing, I say, "Yeah."

It isn't like I actively wait to catch him sneaking out, but I can't help it when insomnia plagues me after a long day of napping from fatigue. It's better than watching the neighbor's cat lick itself in their lawn or the stray dog down the road sniff around for food.

One day, I'm going to sneak it in and hide it in my room, hoping Dad will let me keep it.

"Don't feel like going out."

I just nod.

"So?" He pushes off the frame. "Movie?"

Surprisingly, I'm not tired. The headache that likes to grace me with its presence hasn't bugged me in almost two days, and besides a little hip pain, I feel decent.

"Can I change first?" I don't feel like watching a movie in my scratchy jeans, and even though I'm toasty warm in my sweatshirt, the drawstrings will probably choke me to death if I fall asleep in it.

He tells me he'll grab his laptop while I change, so I quickly grab a pair of gray Hollister sweatpants and a long-sleeve white shirt before washing up and getting ready for bed. Not bothering to run a brush through my staticky hair, I give myself a quick once-over in the mirror to make sure my face isn't too red. It isn't like I care what Kaiden thinks but having someone close to you with a lupus rash on your cheeks and nose is embarrassing. It's no different from them getting to see your acne breakout close up.

Noticing some blood on the toilet paper after finishing my business, I realize I must have somehow forgotten my birth control pill at some point this week. Grandma took me to get the pill two years ago to regulate my period, and I take it religiously along with my other meds. I've learned that each cycle triggers a new flare that aggravates my body. Maybe I could do a continuous pill to skip them altogether. Maybe then I'd feel a little better. But would my doctor listen?

Kaiden has made himself comfortable on my bed when I walk back into my room. His black shorts look more like something he exercises in than something to sleep in, but he looks comfortable, and the tight blue tank shows off muscular arms I didn't quite know he had. It shouldn't surprise me. I hear Rachel and her posse drone on about how much time the jocks spend in the weight room after school.

"What do you want to watch?"

I'm hesitant to climb onto the empty spot beside him. He's already sprawled across the usual side I sleep on, and he looks like he has no plans on moving any time soon. He's scrolling through Netflix and waiting for a reply, which has yet to come as I stare.

"Well, Mouse?"

"Can you not call me that?"

"It's fitting. Plus, you like it."

I do. "Not really," I murmur.

He pats the bed. "Come on. I could call you far worse. I'm sure you have plenty of nicknames for me."

My face heats over some of the choice words my mind conjures. He snickers when he sees me, knowing exactly what I'm thinking. It doesn't seem to bother him, so I force myself on the bed and sit cross-legged.

"None of that Disney shit," he warns, passing me the laptop.

It looks old. The letters are worn down, some of them not even visible anymore on the keys. There are scratches on the screen, an area on the bottom right that looks like it held a few different stickers, and a missing key off to the side of the board.

"I've had it for a while." My eyes meet his, but his are trained on the laptop that I have draped on my lap.

My fingers run across the sticker residue. It looks like it's shaped a certain way, so it can't be the branding the company uses on display models.

Kaiden clears his throat. "Used to have Power Rangers stickers on there. Like I said, it's fucking old."

"Why not get a new one?"

He pauses. "My dad got it for me."

"Oh." Instead of dwelling, I start searching through the different categories. It always takes longer to find something to watch than it does to actually watch it.

I point toward a comedy. "What about this one? It has Adam Sandler in it."

I'm not sure what he likes, but he didn't specify about preference. He just nods and has me start it, then rests it between us and angles the worn screen so there's no glare.

For the first twenty minutes, I'm fine staying seated with my legs crossed. After thirty pass by, I can't feel either ankle and need to stretch out my legs.

Kaiden cusses and moves the laptop out of the way before turning his attention to me. "I can't keep watching you fidget. It's distracting me from this borderline-awful movie."

"You could pick something else."

"I'm invested now."

Rolling my eyes, I wince as my stiff knees crack and extend out. They feel better once straightened, so I stack a couple of pillows behind me and scoot back against them.

"Are you finally comfortable?"

"Not when you're in here," I admit, not really meaning to say the words out loud.

He chuckles. "Don't worry, Mouse. I don't do virgins."

I gape at him. "Wh…how…you can't just say stuff like that! And what does that even mean? That's the stupidest thing I've ever heard."

Now he's full-on laughing, leaning back and shaking the mattress with his rumbles.

I smack his chest. "You're going to wake up our parents. Be quiet."

"What?" he muses, grinning. "Are you afraid they're going to find us alone in your room together? What will Daddy Dearest think?"

He's making fun of me.

I reach for his laptop and start to close it, but he stops me with a heavy sigh. "Would you relax? They don't care. It isn't like I'm some random guy in your bed."

My brows go up to say *Aren't you?*

He bumps my arm with his elbow. "I already told you, I'm not going to ravish you. You're not my type, Mouse."

My eye twitches, the insult sinking a little too deep. "I'm sure."

Resuming the movie, I try to focus solely on that when he pauses it again. "What's that supposed to mean?"

"What?"

"You look pissed."

"I'm not—"

"Don't bullshit me."

I sigh loudly. "All I'm saying is that I've heard the rumors at school. You're the sports star who can get any girl he wants. If you do decide to play in college next year, you'll probably make it big if you want to. Go pro or something. You've got the world ahead of you that you're already mapping out by getting college credits and doing something you love. So I'm not surprised that I'm not the kind of girl you'd go after."

"Because…?"

Because I don't know if I'll be able to map out my life the same way.

I don't say that. "For one, I'm your stepsister. For another, I don't look anything like the girls I see you flirting with. Oh, and regardless of you insisting you don't hate me, you're not the friendliest person to me."

He shifts his body toward me. "First, I don't really do the label thing, so don't call yourself my stepsister, Cinderella. Second, you're right. You need to gain at least thirty pounds to look like the girls I hang around. And third, I'm not friendly toward anyone."

I guess he has a point about his demeanor toward people, so there's no point in arguing it. Before I can even try, he's tilting my chin up with two of his fingers and grinning wickedly. I hate the tingly feeling I get in the pit of my stomach from the contact or how my heart goes into overdrive when I see his dark eyes lighten when he's up to no good.

I tell myself it's because I'm not used to people touching me like this—being close. I'd react this way to anybody who would do the same thing. Yet my brain tells me otherwise. I could meet someone tomorrow who would dare to defy Kaiden's instructions just to speak to me, and I wouldn't feel airy and light and nervous and numb all at the same time with them.

"Frankly," Kaiden murmurs in a tone so low it caresses my skin, "the only reason I'm not going to fuck you senseless is because I've seen what one little touch does. Imagine what I'd do to your body if I got between those pretty little legs of yours."

I stop breathing.

"I'd ruin you, Em."

My eyes widen.

Then I blink and think the only thing I can muster in the fogginess he's created in the depths of my mind.

I'd ruin you first, Kaiden Monroe.

Fifteen

KAIDEN LEAVES SHORTLY AFTER his brazen remark. I'm bothered in a lot more ways than I anticipate, so I brush it off by picking up a book and reading until I fall asleep.

Unfortunately, I dream of Kaiden. And not in a friendly or brotherly way. I dream about him like I'd dream of one of my many book boyfriends who want to devour and claim me and love me in ways Kaiden certainly doesn't.

And that's…well, that's a problem.

A *big* problem.

Because he may not do labels, but I do.

Like stepbrother.

And stepmother.

And fatal.

Fatal attraction.

Fatal affection.

Fatal disease.

He thinks he'll ruin me, but he has no idea what unstoppable forces are in my arsenal. I'm my own weapon, a nightmare that lives in reality. It isn't something I can control, and he has no idea. I don't think getting close to him will do any good, whether it's friendly or not.

If he still struggles with his father's death, what would mine do to him?

I'm not sure I want to find out.

For once, I wish I was seeing Mama's teary golden eyes instead of Kaiden Monroe's. I wish I was listening to Lo's playful laughter instead of Kaiden's husky words. Wishes don't come true though, because this isn't some fairy tale.

It's reality.

And reality is a mean bitch.

Sixteen

TOMORROW IS THE DAY before October break, and everyone is loud and eager to have a week off. I already heard at least half the senior class mention skipping tomorrow and starting early, especially because Halloween is on Saturday. Apparently parties are common for the holiday, costume or not, and I even heard one guy mention going out after midnight redecorating people's houses with toilet paper and who knows what else.

When Mr. Nichols realizes he doesn't have everyone's attention at book club, he reminds us to start reading the next book for the week after break and then lets us go. Considering it's my selection, I probably won't spend a lot of time gathering quotes and ideas for discussion, especially since Dad agreed to take me to Mama's for the week.

Honestly, I'm nervous. I called Grandma asking if she thought it'd be okay, and she seemed excited. That doesn't mean Mama will feel the same, and I'm not sure how she'll react when she sees me.

It'll be good. That's what I keep telling myself. It gives me time back home to visit with everyone, especially Logan. Plus, it gives me a chance to breathe. Things with Dad haven't been bad, but that doesn't extend to Kaiden.

Ever since our impromptu movie night, he finds ways to make me blush—winks, hand brushes, and crude comments. Usually, he doesn't pay me much attention if we're both home. He does his thing and I do mine. Once in a while, he'll barge into my room while I'm doing homework and ask me pointless questions, pestering me because he can.

It makes Cam smile.

You're like siblings, she told me.

I haven't gone to the tree since that day either. For the past couple of weeks, I've gone to school with him, drove home with him, and locked myself away in my room. It never stops him if he wants my attention, and I can't help but wonder what the point of it is.

When the late bus drops me off in front of the house, I'm tired and ready to change into my sweatpants for the evening. To my surprise, the front door is locked and the key on my chain is missing. *Strange*. Thankfully, I vaguely remember Dad telling me there was a spare key hidden somewhere.

It takes a long moment to search through the fogginess of my memory before I'm looking under the rim of the flowerpot he mentioned it being under.

Nothing.

I check another one.

Nothing again.

Sighing, I turn and knock on the door. Kaiden's car is here, so he must have finished in the weight room early. I wait a minute before knocking louder until my knuckles hurt. The doorbell doesn't work. Cam keeps saying she'll get it fixed but never calls anyone.

I back up and glance at the windows, trying to see if there's a light on. There doesn't seem to be, so I go around the back to check the glass door leading to the kitchen.

Someone locked the fence door.

I don't remember it ever being locked.

My phone died twenty minutes ago, so I can't call anyone. I'm not even sure what the home number is here, because I never hear it ring. I'm pretty sure the landline is there for decoration only, because I see Dad and Cam on their cell phones more than not.

They'll come home soon and rescue me from the chilly air that's beating against my skin. My fall jacket is nothing more than a protection against a subtle breeze, but it does little against the nip of air that's getting colder as the minutes pass.

I sit on the front steps and tuck my knees against my chest for warmth.

Five minutes pass.

Ten.

Fifteen.

The tips of my fingers are starting to go numb, and I notice the discoloration of a few. They're turning blue. Lo had something like this when it got too cold. Her circulation wouldn't work right, and her fingers and toes would turn a deep purple until she got them warm again.

I try sitting on them to heat them up but wince at how tender the joints are. Sharp pain shoots down my wrists and settles into my elbows, causing me to tear up. My jaw quivers as the breeze hits me, and there's nothing blocking it from hitting where I sit in front of the door.

After what feels like forever, Dad pulls in. He seems stunned I'm sitting there and quickly gets out with his work bag and a small frown on his face.

"Emery?" When he gets closer, his eyes widen at my shaking form. I can't sit still. My nose is numb, my cheeks sting, and my hands are now swollen and blue despite sitting on them for over half the time I've waited for somebody.

He cusses under his breath and quickly drops his things to peel off his coat. It's thicker than mine and feels like heaven when he drapes it over my shoulders.

"I g-got l-locked out," I stutter, forcing myself to stand. The cold already settled into my joints, causing both my knees to lock up and make it difficult to get out of his way to unlock the door.

He looks at me with concern lingering in his eyes, and it warms a part of my chest that I didn't think a glance from him could. "Isn't Kaiden home? Did you forget the spare?"

I shake my head, too cold to answer. As he pushes the door open, I hear music and giggling and something crash. Dad swears as he guides me in, putting an arm around my shoulder and rubbing my arm for friction.

"What the *hell* is going on here?" Dad has never sounded so angry before, and the bite to his tone even has me wincing.

Not as much as when I look at Kaiden and Rachel in the kitchen. He's covered in flour, she's sitting on the island, and it looks like whatever they were trying to bake has more ingredients on the floor than in the bowl or pan.

The music playing is coming from a distance, his room

upstairs by the sounds of it. Rachel brushes hair behind her ear and glances down, like she can't meet Dad's eye.

Kaiden looks at me. "What's up with you?" He glances at the clock and makes a face like he's surprised at something. "Aren't you usually home earlier?"

Rachel slides off the counter. "I should probably get going. It was fun, Kaid." She kisses his cheek and gives me a once-over before gliding past us toward the door.

Dad's grip on me becomes protective. "I have a lot of things I'd like to say to you right now, but Cam isn't home. What I'm concerned about is the fact Emery was locked outside, half-freezing, while you made…brownies?" He eyes the mess, jaw tight. "You better clean up this mess now and apologize to Emery."

"D-Dad—"

Dad turns to me. "You need to go take a hot shower and warm up. I'll make sure the heat is turned up, and I'll get you something warm to eat." His eyes catch something on the side table by the kitchen entrance. Keys. Two of them. One of them has a little pink protector on the top that matches the missing one from my key chain. "Why the hell are the spare keys to the front door inside?"

My lips part.

Did Kaiden purposefully lock me out?

My nostrils flare, and for once, I do what Dad tells me to without much thought. Leaving them to argue, which Dad quickly starts doing as soon as I'm out of view, I close myself in my room. It takes a bit for my muscles and joints to cooperate enough to peel my clothes off, but once my body hits the hot water and steam in the shower, I finally start to ease.

Until I realize what Kaiden did.

Then anger settles where the stiffness did.

As the water cascades over me, the shakes turn into something entirely different. I'm sore, bitter, and emotional. I thought Kaiden and I were becoming friends, if not something close to that.

I don't realize I'm crying until I let the water hit my back and feel the teardrops slide down my cheeks. Brushing them away, I run my fingers through my hair and wince at the way my shoulders tighten from the movement.

Resting my arms to the sides, I notice what's wrapped around a few of my fingers.

Hair.

Lots of it.

More tears.

More anger.

Not just at Kaiden.

At life.

He's there when I step out of the bathroom, wet hair, sweatpants, oversize sweatshirt, and all. No longer is he sporting his dirty clothes but something new as he sits on the edge of the bed with his elbows on his jean-clad thighs.

I don't say a word.

But he does. "Are you okay?"

I want to ask him why he cares.

I don't grace him with anything.

"You look a little better."

I scoff.

If he only knew how triggering those words really are. I've heard people talk about my image for too many years. On days when you feel closer to death than ever, they're a blow to the gut. It's always about looks. You either don't look sick enough for anyone to believe you, or you look so sick people feel the need to point it out.

For his sake, he's probably right. My fingers aren't blue, and I can feel my extremities. Before leaving the bathroom, I noticed my cheeks and nose were a little red, but nothing unusual because of the scalding water I'd stood under for longer than I probably should have.

"Emery—"

"You should go."

I want to lie down with a book or watch something on my laptop. Maybe go to bed early. Anything that means him going away.

"I didn't—"

"Kaiden," I say, cutting him off, "I don't want to talk to you. I don't want you in my room. I don't want..." I shake my head. "I just don't want to deal with this right now. I don't want your company."

"This was my room first," he points out.

I put my hands on my hips. "If you want it back so bad, then fine. You can switch our stuff when I'm gone next week."

His lips twitch. "It's just a room." Before I can reply, he adds, "You're getting quite the backbone. Maybe I shouldn't call you Mouse anymore."

"Mice are courageous," I argue, not that it really matters. "For something so tiny, they risk a lot around people who want them gone."

"They usually get killed."

I think about the one time Lo and I had a mouse in our room. Mama swore putting peanut butter on the trap would lure it in and get rid of it, but the mouse was smart. Somehow, it licked the peanut butter off without getting harmed.

"Not all of them."

We're silent.

"I didn't know you were out there."

"Doesn't matter."

"The hell it doesn't." He stands, combing his fingers through his hair. "If I'd known, I would have opened the damn door. Rachel and I were listening to music and—"

I hold my hand up. "I don't want to know what you two were doing. In fact, I'd like to think about anything but those possibilities. If you don't mind, I've got things to do."

He snorts. "Like what? More homework? Got another book to read? Is this one about a cowboy or army vet?"

Blushing, I throw back my blankets. I remember Mama reading books with guys like that on the cover of them, but not so much me. I don't feel like correcting him though.

"I'm tired."

"It's not even six thirty."

"The cold does that to me," I snap, eyeing him as I slide my feet under the comforter.

He's silent, teeth grinding.

I want to tell him that the cold does a lot more to me. It causes me bone-deep pain that leaves me uncomfortable for days, makes me so fatigued I sleep for fourteen hours straight, and irritates my already sensitive skin. Instead of giving him those details, I lie on my side with my back facing him.

It hurts my shoulder and hip, but I don't care. For once,

I want to hurt *him*. I want to stop feeding into the way he treats me like I deserve it. For once, I just want someone to feel the pain I do so maybe then they'll truly understand.

I'm sick of being selfless and understanding for the sake of everybody else's sanity.

"You at least need to eat."

"Not hungry," I murmur.

I think he cusses under his breath, but sleep draws me away. I hear the door close behind him and I drift off.

When I wake up a couple of hours later, it's to the smell of something salty. When I sit up and rub my eyes as they adjust to the dimly lit room, I see a plate on the nightstand with a thermos and a Post-it.

The thermos has soup.

The Post-it has a picture of a mouse.

Seventeen

GRANDMA GREETS ME FIRST outside the house. It seems so different to me now. It's stupid because nothing has changed. The front door is still painted white, the light-blue siding is still chipped, and the walkway leading up to the main door still has moss growing between the stones.

The grass on the front lawn is longer than I'm used to, like someone hasn't cut it for a little while but still tries to keep it up. The kiddie pool that used to rest to the side by the lilac bushes is upside down and grimy from dirt, mud, and who knows what else. I'm surprised it hasn't deflated. And the tire swing Lo was adamant on having is hanging unloved, with the rope fraying on one side from the weather.

Grandma pulls me into a tight hug while Dad sets my bag down beside me. He gives Grandma a smile and kisses my cheek. My heart sings a little from the tiny gesture. He used to kiss our cheeks goodbye before work.

"Call me if you need me, okay? "I will" is my response,

despite being positive I won't pick up the phone once while I'm here."

The ride here was long and quiet. He would sometimes ask me questions out of obligation more than curiosity. Like what music I like to listen to, so he could drown the silence. I remember his. Classic rock—'70s and '80s bands with big hair and bigger voices. Dad used to play guitar in a garage band that went nowhere because Mama said they weren't any good.

I told him country was fine.

He liked that too.

Grandma thanks him for driving me before taking my bag and guiding me toward the house. I hold my breath as we walk in, unsure of what or who I'll find.

Pictures still litter the walls in the entryway, though noticeably fewer of Lo and me. I wonder if Mama ever found the hoard of them in my old room. I never moved them when I packed up, because Mama rarely stepped foot inside the tiny space.

I don't blame her.

Staying in the room my sister died in was hard. I can't imagine what walking into it would be like for Mama, knowing it's completely empty now.

Grandma notices my gaze and gently squeezes my hand. "Don't think about it, darling girl. You're here to enjoy yourself."

Am I?

I focus on the thin layer of dust coating the shelf off to the side. I can tell something is missing from it, but I can't remember what. A bowl? A vase? Racking my mind comes up empty, so I let Grandma walk me through the house.

It's clean, not that I'm totally surprised. Mama would go into cleaning frenzies all the time. I just assumed she stopped once she didn't have to worry about anything triggering our flares.

"It looks the same," I murmur, feeling guilty over assuming the worst.

I keep doing that, thinking their life here would have gone to ruin as soon as I left. Deep down, I know it's the opposite. Their lives were unpredictable when I was here, waiting for the other shoe to drop before needing to stop what they were doing to help me out.

You left to give them some peace.

Grandma laughs softly. "Your mother has been keeping busy at her new job. She doesn't have time to obsess over cleaning and reorganizing like she used to. Did she mention it to you?"

New job? I make a face, wondering if Mama has been telling Grandma that we've spoken. It's been too long since we've exchanged words, and something tells me Grandma isn't aware.

She sighs. "Emmy…"

I press my lips together. "Where does she work?"

Grandma walks over to the couch and pats the cushion next to her. Without hesitation, I drop down on the familiar worn seat, sinking into the material and remembering all the times I'd snuggle with Mama here.

"She works as a nurse for the local high school." Grandma's hand rests on my knee, giving it a tiny pat. "She used to love working in pediatrics, but the way she left made them hesitant to hire her back."

I start to let the guilt consume me when Grandma shakes her head. "Don't you dare blame yourself, Emery. Truth be told, I don't think your mother could handle going back there and seeing sick kids. Not when she still pictures Logan so little. Where she is now is a great first step for her, and it gives her time to work and heal until she finds something else. I promise you, she's doing better."

I'm quiet.

Mama would sometimes have to work the floor on Saturdays at the clinic. After Dad left, she would bring Lo and me with her to play in the little area the hospital set up for the kids. There was a big plastic toy house that Lo, I, and some other children would play in until they had to go to their appointments.

Before Dad made his grand exit, he would visit us in between whatever job priorities he had on summer days when we were at the hospital with Mama. He'd take us to the ground floor where there was a long tunnel connecting the two different buildings from underground. He'd take us to the vending machines down there and let us run around to burn off the sugar.

I visited the tunnels shortly before leaving for Dad's. It wasn't as magical as I remember. The food in the vending machines was overpriced, and half the time when you'd click on one candy bar, a different one would fall out. Lo wouldn't care if she got a Mounds or Almond Joy because she ate anything.

But I cared way more than I should because it wasn't what I wanted.

It's not what I wanted.

"Emmy?"

I break away from my train of thought, blushing over zoning out. "Sorry. Does she…is she okay? You know, with everything?"

Her shoulders draw back a little. "Your mother is stronger than even she believes."

Why don't I believe that?

We order pizza for dinner. Hawaiian for Mama, and pepperoni, sausage, broccoli, and onions for me and Grandma. We could have easily gotten a cheese and split it between us, but Grandma says Mama likes bringing leftovers to work.

When I hear the car pull up in the driveway, my body tenses on the couch. The pizza is in the kitchen, waiting to be served, and the television is on some soap opera rerun on a channel I've never heard of.

The door opens.

I hold my breath.

Is it possible to swallow your heart? It feels like it's lodged in my throat, choking me. All because of the woman turning the door handle.

Grandma gives me a reassuring smile from the armchair she's sitting in. She's into the soap opera; I'm too in my head to figure out if the man really slept with his brother's wife. It seems likely.

The door fully opens and Mama steps in, seemingly not realizing I'm now standing in the middle of the living room. My heart hammers rapidly and I hold my breath until she looks up from the purse she holds.

She's in scrubs.

Her silver-blond hair is a mess.

But it's her.

"Hi," I whisper, too afraid to step forward. I take in the

little yellow ducks on her blue shirt. It's the kind of top she'd wear at the hospital. The school probably doesn't require them, but she's got a closetful to choose from.

She remains by the door, her eyes sliding over me and then traveling back up to my hair. I wonder what she thinks of it. The style has grown on me, and Cam plans to take me every six weeks when she gets her hair trimmed to keep mine up.

I'm terrified when her lips part. I tell myself it's been long enough—she won't make the same mistakes she did when she was stuck in grief.

"Hi, Sunshine."

Relief floods my chest when I hear those soft words until I'm practically running toward her. She wraps me in a tight hug, and I soak in the sweet smell of vanilla and lavender, her two favorite scents.

I pull back and stare at her face. She looks tired, like she's somehow aged, but I notice something vital that allows me to breathe.

Mama's eyes aren't golden.

Eighteen

MAMA AND I SPEND the night talking about her new job and hobbies. She seems happy, lighter than I remember. The relief knowing she's doing okay is short-lived because of my conscience telling me she was only hurting because of me.

But you knew that.

Knowing Mama likes her new job and joined a crafts club at the community center makes everything easier to handle. She needed to find herself. To get through the loss of Lo and, in many ways, the loss of me.

I'd almost forgotten what Mama's smile looks like. It's the same type of foreign anomaly as her laugh—airy and eager, like bells. I want to tell her how much I love the sound, but I'm afraid it'll make her stop.

Before Grandma comes back, Mama notices my bracelet. Her smile doesn't falter. That's how I allow myself to hope that we can be like how we were.

Emery and Mama.

Sunshine and blue skies.

You're my sunshine, baby girl.

Then you're my blue skies, Mama.

Logan would always be the rainbow, colorful and happy and effortless no matter the storm.

I want to play the song, but I'm afraid.

I want to ask about Lo, but I'm afraid.

I want to be there for Mama, but…

I'm terrified.

I'm terrified that talking to her about anything other than our lives as they are now will break her. Will she shut down again? Cry? Freeze? Go silent? Will she stop seeing me as Emery and start calling me Logan again?

I want to know about her job and what she has for breakfast and what she does with her spare time. But I also want to know if she visits Lo and talks to Grandma and sees a grief counselor like everyone has suggested.

But I can't.

Because Mama's smiling.

Because Mama's eyes are green.

Because I love her too much to hurt her.

In my head, I sing the song.

In my head, Mama sings with me.

Instead, she touches my bracelet, stares at the letters, and then kisses my cheek before going to bed. It's early, but not as early as she usually went to sleep. I wonder if she still takes sleeping pills.

Grandma doesn't come back right away, so I clean up the kitchen and living room before heading back to the place I hold the most memories. My bag rests on my old bed—the new white-and-blue comforter set on it is one I haven't seen before. It's tucked in and folded at the corners like you'd see at a hotel, and I know it's Grandma's doing because she used to be a housekeeper.

The room is exactly as I remember it. By the nightstand is a dent in the wall from the time Lo and I were jumping on my bed and I knocked over the lamp in the process. It smashed against the drywall before shattering on the ground. It was Mama's favorite.

It hasn't been repainted; the off-white I remember it once being now looks more cream. The entire house could use some upgrades like Dad always told Mama he would start when we were little. She wanted a new apple-themed kitchen, something red and bright and welcoming.

Pushing the thought away, I examine the bookshelf. I had books galore covering every inch, along with a hidden picture of Lo in between books I knew Mama didn't want to read. The ones I left behind aren't on the shelf anymore, which makes me walk over to the closet.

It's empty.

Heart hammering, I look under both the beds for any of the frames I'd taken down for Mama's sanity. They used to haunt me while I slept, guilt seeping into my bones worse than the aches did. Now they're gone, the space under my bed dust-free, like someone cleaned it special for me.

I vaguely hear the front door open, and Grandma calls our names. Panic buries itself in my chest as I open dresser drawers and plastic storage bins to see what happened to Lo. Every memory taken of her is missing, and I need to see them. I need to know they're there.

"Emmy?" Grandma's voice is closer, but I struggle to hear it. My chest is so tight I think I might be dying from suffocation.

Someone shakes me.

Someone calls my name.

"*Breathe*," a soft voice commands.

Not Grandma's.

Mama's.

I'm crying into her chest while she sits next to me on the floor, rubbing my back and hushing me like she used to a long time ago. She is humming. It isn't our song.

It isn't our song.

It feels like forever by the time I'm able to pull away, and I only do when she somehow produces a tissue and wipes down my face. It makes me want to cry harder because I never liked being this way with Mama, even if I dreamed of her comfort.

Where were you then, Mama?

I needed you.

I choke down the words because they mean nothing now. Not when Mama is here and holding me and comforting me and being the woman I want her to be. I left her like Kaiden said, but only because she needed me gone.

Kaiden is wrong though.

I need Mama more than she needs me.

"I don't want to forget." I hiccup and glance at all the empty space in the room. "I don't want to forget her, Mama."

Her eyes glisten and the familiar tone of gold breaks through. There's anguish and something more, something deeper. Guilt.

"You will never forget her," she whispers, brushing the pad of her thumb across my cheek.

Grandma walks back in holding a large leather book. She passes it to Mama, who opens it slowly and smiles at the contents. When she turns it to me, my heart dances.

It's a photo album of Lo.

Of all the pictures…

I look at Mama and wonder how I got to the conclusion that has made me doubt her so much. When I think of her, I think of her sadness, reclusion, and brokenness. I don't see the woman who sang to me or baked me cookies because I was sad or told me how much she loved me because she could.

I've judged her.

Criticized her.

Wondered why she let me leave.

She knew you'd be better off…

"You put them in an album" is my quiet response. It isn't a question, just a surprised statement.

Did Mama know how I felt about her?

Another tear falls.

"Baby," she whispers.

I close my eyes.

Mama falls asleep next to me in my bed that night, holding me and combing her fingers through my hair. The motion hurts, but I don't tell her that my scalp aches or that I wince every time her nails get caught and tug. I try to remember what it felt like before the pain. It comforted me. Lulled me. Eased me.

When we wake up in the morning, she sees the hair on my pillow first.

Her lips part.

Her eyes widen.

She whispers, "Not again."

She chokes on tears and fear and worry as she sits up and stares at the chunk of hair resting beside me on the cotton pillowcase. Her eyes can't travel anywhere else.

"Not again, Logan."
And I know the truth.
I'm going to wreck Mama.
But not as Emery…
Because Emery doesn't exist.

Nineteen

I SKIP BREAKFAST AND escape to the one place I can find peace. Grandma tries to stop me and tells me to at least take a granola bar, but my appetite is diminished by the truth embedded in the walls that surround me.

It isn't like the concept of pain is foreign to me. Pain is a constant in my life—the one thing my body is used to. But the feeling in my chest is deeper than anything my disease can cause, despite it being the very reason for the ache in the first place.

Nobody wants to break their mom's heart…

When I see Lo's grave, my heart gives in to the hurt. The stone is clean, not a speck of grass, dirt, or bird poop on it like last time. The area around it is kept up, unlike the lawn surrounding the house. Someone has been here, maybe even Mama.

Dropping on the uneven ground, I run my fingertips over the edge of the smooth granite before tracing the letters of her name. They're rougher, the indentations causing my skin discomfort, but I pay it no attention.

Logan Olivia Matterson.

Beloved daughter, sister, and friend.

I drop my hands into my lap and just stare at the stone like something will happen. Maybe if I believe hard enough, I'll see Logan. It can be like one of the books I've read where the loved ones get a second chance with the deceased.

"This isn't a book," I whisper to myself.

The breeze picks up and causes me to wrap my coat tighter around me. There hasn't been any snowfall yet, which seems odd for early November. At least here. Dad told me that they don't get nearly as much snow in Exeter.

I settle on my butt, crossing my legs under me and stuffing my hands in my coat pockets. "I'm sorry I haven't been here for a while. I decided to live with Dad for senior year." Shifting on the ground, I chip at a stain on my jeans. "I know you're probably wondering why I'd want to do that after what he did, but..." I shake my head. "Actually, you're probably not. You've always been forgiving of people. I guess it doesn't really matter, huh?"

I'm not sure why I pause like she can respond. Sighing, I glance at my ragged nails from my constant picking and biting.

"Dad tries, so I can't really fault him for anything. You would have told me it isn't worth holding a grudge over. Anyway, he's got a new wife and stepson and they're...nice."

The wind blows a little harder, then dies down completely until nothing but bitter air remains as usual. I wonder if that's Lo telling me to keep talking.

Licking my lips, I say, "Our stepmom's name is Cameron, but she goes by Cam. Dad really seems to love her. I don't think I ever saw him look at Mama the same way. She cares,

Lo. She knows about us, about *you*, and she wants to help however she can. She even took me to get my hair cut."

I drag in a deep breath. The air hurts my lungs, but I suck it up as I touch the tips of my hair. "Sometimes I wish that Mama would come visit me there, or call more, or…just be there like Cam is. She misses you so much, Logan. She's hurting and I can't fix her. It takes one little reminder that I'm sick for her to spiral, and I know that means being here won't do her any good.

"Kaiden, Cam's son, made me wonder if I was being selfish by going away, but I realize now I'm not. Hopefully you can forgive me. I know I promised I wouldn't leave you, but you would have too if you saw Mama."

There's no wind.

No subtle breeze.

I hold my breath.

Selfish people don't put anybody first.

Selfish people don't sacrifice everything.

They never come second.

They never feel torment.

My torment is in a five-foot-five form with blond hair streaked with silver and mossy-green eyes filled with sadness in every crevice. I want to believe facing the torment means building my strength, when really it tears me down a little more each day.

Because Mama is selfish.

"*Mama* is selfish, Logan."

Once the words are uttered, my body reacts. It's like an anvil is about to crush me before someone saves me in the last second. It's a weight I don't need burying me under everything else that's already trying to put me in a grave next to Lo.

I stare at the ground.

At the grass.

At the dirt.

"I don't want to die," I whisper.

My family has never been religious, never even gone to church. Mama said when she was little, she'd been dragged every Sunday and hated it. Dad never went a day in his life. They told us we could decide when we were older if it's something we wanted to do, but it seems pointless.

What good comes out of praying to someone nobody truly knows exists? Faith shouldn't be blind if it's meant to be followed. Where's reason? Where's proof that believing in God actually makes death any less terrifying?

Maybe you'll see Lo.

Maybe…

It's not enough though.

Doubt creeps into the cracks that one day may allow me to see Lo. Doubt is fear's best friend—the little demon I'm well acquainted with that rests on my shoulder and whispers everything I have to be afraid of in my ear.

What if death is death?

What if I never see Lo?

What if Mama loses it completely?

What if.

What if.

What if.

I'm fed every insecurity and internal dread that can beat me down. One day, I may not get up. I may not survive it. It could end me.

Exhaustion swipes over me as I stare blurry-eyed at Lo's headstone. I want to reach out and touch her name like I'm touching her hand, her hair, her face. I want to hug her just one more time.

Just one more.

I curl up on my side on the ground, right over her grave, and pretend she's right here with me like I've done in the summertime.

"I wish you were here" are the finals words I tell her before letting nature fill the silence between us.

Sometime later…I fall asleep.

There's cursing. Cursing and shivering.

Why am I so cold?

Suddenly I'm being cradled in warmth, floating in air. Everything hurts. My limbs. My face. My muscles. I think my teeth are chattering but I'm too numb to know for sure.

Forcing my gaze over the muscular shoulder of the person holding me, I see Lo's headstone fading away. I squirm, cry out, and plead for the person to set me down.

"Lo!" My voice is hoarse as I reach out behind me. "Logan!"

"Stop, Emery," a familiar voice demands. The grip on me tightens, keeping me in place against him. "Dammit, Mouse. What the hell were you doing sleeping out here? It's fucking forty degrees."

Mouse.

Slowly, my gaze lifts up to meet his face. He isn't looking at me though. He's facing forward with a locked jaw that's popping in anger. If he looks down, I bet his brown eyes will be dark, hard—full of judgment.

"W-wanted…L-Lo."

He scoffs, walking the path in front of him like he's done it thousands of times. When my shaking becomes too much, he swears again and holds me closer, his breath warming the tip of my nose as he picks up the pace.

"You would have been with her for good if you stayed out here any longer," he murmurs, shaking his head. "The temp is dropping. It's supposed to be below freezing soon, you idiot."

I want to laugh. If he'd known what I'd been thinking of before I fell asleep, he would see the dry humor in that too.

Burying my face in the crook of his neck, I feel him tense. I want to ask him if he believes in the afterlife or heaven or hell. Does he think he's going to one or the other? Does he not believe at all?

I bet Cam took him to church.

Instead of asking him anything, I absorb the heat his body offers me. We're silent, though I'm sure he has lots to say to me. I'm grateful he doesn't say any of the things he's probably dying to toss at me—to yell, to call me out on.

When he makes it to the front door, a loud gasp sounds. Grandma. She ushers him in and tells him to put me in my room. He stumbles and stops and glances around until Grandma points him in the right direction. Momentarily, I wonder if the hair is still on the pillow. I didn't move it. I couldn't.

Before he rests me on the mattress, I notice there's nothing on the pillowcase. Releasing a silent breath of relief, I flutter my chilly eyelids until I'm watching his grim features.

He isn't looking around the room.

He isn't snooping through my stuff.

He's staring at me. Watching.

He's...worried.

"Wh-what are y-you doing here?"

Grandma comes in before he can answer, ushering him out. "I need to get her out of these cold clothes. I'll let you back in when she's changed."

She closes the door on him just as he steps over the threshold into the hall. Grandma scolds me under her breath as she peels off my coat and shoes, then carefully helps me slide out of my jeans and socks and slips off my shirt. Beside her on the nightstand is a wet washcloth, and my body eases into the warmth of it when she starts carefully pressing it against my skin.

"Don't ever do that again, Emmy." Her voice cracks, and for the first time, I realize just how much she's gone through.

I've always worried about Mama.

But so has Grandma.

Only she's had the burden to worry about me too, and that was never fair to her. She shouldn't have to concern herself over two generations of broken women.

I swallow. "I miss Logan."

She pauses what she's doing, setting the washcloth down and blotting me with a dry cotton towel. "I know. We all do."

"I miss Mama too."

She grabs my pajama pants and helps me put them on. The fuzzy material feels perfect against my skin. The long-sleeve top she chose matches the floral bottoms, and she makes quick work of putting the blanket over me once I'm fully dressed, tucking the edges under my body.

"I think your mother misses herself too."

Twenty

I WAKE UP IN a haze. Something feels off. Blinking my eyes to adjust to the dim lighting, I attempt to move only to find something holding me down.

Pressing my lips together, I slowly gaze downward at the toned arm draped around my midsection. Eyes widening, I try remembering what happened before I fell asleep. Grandma had brought me grilled cheese and tomato soup, Kaiden told me tomato soup was gross, and—

Kaiden.

Just as I'm about to wiggle my way out of his grip, he tightens it. "It's too fucking early," he mumbles, voice muffled by sleepiness.

"What are you doing?" I hiss, trying to get out of bed.

He won't let me. "I'm trying to sleep, but you're being annoying."

Scoffing, I try prying his arm off me again. "I can't believe you're in my bed. You do know there's one *right* over there if you want to sleep!"

He grumbles and pulls me against his body. Being pressed against him is like having my own personal heater, which I normally wouldn't complain about. My back is against his solid front, and I wonder how much time he puts into working out. When his lips brush my ear, I freeze in his hold. "Do you really want me on that bed, Mouse?"

I'm about to tell him off when I realize he probably doesn't mean it in the way I think. His voice isn't cocky or slimy; it's knowing. Closing my mouth, I glance at Lo's made bed. It isn't even the same one she slept on. The one she passed away in was taken away a few days after the funeral. I'm surprised they even put a new mattress in the room. It's not like anyone would need it.

"That's what I thought," he says, letting out a tiny breath that tickles my cheek. "You were shivering, so I thought this might help warm you up. Now stop talking."

He makes himself comfortable, his nose nuzzling in the crook of my neck and causing my arms to pimple with goose bumps. I wish I were uncomfortable, but there's not even a lick of pain I could use to get him away. As if he knows that, his arm hugs me to him, molding my body to his.

Oh my God.

Is this spooning?

My heart is going haywire in my chest. I've never cuddled with a boy before, much less slept next to one. The fact that he's so content only makes my anxiety worse.

"Kaiden?"

"Go to sleep."

"What are you doing here?"

I jerk when I feel his teeth nip the top of my shoulder. "I thought we established that. I'm—"

I wiggle away from him only to press my butt against something hard. "In my hometown, Kaiden."

He groans and holds my hips still. "I need you to stop moving around unless you're willing to help me out."

Brows pinched, I consider his words in silence while his breathing evens out. When I put two and two together, my throat thickens, and I carefully scoot away until I'm on the edge of the already tiny bed. Gripping the mattress, I stare at the carpet and wait for him to answer.

"I was bored."

"Most people watch television or, I don't know, hang out with friends." Trying to get comfortable leaves me struggling for balance, and I almost fall on the floor until Kaiden hooks his arm around me and yanks me over to him.

Body heating when he moves to hover over me, I try looking at anything but him. His large frame takes over my senses though as he cages me in. All I see is how his red cotton shirt drapes from the collar just enough to see the sculpted muscles underneath. His natural woodsy scent reminds me of the trees I climbed once upon a time. But it's his eyes, dark and penetrating, that get me the most. Once I lock my gaze on them, I'm stuck there.

Licking my dry lips, I murmur, "It isn't like you don't have a following of minions you could force to hang out with you. If you were that bored, you could have asked Rachel. I doubt it would take much."

His lips curve. "That sounds oddly like jealousy, Mouse. For the record, I'm still pissed at Rachel for pulling what she did. I didn't know she took your key at school or grabbed the one outside."

We stare for a moment.

Then I shrug.

I vaguely remember Rachel bumping into me at school. I dropped my things and watched as she picked a few of them up. Silly me for thinking she was being nice.

He flicks my chin. "Rach and I used to be close when we were younger. Honestly, she annoys the shit out of me now."

I hesitate to reply. "So why do you hang out with her?"

He doesn't answer.

"Kaiden."

His smirk is wide. "Have to say, Em, I like my name on that mouth of yours."

I suck in a breath when he dips down, thinking he's about to kiss me. I don't want my first kiss to be on my old bed in the room my sister died in. And I shouldn't want it to be with Kaiden.

Instead, his lips brush the right side of my mouth, then trail to my ear. "Nostalgia."

I blink.

He pushes himself back up. "Rachel reminds me of what it was like before I let everything get to me. Before your dad came into the picture, Mom was always on my ass about my feelings and shit. It was…" He paused. "Rachel helped me forget about it all."

Frowning over his response, I soak in the way his features softened. He likes Rachel, respects her maybe. Yet it seems like whatever they have going on is on two different levels of understanding.

"I don't like your father," he continues, brushing his knuckles across my jaw. "But I don't hate him either. He distracts my mom."

Swallowing is hard with my heart lodged in my throat.

"You talk to her more. That must mean you want something from her. She loves you so much."

His touches stop, his knuckles lingering against the edge of my chin. He doesn't make eye contact with me, but his gaze drifts across every piece of my face like he's looking for something, searching.

"I do it for you," he hums under his breath.

Without another word, he settles on his side and draws me into him. My shoulder presses against his chest, and I don't bother fighting him when he repositions us so we're both lying on our sides. This time we're facing each other, but I can't look at his expression.

I focus on his shirt, the way his chest rises and falls, and I exhale slowly. "Why did you bother coming here? Be honest."

His hands find mine between us. He guides my palms to his chest and leaves them there, curling one of his arms around me until our bodies have no room left between us. Without mobility of my hands, I can't push him away.

Do I want to?

We spend a while listening to each other's breathing. After enough time passes, I settle into the bed, letting one hand drape around his side and the other fall onto the mattress.

"You didn't say goodbye," he whispers.

I close my eyes and breathe in his scent.

"I was coming back."

His silence tells me what I already know.

He doesn't do well with goodbyes either.

The longer we lie in silence, the more my body settles back into comfort until my lids get heavy. I'm half-asleep when I feel his hand go to my hair and brush some behind my ear. I'm too tired to worry about what his touch will do to the fragile strands.

He leans toward me. "I was worried about you, Em. That's why."

His voice fades.

The room fades.

But his warmth lulls me to sleep.

Twenty-One

I WAKE UP ALONE by the time the sun is finally up. It takes me a while to get my stiff limbs to cooperate enough to stretch and climb out of bed. After changing into leggings and a sweatshirt, I head to the kitchen, where I smell bacon.

To my surprise, Kaiden is at the table with a plate of pancakes in front of him. Grandma smiles at me when I walk in and transfers a few of the fluffy cakes on a plate for me, along with some fruit on the side. Glancing at the empty seat next to Kaiden and the one at the opposite end that Mama usually sits in, I weigh my options.

I sit in Mama's seat.

"How did you sleep, Emmy?" Grandma finishes cooking before turning off the burners and joining us at the table. She sits between Kaiden and me, poking at the eggs on her plate.

"Um..." I clear my throat, not making eye contact with Kaiden. "Good. I slept good." I stab a strawberry and pop it into my mouth, looking over my shoulder at Mama's open bedroom door. "Where is Mama?"

Grandma hesitates. "She left for work already. She mentioned something about an early meeting with the school."

I press my lips together and nod.

I focus on my pancakes when Grandma adds, "Tomorrow is the last day before break for them, so she'll be home the rest of the week."

There's so much hope in her voice, and I wonder if she believes everything will be okay. Mama has always been great at avoiding me when she wants to, and I doubt now is any different from when I lived here.

My voice is quiet. "Good."

Kaiden sees right through my false brevity. When I glance up, his head is tilted to the side as he studies me. His plate is already half empty, so I wonder how long he's been up.

I fidget in my chair. "What are your plans today, Grandma? Do you still see Betty across the street?"

She smiles. "The two of us planned on doing some shopping later today. If you're interested in tagging along, I'm sure she'd love to hear all about your new school." She gives Kaiden a small nod. "You're welcome too, of course."

To my surprise, he smiles back. It looks weird on his face, considering there's usually a scowl in its place. "Em actually told me she'd show me around town."

Grandma's sculpted white brows arch before she looks at me. "Did she, now?"

Kaiden's lips waver. "Yeah, she told me she'd show me her favorite spots. I've been looking forward to it since she said something last night."

Closing my eyes, I internally sigh. I don't go anywhere besides the bookstore, and that's been closed for a month now according to their website.

Grandma hums out a noncommittal reply, amusement evident on her face. The corners of her lips are crinkled in a barely there smile, but I know she knows.

I cut my pancakes. "These are good."

"You say that a lot," Kaiden responds.

I peek up at him. "Say what?"

"Good."

"What's wrong with good?"

"It's a lie."

Grandma laughs. "You two are interesting together, I'll give you that." She scrapes her chair backward, grabbing her plate and standing. "I'll leave you to it, then."

Together? "Grandma—"

She gently pats my shoulder before walking out of the room.

Kaiden is grinning from across the table.

"What?" I grumble, picking at my food.

"So you slept well, huh?"

I'm silent.

"Didn't wake up at all?" he presses.

My shoulders drop. "Why did you tell her I was showing you around? She knows that you're lying."

He seems genuinely surprised. "How would she know I'm lying?"

Shaking my head, I push around the fruit before setting my fork down. "I never got out much when I lived here, okay?"

He snorts. "Did you ever have a life? You don't do anything in Exeter either."

My nostrils flare. "There are reasons."

His fork clinks against the glass plate, causing me to stare at his waiting expression. "I have all day, Mouse. What aren't you telling me?"

Narrowing my eyes, I scoff. "What aren't you asking, Kaiden? You're so worked up over your own bullshit that you don't ask anyone about themselves. You assume."

"That isn't—"

"Don't lie," I cut him off. "You make stupid assumptions about everybody and everything. You shut down when things don't go your way and you blow up when people try to help. Yet you never ask anybody about anything that's relevant because you're trapped in your own little world."

His lips part, but nothing escapes them.

Taking a deep breath, I focus on finishing breakfast before tackling the rest of the day. I don't want to go shopping with Grandma and Betty, but I also don't want to chauffeur Kaiden around. He'll complain about how little there is to do here or give me crap about my only true happy place being a musty old bookstore that has more dust than books on the shelves.

When I'm finished, I take my plate to the kitchen and start washing it off. Kaiden nudges me out of the way and drops his plate in the sink before grabbing the sponge from me and taking over. I gape as I watch him scrub down and rinse off our stuff before placing them strategically in the plastic drainer.

"You act like you've never seen a guy do dishes before," he grumbles, turning the water off and drying his hands with the dish towel.

Dad would sometimes do dishes when we were little, but mostly it was up to Mama or Logan and me. Especially when Mama would give us treats or coins for helping.

"I just didn't expect *you* to do them," I murmur, shrugging.

He doesn't respond right away. Then he turns to me, resting his hip against the counter. "I prefer keeping out of people's business if I don't think I belong in it."

I snort unattractively. "Really? If memory serves, you think it's necessary to rule the school like you're the king. Kings are in everybody's business. I can't even eat a salad in peace without you making a scene."

"That's different."

"How?"

His tongue clucks. "High school is a nasty place, especially Exeter. There was a guy who graduated about a year ago who held my position. Everybody knew him, respected him, and listened to what he wanted. You know what that was? For everyone to get along."

I roll my eyes. "Not everybody is going to get along all the time. So what? High school is just four years—a blip in the grand scheme of things. You're wasting time trying to get everyone on the same page."

He looks away.

I contemplate telling him my own experiences from the only other school I've known. "Logan and I have always been opposites. Everyone loved her because she was outgoing and fearless. I was picked on because I hated interacting with people. I've always preferred being buried in a book where nobody could bother me. But even on the days when people teased me and gave me crap, I got through it."

He still doesn't look at me.

"There are worse things in life than being picked on. It's

draining to try fitting in. Lo and I were different, but I loved us because we were who we were. People may not have understood that, but only our opinions mattered."

"So, what?" he finally asks, crossing his arms on his chest. "Would you like me to let them talk shit about you? Do you want guys to hit on you, catcall you in the halls, or worse?"

Worse? "What…?"

"You don't want to know."

My eyes widen.

"Exeter High is a hunting ground," he says quietly, stepping closer. His tone drops. "I've seen bad things happen to people like you all the time. I do what I can to keep the predators away, but they're around and they love fresh meat."

I swallow.

He flicks a strand of my hair. "You're not wrong though," he adds, shrugging. "It's tiring to give a shit about what people do and think. It's necessary though."

One of my brows arches. "And what would people like me be?"

He smirks. "The mice. The quiet ones who don't bother anyone. That's who they go after, you know."

I blink and whisper, "I can take care of myself, Kaiden."

He glances around the room, lips pressing together, and then nods. "Yeah, Mouse. I can see that now."

Twenty-Two

KAIDEN MONROE LOVES FROZEN yogurt. Like smiling, it seems odd for someone as intense as him. He's content as he spoons some of the cake batter Froyo from the bowl, picking through the gummies he added to the top. *Gummy bears!*

The girl working the register keeps looking over at our table. Kaiden is oblivious, but I roll my eyes. I vaguely remember seeing her in a study hall held by one of my old math teachers a few years ago. She's graduated already like most of my former classmates, I do know that much.

Kaiden notices my barely touched dessert and points toward it with the neon-pink spoon. Considering the other option was purple, it makes me giggle. "You going to eat or what?"

I'm not sure why he cares. I insisted on paying, so it isn't like he's out any money if I decide to throw it away.

His eyes narrow. "What's your deal?"

I shake my head, raising the spoon of chocolate fudge–flavored yogurt to my lips to appease him. He grins and starts eating again, having over half his gone before I even eat a third of mine. It hasn't even been three hours since we ate breakfast, so I'm not hungry.

Grandma insisted we take her car and ride around, so I showed him the old bookstore, and we walked around the small strip mall containing only a few stores and a tiny theater, but considering the stores in town rarely stay in business long, the mall attracts a lot of people. Otherwise, everyone would need to travel two hours to go shopping.

We spent most of the morning in silence. Sometimes he'd make a comment, or criticism in his case, over something we saw in passing. More times than not, he just matched my pace and walked beside me without a word to say.

Yet it was…peaceful.

The cashier looks our way again.

Kaiden chuckles. "Friend of yours?"

He's known the whole time? "No."

He gives her a quick once-over, in which she blushes and wiggles her fingers, before looking back at me with no interest in his features. "It's a small area. You probably know everyone."

I eat more of my yogurt. "Is that your way of asking for an introduction? Sadly, I don't know her name."

That's not true. It's Marigold. I remember now because her hair is the color of one, and her sisters are all named after flowers. Rose, Lily, and Marigold. Mama said her parents are hippies or something.

He pushes his empty bowl away from him. "No need to be jealous, Mouse. I'm all yours."

"What if I don't want you?"

He shrugs.

That's it.

Ignoring him, I eat about half my dessert before I'm full. Blotting my lips with a napkin, I ball it up and throw it into what's left of my dish.

"You're seriously not eating it all?"

"I'm full."

"You barely eat."

"You barely shut up," I counter.

His head tips back in a loud laugh that makes his chest shake.

Marigold glares at me.

I hold her gaze.

She goes in the back.

Brushing hair behind my ear, I wet my bottom lip and study the little crumbs on the tabletop. "I thought I'd like being home. I even thought maybe Mama…" I swallow my words and toy with the spoon in my dish. Taking a deep breath, I close my eyes. "I thought Mama was okay. Or better. Something. I don't think she'll ever be okay, Kaiden."

"She seems a bit off," he agrees.

I lift my gaze. "You met her?"

He leans back in his seat. "After you fell asleep, she came to check on you. She wouldn't walk into the room. I told her I'd leave you two alone, but…"

"But what?"

He doesn't say.

"But. What?" I enunciate my words clearly, an almost growl.

"She said she couldn't be what you need right now," he answers dryly. "Not sure what the hell that means, but she wouldn't even fucking look at you when she said it. She kept looking at the other bed."

"Lo's bed."

He grunts.

"Now do you get it?" I ask.

Do you get why it's better?

Do you get why I had to leave?

Do you see I'm killing Mama?

"Yeah, Mouse," he murmurs. "I get it."

This time when we visit Lo's grave, Kaiden sits beside me like I'm going to try falling asleep again. It's colder now. I don't want to stay long, much less curl up on the cold, hard ground.

Legs crossed under me, I tuck my bare hands in the soft lining of my jacket pockets. "I used to love coming here and talking to Logan about my day. If our old friends did something that annoyed me, I'd vent to her about it. After she died, everyone just moved on like it was no big deal. It seemed like I was the only one who really missed her."

One of Lo's closest friends was part of the cheer squad with us. Ria Chaplin. I always thought she was annoying, but Lo loved her. Sometimes I think more than me. I even remember Lo ditching our plans after school to hang out at Ria's house with some of the other girls from the squad. They never invited me, but Lo would always tell me about the silly games they'd play and gossip they'd hear from Ria's older sister after Mama brought her home.

Ria used to tell Logan she thought I was holding her back. I overheard them talking after practice one day about me not being as talented. I never wanted to join the team; I did it for Lo. She begged me to do it with her. There was no denying that my passion for cheer didn't come close to matching hers.

I shake my head, running my tongue over my top teeth. "This one girl went to the funeral with her mother, but she wouldn't even come over and talk to me. Some of the girls from the squad were in the back, and all they talked about was how they wanted to leave."

Kaiden shifts, resting an arm over his knee. "Maybe they weren't handling it well."

My jaw twitches. "They handled it just fine. Ria mentioned wanting to go to McDonald's to get a shake before they all went home. I couldn't eat for a month, and she wanted to go get a *shake*."

He's quiet.

My eyes graze over Lo's grave before slowly making their way back to Kaiden. He's watching me with no clear emotion on his face. At least there isn't pity.

"Do you visit your dad?"

His eyes cast downward. "Yeah."

I nod.

"Maybe you're right." I sigh. "Maybe the girls just didn't know how to cope, and I've been irritated with them since. Does it make me a bad person to like bad-mouthing them to Lo? She thought Ria and them were great."

He chuckles. "Nah, there's worse you could say about people."

"Like?"

He simply shrugs again.

I pull my knees up to my chest and rest my chin on them. "I think Logan is around sometimes. Like when I'm having a bad day or something, it's like I feel her. In the wind. The sun. In music." I angle my body toward him slightly. "Do you ever feel that?"

His eyes are unblinking. "No."

I can't tell if he's lying or not. I wish there was a telltale sign, like a twitching eyebrow or a lingering gaze. It's almost like he's mastered the skill—like he's had years of practice. How long has he lied to himself?

My head tips back up to the sky. "I read an article about people coming back as other things. This one time, a woman was doing a maternity photo shoot and a ladybug landed on her. The photographer snapped a picture when the woman explained her late mother loved ladybugs. Then, during the baby's cake smashing photo shoot over a year later, a ladybug landed on his overalls. They got a picture of that too."

He scoffs in disbelief. "You can't honestly believe the woman's mother was the ladybug, can you?"

"Why can't I?" I challenge, staring only at Lo's grave. "Sometimes we need those types of beliefs to get us through the day. Like when I see a rainbow, especially without any rain, I like to think it's Logan."

"That's impossible."

I question a lot of things—God, the afterlife, what comes after death. Everything about never existing anymore terrifies me. What if we take our last breaths and then that's it? What then?

I scoot forward and put my hand on the cold marble stone in front of me. My fingers curl over the top, as though I'm holding Lo's hand. "Maybe it is," I agree softly. "But maybe it isn't. Who's to say what's out there and what isn't? None of us really know."

So we pretend.

We pretend our loved ones are still close to us.

We pretend we're okay.

It's not denial.

It's coping.

It's reassurance.

It's how we get through another day.

My hand is cold. "Ready to go inside? Grandma is probably going to be gone for a little while longer, which means we have the TV to ourselves."

His head tilts. "You want to watch TV?"

"What else would we do?"

His lips quirk in a devious smirk. "I can think of a lot of different things, Mouse. A house to ourselves can get us into a lot of trouble."

My heart does a little jig in my chest, but I silently tell it to stop. I stand up, brushing my leggings off. "I guess it's a good thing I was never a troublemaker then, huh?"

Amusement lingers on his face as he joins me, standing a little too close. Then again, we literally slept pressed against each other, so I suppose the minimal distance between us now is welcoming.

"Admit it, Mouse."

My brows pinch. "What?"

He leans in, his lips grazing my ear until the warmth of his breath causes me to shiver. "I think you want to know what trouble tastes like."

I allow myself to close my eyes for a split second and absorb the moment before turning my head toward where his lips linger. If I move ever so slightly, our lips will touch. It could be my first kiss, and I bet it would be a good one. Kaiden seems like he knows what he's doing, not that I want to think about him doing this with other girls.

How many people does he travel to see on school break? He already admitted he doesn't usually take people to his special spot at the sycamore. Yet for me, he does.

I let my heart absorb the win.

Then I bury it deep, deep down.

His breath caresses my mouth, invites me in. My nose nuzzles his cheek as I take in his masculine scent.

I exhale. "Pass."

Then I walk away.

Twenty-Three

At some point during *America's Funniest Home Videos* reruns, I fall asleep next to Kaiden on the couch. I don't remember curling up or using Kaiden's thigh as a pillow, but it's how I wake up. His arm is draped over me casually, his breathing even.

I hear Grandma from the kitchen, talking and rattling around dishes, and realize she's speaking to Kaiden. Pretending to still be asleep, I flutter my lids closed and try not to think about the hard muscle under my cheek.

"I think it'll be good for them," Grandma says quietly, her footsteps nearing. "I want nothing more than to see them get along like they used to. It's been…tough."

Kaiden doesn't seem to buy it. His arm around me tightens gently. "And whose fault do you think that is?"

There's a pregnant pause. "I'm not dismissing my daughter's actions, young man. What I'm saying is that I want them to find happiness again."

I feel eyes on me, so I force myself to remain still. The

sweet smell of cinnamon wraps around me like an invisible blanket, causing my muscles to ease into him despite the tense conversation.

"I've made dinner reservations for the four of us tonight." Something ruffles and then I see Grandma's navy-blue orthopedic shoes come into view through the narrow slits of my eyes. "It's their favorite restaurant, and I'm sure you'll find something you like as well."

She kisses my temple lightly.

"I love them both," she tells him softly, her hand gently brushing through my hair. I fight back a grimace from the way my scalp reacts. "I just don't know how to fix them."

Kaiden's thumb brushes the bare skin of my stomach where my shirt must have ridden up during my nap. I bite back making a noise, but the slightest jerk of my body in his hand causes him to press down knowingly.

"Do you think forcing them to eat dinner across from each other will really help?" he says with doubt.

"What else can I do?"

"Sometimes we can't do anything."

Grandma moves away, her touch disappearing along with the cherry blossom scent from her lotion. "I don't believe that. When you love people as much I love these two, you find ways to help heal them."

"What if the damage is too much?"

Grandma's steps stop. "Healing doesn't mean the damage never existed. It just means that it can no longer control our lives. I sincerely hope you remember that. I know a hurt soul when I see one, boy. You and Emery are one and the same, which means you're also tough. It doesn't matter what battle you're fighting. It only matters that you're willing to fight."

"And what is Emery fighting?"

Grandma doesn't answer right away. "I suppose if you don't already know, it's not my place to tell you. You came here for her. You care. Give her time to tell you herself."

I swallow and try to calm my pounding heartbeat. Can Kaiden feel it? Hear it? My anxiety over him knowing the truth drums the beat louder until my ears thump along.

Grandma leaves the room and I remain still. My eyes open to a muted television screen. The show on now is one I don't recognize. The time on the clock says it's almost four thirty.

"You can get up now," he says.

I lick my lips and sit up, sneaking a peek at him through my lashes. "I didn't mean to fall asleep on you."

His arms go to his chest. "Your grandmother seems to think we're the same person. Not sure if I should take that as a compliment or not."

I frown. "Am I that bad?"

He levels with me. "You're holding something back from me."

His accusation makes me roll my eyes, which he doesn't find amusing. "Just because I don't tell you everything doesn't mean I'm holding it back. There's a lot we don't know about each other, Kaiden."

His lips twitch. It's almost like he's weighing his response options. He can't disagree with me, because I'm not wrong. But that won't stop him from commenting something snarky back, because that's his defense mechanism.

"I suppose this is where we exchange boring facts about ourselves?" he guesses, deadpan. "Am I supposed to tell you that my favorite color is black and that I listen to emo music and self-loathe in the darkness of my bedroom?"

My brows go up and I stifle a giggle. "I don't know. Do you?"

He eyes me.

I smile and shrug. "You're probably the kind of guy who loves the color gray even though it's boring. Heather gray, not light. And you don't listen to emo music, whatever that is. You listen to rap. Probably R and B too. I bet you loathe country music based on principle alone and that the only thing you do in the darkness of your room is—" I stop myself and blush. "Uh, well, you know."

"I don't know." Leaning in close to me, he whispers, "What do I do in the darkness of my room, Mouse?"

His breath tickles my nose, causing me to wiggle it. "What every guy probably does."

"Which is…?"

My eyes widen. "You can't honestly expect me to say it. My grandma is in the house somewhere."

His eyes dance with mischief. "Tell me what I do in my room."

I swallow. "Sleep."

"And?"

I try glancing away, but he won't let me. He turns my head to face him, our eyes locking. His fingers remain on my chin so I won't look anywhere else.

"Watch movies?"

He smirks. "Wrong."

"Do homework?"

"Try again."

My whole face heats up.

"Say it, Mouse."

"T-touch yourself?"

His whole face lights up. I try moving away, but he keeps me locked in place. "Tell me something. Do you touch yourself?"

My jaw drops.

There's no way he just asked me that.

Except…he's Kaiden.

"I'm not answering that."

He lets go of my chin. "That's a yes, then."

"What? No, I—"

He winks. *Winks*. "We all do it. The fact that you're too embarrassed to say you get yourself off just confirms it."

My neck tingles.

Not wanting to egg him on, I swing my legs over and plant my feet on the floor. "I should probably see if Grandma needs help with anything. So—"

He tugs me back down onto the couch when I'm halfway to standing, making me flinch. I draw my arm back and rub it, causing him to study me. "It's your turn."

My…?

"You're not a girly girl, so it's safe to say pink isn't your favorite color. My best guess is that yellow is, since you wear it most often. I know you're obsessed with that happy-go-lucky song about sunshine and shit, so you're probably into indie rock and country too. Mainstream pop. You're a nerd, so I know you spend most of your time in your bedroom doing homework and reading. When you're not touching yourself, of course."

I grab a pillow and smack him in the chest with it. "Would you stop? I do *not* touch myself!"

Grandma walks in at that exact moment, her lips turning upward. "Interesting conversation to walk in on. Emmy, your mother just called. She's going to meet us at Le Sal's restaurant in half an hour."

Trying to pretend Grandma didn't just hear me tell Kaiden about what I do or don't do in the confines of my bedroom, I nod. "That sounds like fun. I've been craving their chocolate mousse for a while."

She grabs her car keys. "I'll warm up the car. If you want to change, I think we'll leave in about ten minutes. We need to beat traffic."

I nod and watch her button her coat before leaving Kaiden and me alone again. He's still clutching the pillow I hit him with, so I grab another one and smack him again. "You're a jackass."

He just smiles.

I sigh and throw the pillow back onto the couch beside me. "For the record, I love most music. I grew up on classic rock though. It's a preference of mine."

His eyes scan over my face. "I can probably guess a lot more about you."

Please don't, I silently groan.

I know asking him not to will only make him want to torture me more.

"You've never been kissed."

My eyes bulge.

He scoots closer. "You've never slept with anyone before."

His knee brushes my leg.

"You haven't lived yet, Em."

Pressing my lips together, I lean back to put a little distance between us. "And that stuff is supposed to help me live?"

His lips quirk. "They're a start. It's better than the existing thing you're set on doing."

"Technically," I point out, "I did sleep with you, so that scratches one of those items off the list."

His eyes spark. "Is that an invitation to help you scratch off more?"

"Dream on, buddy."

He taps my nose. "I'm sure you'll be a welcoming feature in them tonight. Especially if you press your ass against my—"

The front door opens, and I death-glare Kaiden into silence. His smirk tells me he's saving this conversation for later, something I don't look forward to.

Grandma glances at us as she peels off her coat, not saying a word. I'm not sure she needs to because her eyes dance with as much amusement as Kaiden's does. Standing up, I flatten my shirt down and inspect my outfit. Too lazy to change, I head into my room and put on a pair of socks and shoes before grabbing a scarf and my jacket.

Kaiden and Grandma are talking but stop when I show back up.

Grandma smiles.

Kaiden winks.

Twenty-Four

LE SAL'S IS THE town's best-known restaurant. It doesn't have any limitations; they serve everything from pizza and wings on game days in their bar area to lobster in the main dining room. In the summer, the patio is full of people surrounding the glass tables, under cover from the sun's rays using the beige umbrellas as they talk among themselves.

Even Dad loved coming here. He'd always order the steak and potatoes no matter how much Lo would tell him to try something new. She was never better. She and I always got chicken tenders and fries, though sometimes instead of honey mustard, she would ask for ranch.

It's busy when we arrive, so Grandma says she's glad she made reservations. As we wait to see the hostess, I glance around the room with Kaiden nearly pressed against my back. The noise is overwhelming in the front dining area, the main one, so I hope we get put in the back. Mama usually hates it there. She thinks the waitresses forget us, but it's all I hope for to avoid getting another headache.

Kaiden dips down behind me. "Swanky place for such a small town."

I giggle. "Did you just use the word swanky?"

He grins in return.

We step closer to the hostess station. "I used to love coming here. We'd make it a tradition to come at least once a week. Thursdays always worked best because it wasn't as crowded."

When the hostess asks us if we have a reservation, she searches our name and tells us Mama is waiting. I'm relieved when we're guided to the back dining room, where Mama is tucked away in the corner.

As soon as she sees us, her lips twitch into a tiny smile. It doesn't last very long, and I wonder what she's thinking.

Do you really *want to know?*

The hostess gives us menus and makes sure we all have silverware at our seats before telling us our waitress will be right with us. Before I can put much thought into where to sit, Kaiden pulls out the chair next to me and gestures for me to take it. Grandma sits next to Mama, so I shrug off my scarf and jacket and drape them both over the back of the chair before sitting.

We're quiet while we scan the menu for drinks and food, and in no time we all have our orders in with a bubbly brunette who keeps smiling at Kaiden like he's the only one at the table. When she scribbles down my chicken tenders and fries, I'm not even sure if she hears what kind of dipping sauce I want because she's batting her lashes at him.

The bitter feeling returns to my chest, and I want to grumble it away. I know what it is. I just don't want to accept it.

Jealousy.

When she's gone, the quiet continues. Kaiden looks at

me and then Mama, not saying a word. Maybe he's expecting her to start the conversation.

I play with the wrapper from my straw, folding it like an accordion before flattening it back out.

Grandma starts the conversation. "So how was everybody's day? Kids, you should tell Joanne about where all you went."

I squirm in my seat and toy with my napkin. "I just took Kaiden to the mall and we got some Froyo after."

Mama nods, seemingly interested. "Did you buy anything?"

I shake my head.

There were a few books I considered getting at a tiny book boutique we went into. Kaiden even offered to buy them, but they were way too much money. I dragged him out before he could go back for them.

Kaiden sinks into his seat, and his comfort tells me he's getting ready to settle into a conversation I don't want him to begin. "Why didn't you call her?"

I tense.

Mama's lips part slightly.

He reaches out and sips his water. "Just seems strange that you'd let your daughter move in with a man who left his family."

I kick him under the table, but he doesn't even flinch.

He sets his glass down. "I acknowledge that it's none of my business, but your daughter does live with me now. Since you don't seem to care, somebody has to."

"Kaiden," I warn.

He won't look anywhere but at Mama.

She blinks rapidly, and when her head moves, I see the slight shine to her teary eyes. I close mine, not wanting to see the color change.

"You're right," she says softly.

My eyes snap open.

She's looking at him, not me. "I can't sit here and pretend like I've been a good mother to Emery."

Surprise colors my face.

Her eyes shift to mine. "Sunshine, I need to get better. I need…you to get better." I hold my breath, praying she doesn't say more on the topic. She gives me the smallest, saddest smile. "I signed up for a support group a while ago. One of my coworkers left a brochure on my desk, and I couldn't throw it out. I know I should have gone a long time ago, but…"

But what?

But you were scared?

But you were in denial?

But you thought you were fine?

"It's been helping. They suggested I put Logan's pictures in an album and change up your old bedroom for something new. I…I visit her grave a few times a week. They made me accept that I've treated everything since her death so poorly, and I can't apologize enough to you for that. I don't know how to fix it, which is why I thought you seeing your father would be best. You and he…he deserves to have you back in his life.

"Having you here means the world to me, and I haven't shown it," she continues, reaching out to me. "Maybe once I get more of the help I should have accepted years ago, we can try this again. I need—" She closes her eyes and squeezes my hand, and I accept the pain—both hers and my own. "I just need more time. You've given me years and so much love, so I hate to ask for more. But it's what I need."

Time.

Time is my greatest enemy.

Doesn't she understand that?

But then I look at her. Really look.

I see the features I notice on my own face when I chance a look in the mirror. I see heartache and pain and unspoken emotion in the bags beneath her eyes. Her cheeks aren't damp, and people aren't staring, and there's nothing out of the ordinary about us.

We're a family having dinner.

We're a family with problems. We're riddled with imperfections and flaws and struggles like anyone else in the room.

We're just buried in years' worth of pent-up frustration and anger and guilt over it.

She wants time.

I'll give her time.

One more hand squeeze and we're both settled back in our chairs.

We eat dinner in peace—in necessary silence.

Kaiden looks at me.

I don't look back.

When we get back to the house, Kaiden pulls me away from Mama and Grandma. He grabs the blanket from the back of his car and tugs me toward Lo's grave. I don't protest and ask why he's doing this. I just let his hand envelop mine until he lets go to get the blanket situated on the ground.

It is way too cold to stay out here for long, but I somehow welcome the uncomfortable chill. We get too used to finding comfort in things we shouldn't—accepting what is instead of questioning it. So I hug my knees to my chest and stare at Logan's gravestone.

It's already getting dark, which means the temperature will only get colder. Since Kaiden likes to scold me for being outside, I'm sure the sycamore and grave outings won't last once winter officially greets us. The snow will ruin our chances to escape our family, and I wonder if he's as sad as I am about it.

I don't ask.

I sit.

I stare.

I sulk.

Closing my eyes, I rest my cheek on my knee. The warmth from my leggings soaks into my cold skin, and I wrap my arms a little tighter around my shins.

"What did she mean?" he asks, breaking the silence after a few minutes.

I open my eyes to see him watching me.

"She said you needed to get better."

I press my lips together.

"Emery," he all but growls.

I sigh, knowing it was only a matter of time before this happened. The sick girl can't lie dormant forever, not even in the eyes of someone who doesn't want to see a problem.

He treats me like anyone else.

He messes with me.

He's rude.

He's cruel.

Oddly, I don't want that to end.

"Does it matter?" is my reply.

His eyes narrow.

I scoot closer to him. For warmth, for comfort, for anything but the truth he seeks. "I get angry with you a lot for the stuff you do. It's like you don't care about hurting anybody's feelings—Cam, Rachel, me."

My head rests against his shoulder, which tenses for a moment before relaxing. His arm lifts and wraps around my waist, tugging me closer into him. I sigh when I feel his body heat wrap around me.

We both see our breaths.

My nose tingles and numbs.

I bite my lip before letting it loose. "I decided that it's better than people pretending to be good though. There are a lot of fake people in the world, Kaiden Monroe. You may be a jackass, but at least you're real."

His chuckle fills the night air.

I tip my chin up, looking through my lashes at him. His gaze dips to meet my eyes, and we stay like that. Close but not close enough. Distant but not distant enough.

He knows more than I want him to.

But he doesn't know what matters.

I swallow. "Kaiden?"

"Hmm?"

I lean closer, one of my hands pressing against his toned stomach. There's nothing soft about him. He always looks like he's ready to pounce, to fight.

I'm not sure what to say.

I can't ask for what I want because I'm not sure *want* is the right word.

I need it.

His warmth.

His distraction.

He told me I shouldn't just exist.

That I should live.

He can help.

"You remember when I said pass before?" I whisper, slowly rising to my knees so our faces are at the same level.

His eyes darken.

"Can I take that back?"

His nostrils flare as his palm cups my jaw, light but fiery. The anticipation rises in the air between us, setting a fire to the chill.

"What if I'm not any good?" I whisper.

He chuckles. "Then we'll practice."

That's all he says before his lips are on mine, much softer than I expect. They brush mine once, twice, a third time. He distances himself just enough to tease my lips with his breath, angling my head to the side before kissing me again.

This time harder.

Hungrier.

Needier.

I quickly figure out what to do and follow his lead, pressing my fingers into his sides and causing him to jerk. I let go and bunch his shirt in my hands, holding on while he parts my lips with his and drags the tip of his tongue along my bottom lip before his tongue tastes mine.

I gasp when his hands drag down my sides, gripping my hips tightly and then loosening up. He tastes like marinara and lemon water and smells like the woods, and everything about the moment consumes me.

One of his hands goes to my hair.

One of mine goes to his face.

His other hand goes to the small of my back.

Mine goes to his bicep.

I'm not sure where to touch him or not, but he doesn't let me stay in my head long enough to begin doubting my lack of experience. He presses on my lower back until he's pushing me into his lap, positioning my legs on either side of him. My hip pops and makes me wince, but I force myself to focus solely on Kaiden. A startled noise escapes me when I sink onto him and feel something hard press against my inner thigh.

He draws back, but only to begin kissing my jaw until his lips work their way down my neck. I shiver, but not from the cold. My body is overheating as his teeth graze the skin of my neck before suckling just above my pulse. It feels good, too good, the way he nips and sucks and licks the same spot.

"K-Kaiden." I press a hand against the back of his head, wanting him to keep going. He groans when my hips involuntarily move on his lap and his teeth bite into my flesh.

It stings, but then he licks the pain away.

His hands go to my hips, pressing down on them to get our bodies as close together as possible. He doesn't know my hips are a trigger point of pain, but I don't bother stopping this to tell him. I just endure the sharp feeling because there's a new kind of heat burning between my legs, one that gets more and more intense as his nipping becomes rougher and his hands become more demanding. I can deal with this kind of pain.

I move against him, needing friction. He growls and helps me build a rhythm, sliding his body against mine as he rocks into me. His mouth works its way to the base of my neck before my scarf gets in the way.

He doesn't move it.

He doesn't undo my coat.

He just focuses on me.

My warmth.

My need.

My silent pleas.

Our mouths meet again, and his kisses are lighter but just as needy as mine. My tongue dances with his, my hips becoming jerky, and suddenly I'm panting and gripping his shoulders and leaning my forehead against his.

I almost come undone when I feel his hand reach between us and begin rubbing me over my leggings. Nobody has ever touched me there, and the added sensation feels amazing. I move against his palm until he's pressing into me so hard I tip my head back and let the tingling sensation take over until I feel it everywhere.

"Fuck, Em," he groans as I ride out the sensation against his hand. He kisses my cheek, my jaw, and then pecks my lips when my movement creeps to a stop.

Swallowing as I catch my breath, I pull away from him. His eyes are dark, his face flushed, and his chest rises and falls as quickly as mine.

If this is what living is like, I definitely want more of it.

"I've never…" I blush hard, shaking my head and glancing down at where our bodies meet. The admission burns my body. "I've never had one from someone else before."

He grins.

It's devious.

All-knowing.

It's…Kaiden.

"Just wait until it's my cock, Mouse."

My eyes widen.

He laughs…and then guides me back inside like it's just another night.

Twenty-Five

THE BATHROOM MIRROR SHOWS me a new kind of flush to my cheeks. Not one caused by disease or cold air but by Kaiden. Maybe I could have pretended it was early winter's caress when I came in to peel off my scarf and coat, but my swollen lips said something else.

That's why Kaiden is on the couch, with the pillow and blanket Mama gave him. At first, my face burned when she chanced us both a look before passing him things to use for tonight, but then I smiled.

Because Mama noticed.

Mama saw me.

Flushed cheeks, swollen lips, and all.

Now I'm curled in my room, touching my lips that are nothing extraordinary since hours have passed. I kept squirming on the couch when I agreed to watch TV with everyone, because Kaiden kept finding ways to nudge me with his knee or brush my arm with his hand, so I opted to change and go to bed. Mama and Grandma followed suit, telling me good night before we closed ourselves in our rooms.

My phone's reading app is up, but I've been rereading the same page for the past five minutes. I'm distracted, my brain replaying what happened outside over and over until my heart is racing like it did before.

Not even my favorite romance books can get me to stop thinking about what happened.

My first kiss.

With *Kaiden*.

I'm sure by typical standards, I should have been kissed by anybody else—a band geek, a drama nerd, an outcast. Not my stepbrother. Not the person who's isolated me since moving, going hot and cold in an instant like the broken faucet in the kitchen downstairs.

I try focusing back on the book.

Two sentences in, my bedroom door quietly opens.

I hold my breath.

"I shouldn't be surprised you're reading," he muses, creeping into the room after shutting the door with a soft click.

I sit up in bed. "You shouldn't be in here. There's a reason you were given stuff for the couch."

He grins, not stopping until he's leaning over me. "Maybe I'm just making sure you're all tucked in for the night. Hmm? That would simply make me a concerned family member."

I blanch. "Don't refer to yourself as my family member. Not after..." Waving my hand around, I shake my head and avoid his gaze.

He sits on the edge of my bed, picking up my phone and glancing at the screen, making a disappointed face. "I'm surprised you're not reading something smutty. I hear people love reading all about different sexual positions and calling it research." He tosses the phone back onto the mattress. "Is that why you read, Mouse?"

I roll my eyes. "I read because I love books. Get your mind out of the gutter."

"Can't. It's a permanent residence."

I flatten the comforter around me. "Well, as you can see, I am already all tucked in. Your job here is done."

His head tilts. Without a word, he turns himself around and practically forces me to scooch over. By the time he's settled in, he's taking up most of my bed, one arm bent behind his head in support and the other opened as if he's inviting me to use him as a pillow.

"What are you doing?" I whisper, having déjà vu from last night. My eyes go to the door, worried someone will notice he isn't on the couch. Usually Mama is the one who will get up in the middle of the night, especially if she doesn't take her sleeping pills.

Instead of waiting for me to move over, he pulls me into his body. I'm practically lying over half of him by the time he wiggles his way into the mattress and drapes an arm around me.

"Seriously?"

He looks over. "Don't act like you hate this. Can you honestly say you were restless last night? Do I make you uncomfortable? Or did you sleep better than you have in a while because you were *too* comfortable?"

I don't answer.

He turns his head so he's facing the ceiling. His breathing is even, calm. "I hear you tossing and turning at night at home. You don't sleep through it very often, do you?"

How does he know that?

I don't have to ask, because I realize he's always sneaking in and out of the house. He'd have to pass my room, and Mama always told me I was noisy when I got restless. I guess it's only gotten worse.

Quietly, I admit, "I get nightmares."

To my surprise, he doesn't reply right away. His hold on me tightens a little, almost like a comforting squeeze. It's his version of a hug—telling me he's here.

"And last night?"

I lick my lips. "I didn't have one."

"Do they happen every night?"

Pausing, I debate on lying. If he knows I get them almost every night, he'll ask what they're about. Anyone would be curious over what haunts a person's thoughts so often.

"Not every night," I settle on.

He knows enough to slowly nod. "I'll stay for a while. Should probably slip out before your grandma or mom finds me in here."

I hum out my agreement.

We're silent for a long while, just listening to each other's breathing, heartbeats, and other old-house noises. I can hear the freezer running as it produces ice, and if I focused hard enough, I'd hear the slightest drip coming from the bathroom sink.

Deciding to break the silence first, I rest my cheek on his chest and let out a tiny sigh. "I don't know why you're being so nice to me, or as nice as you can get, but thank you."

His chest starts moving, and I'm confused until it registers that he's laughing at me. Peeling myself off him, I glance down with pinched brows.

"I assure you," he murmurs, voice low and eyes dark, "my intentions aren't *nice*, Mouse. But if you want to thank me for being your first kiss, then you're welcome. It's unfortunate though."

He thinks kissing me was unfortunate?

Tensing, I lie back down and don't say a word. He must sense something is wrong, because he draws me away until I'm staring back down at him again.

"Don't get self-conscious on me."

My jaw ticks. "You just told me that—"

"Other guys aren't going to get you off like I did, Emery." His words silence me. "They will take, take, take, but they won't give. Any other guy will be ruined for you because of me."

Maybe he thinks I'll swoon or kiss him or thank him again. I don't do any of those things. Instead, I fight off the laugh that wants to bubble from my lips.

His eyes narrow.

I shake my head and pat his chest. "I'm sure you're right, Kaiden. But I've read that very line in, like, forty different books. The truth may be the same, but the delivery could get worked on for the full effect."

Now he's silent.

Then his chest starts shaking again.

I fall asleep shortly after he pulls me back to him, not bothering to worry about his warning.

It won't matter anyway, because Kaiden is…Kaiden. *My* Kaiden. The very person I need in my life to put things in perspective.

Nobody compares.

Nobody will get a chance to.

Twenty-Six

KAIDEN SLIPS INTO MY bedroom almost every night since break. There are no expectations, just dreamless sleep and the occasional fondling that I'm sure isn't accidental. It's nice, welcoming even, when I hear the door crack open and feel the bed dip beside me. Sometimes I'll wake up to trailing kisses or hand-holding. Other times to soft snoring that makes me giggle.

December has hit in full force, with winter snowfall coating everything in white. I never liked the season, even when I was little. Lo would always drag me outside to build snowmen and snow forts, but I'd protest every time until Mama said it's good to get out.

Now I loathe the cold weather for justifiable reasons, not that anyone truly gets it. When the temperature drops, my joints become so stiff I can't move them for at least an hour after waking up, and there's always a dull ache that lasts throughout the day unless I wear gloves and try to keep warm. Wearing gloves during classes isn't an option though, so I endure the struggle of holding a pen while jotting down notes.

Even my space heater doesn't do as much as Kaiden's warm body wrapped around me does. I go to bed wearing layers, sometimes even sleeping in my fluffy bathrobe for extra comfort. But it doesn't always help. The single-digit temperatures do my body in, and it reminds me of the days Lo struggled to get out of bed because her body was so swollen and locked up that she had to be tended to from our room.

School has become a welcome distraction from the aches and pains and late-night rendezvous with Kaiden. Most girls would probably be irritated over being ignored by him in the halls, but I prefer it. Nobody sees him for who he is here. He lets down his walls for me at home, sharing silly stories about our pasts that mean more than he could ever know.

During Thursday Book Club, Annabel sits by me instead of in her usual seat. She kept looking at me in history but never said a word. I was almost tempted to ask her to sit by me at lunch, but I've gotten used to the empty table that graces me for forty minutes.

Annabel brushes hair behind her ear as she settles into her seat. "I don't think the others like our book choices."

Three of the girls stopped showing up almost two months ago. Apparently staring at Mr. Nichols wasn't worth the effort of reading and talking about the books.

After break, we discussed Jodi Picoult's *My Sister's Keeper*, which one of the girls protested because of its content. Both Mr. Nichols and Annabel defended my choice by arguing it should be discussed regardless of what happens to the characters.

Nobody wants to read about reality.

Mr. Nichols had asked Little Mermaid why she thought so, which she scoffed at. She doesn't want to talk about books or why she doesn't like reading them. But I know the answer she won't verbalize.

People are afraid of the truth. They don't want to accept that bad things happen to good people every single day. People struggle. People die. It's life.

Little Mermaid called me morbid.

I called her naive.

Mr. Nichols told us to be respectful.

The more we talked about the book, the more heated it got. It stopped being about the content and about why authors write about realistic topics.

Fiction is the perfect platform to talk about the things nobody wants to have conversations about in real life. When you're reading about a character's struggles, you find ways to relate from a distance. It doesn't always hurt as much, but that doesn't mean it doesn't hurt at all.

Chronic illness is real.

Death is real.

People don't like to read about those things because they know it could happen to them. Distance or not, you put yourself in the shoes of every character you read.

Denial doesn't make the fear go away.

It expands it.

Feeds it.

Makes it impossible to fight.

Annabel pulls out her book choice, Margaret Atwood's *The Handmaid's Tale*, and wiggles until she's settled comfortably in her chair.

I give her a small smile. "The others don't like living in

a world that's beyond creepy vampires who watch women sleep and kids who get put in an arena to slaughter each other. They'll get over it."

She giggles. "We're doing them a favor, if you think about it. Hitting them with reality before reality can."

I grin back at her.

Mr. Nichols walks in and smiles at us. We're the only two in here so far, but a couple of girls are lingering at the computers across the room. They're giggling and joking and probably looking up something they shouldn't be online. I see people do it all the time, hacking through the firewall the school places on social media sites.

"Ready for another group read?" he asks, setting his messenger bag down on the table in front of his chair.

Annabel rolls her eyes. "Do you mean argue with the girls about tasteful literature? Yes. I'm prepared."

Amusement flickers across Nichols's face, but he doesn't buy into the remark. "I've considered adding this book to the curriculum for next year. I'd like to see what discussion we come up with based on first opinions."

Annabel makes a face. "It's the kind of book you'd need students to do research on. It isn't like Emery's book last month. Atwood uses political influence in this."

Nichols sits down, taking out his own copy that has multicolored tabs marking the pages. Something tells me he's already done extensive research on the book, especially if he's interested in teaching it.

Annabel must realize the same thing because she looks apologetic. "Why would you want to teach this, anyway? It gets a lot of backlash, and most students will just watch the television show instead of reading it."

He chuckles softly over her disbelief in his reasoning. "Emery made a good point. Literature isn't always going to give us the content we desire. It's important to change up what's expected of the students, including how political and personal experiences impact people in everyday life."

I can't help but notice how he looks at me while he delivers the last part.

When it's time to start, only a few of the girls join us. It seems like book club won't exist past Christmas break at the rate it's deteriorating. I knew it was going to be tested through the semester, but I'd hoped more people would join.

Halfway through our conversation on first thoughts of what we were assigned to read, my vision grows fuzzy. Blinking past the blurriness as I stare at the girl whose name I can never seem to remember, I take a few deep breaths and sway slightly in my chair. From the not so far distance of my conscience, a headache forms, heavy and unforgiving.

It's been a couple of weeks since one settled into my temples. I thought I was finally getting relief, but maybe Cam's suggestion on seeing a neurologist will give me answers. She's on medicine for chronic migraines, so she's willing to set up a new patient appointment for me.

Rubbing at my eyes, I try to focus on what Mr. Nichols is responding with. He's talking about feminism and the main character's forced submission to her commander.

Survival mode.

I know it well.

Why am I so nauseated all of a sudden?

I try to distract myself, thinking about how to add my commentary in. I could talk about how the women pitted themselves against each other as a new form of feminism. Survival of the fittest and all that.

The idea of opening my mouth right now doesn't seem like the best idea, so I swallow the temptation to throw up and start collecting my belongings with shaky hands.

Nichols mentions the color theme.

Red for the Handmaids.

Blue for the Wives.

Green for the Marthas.

I'm turning green right now.

Annabel stares.

Mr. Nichols says my name.

I bolt out of the library on unsteady legs. Dizziness greets my every step as I run toward the nearest trash can I see in the hall.

My name is being called.

It's getting louder.

I'm getting sicker.

I vomit as my hair is pulled back.

Not by Annabel.

By Mr. Nichols.

I'd swear if I could.

Instead, I empty my stomach and pray that I pass out to avoid further humiliation.

Be careful what you wish for.

Twenty-Seven

I SHOOT DAD DAGGERS with my eyes from the back seat of the car while Mama tries collecting herself in the phone pressed to my ear. Despite insisting I was fine, Dad and Cam dragged me to the hospital for a second opinion where he called Mama as a grouchy old nurse checked my vitals.

The doctor on call looked at my records, checked my temperature, gave me pain and nausea medicine, and referred me to the hospital's neurology department like I told Dad he would. I've spent a lot of time in hospitals, so I know the visit wasn't worth the two-hundred-and-fifty-dollar co-pay my father was charged for his overreaction.

He told me I didn't understand.

It's a parent thing.

I'd be laughing over the ironic statement if Mama hadn't called me crying as we walked out of the emergency room exit. Cam rubbed my back and told me she'd make me an appointment with neurology for as soon as they had an opening, and Dad had the nerve to look apologetic when I answered the phone.

At least Mama called.

After twenty minutes of her panicked worry, I finally get her to believe that I'm okay. I tell her my head hurts less, my abdominal muscles aren't as cramped, and my nausea has simmered.

Lo wasn't like this, Mama.

Somehow, that point calms her. If Lo didn't suffer from it, it must be unrelated. I believe it to be true anyway, so it isn't like I'm giving her false information. The doctor even said migraines are a common occurrence, nothing to worry about.

Doctors also thought you were anorexic.

I shove the thought away.

When Grandma tells me that she'll take care of Mama, I disconnect the call and stare into the night. The roads are coated with a dusting of snow that the streetlights make glisten, and the wind whistles against the ice-ridden tree limbs. The heat controls for the back are on full blast, and I'm sitting on my hands as the seat warmer toasts them.

"You shouldn't have called her."

For a split second, I don't think either of them will reply. Cam glances at me before looking at Dad for guidance. His shoulders tense before he loosens a sigh.

"She's your mother, Emery."

She's your mother.

It's a parent thing.

I shake my head. "You wasted money that could have gone toward the holidays. I told you I was fine."

The car slows for a light. "We needed to be sure. You never know—"

"That's right," I snap. "*You* never know, Dad. I've spent years figuring out how to read my body. Grandma used to get such bad migraines she'd puke and then feel better. Out of everything that's wrong with me, that much is normal."

The car is silent as he continues down the road. As the house nears, he chances a look at me in the rearview mirror. I don't expect to see sadness in his eyes. Maybe if I look hard enough at the dulled color, I'll see the speckle of emerald Mama always told me about.

Dad doesn't say a word and neither does Cam. I remain silent as he turns on the blinker and pulls into the driveway. None of us unbuckle once the car is parked. We just sit there with nothing but the heat and low hum of the radio filling the air around us.

Locking eyes with his in the mirror, I swallow past the sudden onset of emotion building in my throat. Dad is worried about me, maybe even guilty for not worrying more.

His eyes tell me he's sorry—not for calling Mama but for not being there. He's making it up to me, making the most of what he can now.

I'm not making it easy for him.

My lips feel dry, so I wet them. "If it's a parent's job to worry, then I guess it's a kid's job to be annoyed by it."

It's my peace offering—an extended hand. Thankfully, he takes it and gives me a tiny nod before turning off the car and guiding us all inside.

Kaiden is waiting in my room, looking none too pleased. Cam said she texted him to let him know where we were, but he never got back to her. I figured he was out doing who knows what with his teammates.

He rises from the mattress and gives me a furious gaze, lips pressed into a straight line. As he appraises me, I wonder what he sees. The medicine they gave me to ease the nausea and pain have helped immensely, but I probably look as tired as I feel.

"Don't start right now," I tell him, toeing out of my shoes and grabbing my sweatpants and a sweatshirt from my dresser.

He holds his hand out. "Give me your phone."

My brows pinch. "Uh, why?"

His steely voice tells me his patience has worn down hours ago, so I dig out my phone from my back pocket and place it in his palm. He fingers the keyboard, getting past the lock in ways I don't want to know, and then passes it back to me without one ounce of emotion other than anger on his face.

"Use my fucking number."

That's all he says before he walks out.

I stare at my phone screen, the new contact set as the number two speed dial next to my voicemail system. He moved Mama and Grandma to third and fourth, making sure his name was the first I'd see.

Looking over my shoulder at the open door, I shake my head, shut it, and change. After washing up for bed and brushing my teeth, I curl under the blankets and nuzzle the pillow.

My door cracks open sometime later, but the mattress doesn't dip right away. Without turning, I assume Dad or Cam is checking in on me. I appeased them earlier by eating a couple pieces of dry toast from the hospital cafeteria while we waited for me to be discharged. I didn't bother eating more when I got home, nor did I feel like arguing with them on the matter.

According to the hospital scale, I'm a few pounds heavier. It took me by surprise considering my lack of appetite these days, but the ten-pound difference was shown on two different scales when I mentioned my doubt.

Cam said it was my clothes, since I wear more layers this time of year, and Dad seemed happy that I was gaining weight. After dropping too much to be considered healthy without really trying, I suppose it shows that I'm finally turning in the right direction.

When the bed dips after what feels like forever, the comforter is pulled out from around me until a warm body is nestled against my back.

Kaiden's arm wraps around my stomach, and his breath tickles the back of my head. "Are you feeling any better?"

I wiggle into his hold, resting my back against his front like usual. "A little. I've just been getting headaches, that's all."

He makes a disbelieving sound.

We're quiet for a while. "Kaiden?"

"Hmm?"

I let out a tiny breath. "I'm sorry I worried you."

His hold tightens. "You didn't."

Rolling my eyes, I say, "It's okay to be worried, you know. I won't tell anyone. It can be our little secret."

I yelp quietly when he yanks me until I'm on my back and he's hovering over me. "I can think of other secrets to keep between us that are a lot more fun."

Biting my bottom lip, my hands go to his sides and hold on to his loose shirt. "I doubt you want anything right now. I got sick today, remember? Not very attractive."

He lowers his bottom half onto me, his erection disproving my words. "Trust me, Mouse. I want you."

I swallow. He smirks.

"What if I didn't brush my teeth?"

"I can smell the mint toothpaste."

He leans down slowly.

"What if I tell you no?"

"Then I'll stop."

His lips are so close to mine.

Our breaths mingle. "What if I told you that I'm sick?"

"Headaches, right?"

No. Yes…

Gripping his shirt, I meet his lips halfway in a soft touch. He doesn't push or act as animalistic as we did before. Our lips graze each other's a few times before he presses down so his hardness is settled between my legs.

I wince when one of his hands grips my hip, but the pressure of him squeezing it makes me cry out. "Wait. Stop."

Pushing up on his arms, he rolls off me and studies my face. "Em?"

I shake my head, feeling my whole face heat with embarrassment. "I'm sorry. I just…"

He lies down, opening his arm up for me to cuddle in like he doesn't mind me telling him to stop. He told me he would, and I have no reason to think he'd go against his word when he's been uncharacteristically nice to me.

Well, for the most part.

"My sister died of an incurable autoimmune disease," I whisper against his chest. Closing my eyes, I picture Logan. "She never showed it, but I know she was in a lot of pain, especially the months leading up to her death."

His hand rubs my upper arm. "Is that like a twin thing? You sensed her pain?"

It's hard to breathe suddenly. "No."

He keeps rubbing my arm.

"I have the same disease, Kaiden."

His palm freezes.

Twenty-Eight

I'm not sure what to expect, but it's not this.

Kaiden gets off my bed like it's on fire, and I worry that he's one of the many uneducated people who think he'll somehow catch my disease like it's contagious. Except it's not concern or disgust on his face; it's something far darker. It's a mixture of anger and betrayal and a third emotion I'm not sure should be mixed with the others.

Slowly sitting up, I wince when the loud sound of my hip and elbow popping echoes in the silence between us. His eyes go toward the sound, then to my face, before he studies the rest of me.

"Kaiden—"

"Don't." His voice is too sharp to disobey.

Zipping my lips, I watch as he searches for something across my features. His gaze dips downward, sliding over my body. There are advanced cases of some diseases that show just how much they impact people externally, but most times it's an invisible internal battle.

People think sickness has a face.

They think disease is an ugly word.

I used to be embarrassed by it—maybe I still am. Nobody in their right mind thinks disease is a pretty thing. Most people associate it with things that could be controlled, as if it's my fault I'm sick.

I can walk, talk, and go to school.

I must be fine.

"You're not going to find anything," I finally say, brushing my sweaty palms down my thighs.

He finally meets my gaze again.

Then he swears. *Loudly.*

Throwing the door open to my room, it slams against the wall and leaves a hole where the knob strikes. Cringing, I scurry off the bed and follow him into the hall.

"Kaiden, come on. It's—"

He stops halfway down the stairs. "Why the fuck didn't you tell me?"

There's no way our parents won't hear this. His loud, betrayed voice is a reminder of what I knew would happen. They should have warned him before I moved in.

I won't let him blame me though. "When have you asked me?"

He scoffs, walking up three steps so we're at eye level. "Was I supposed to guess that you're sick, Emery? That you're dying or some shit? I'm not a goddamn mind reader."

My jaw ticks. "I'm *not* dying. And you knew my sister passed away! Did you ever think to ask how? Did you ever stop sulking from your own pity party of one to consider anyone but yourself? No!"

The light downstairs flicks on, and both Dad and Cam

appear at the bottom of the staircase. They both stare up at us in confusion, Dad's arm around Cam's shoulder as his brows pinch together.

He asks, "What is going on?"

Kaiden ignores them and narrows his eyes into slits at me. "You could have offered up the information. It isn't like you haven't had ample opportunity since you moved here."

I throw my hands up. "You. Didn't. Ask!"

Cam steps up. "Kaiden, honey—"

He whirls around. "Did you know she was sick? Was this all a big *fuck you* to me while being left in the dark? I bet she was at the hospital for other reasons and you're all lying to me about it."

Cam reaches out. "Kaid—"

He stays out of reach. "This is no different from what you did with Dad. Guess what, Cam? I'm eighteen. I can handle the shit life throws at me."

"Really?" I say with doubt from behind him, practically scoffing like he did. "From where I'm standing, I don't think that's accurate. You're so consumed by your anger that you're not even considering anybody else in the matter. Least of all me, who was trying to be honest with you."

He spins so quickly I nearly fall over but catch myself on the wall. "*After* you lived here for months. Don't turn this around on me like you're innocent."

My teeth grind to the point they hurt.

Dad's voice cuts in. "We all need to take a step back and try calming down."

Kaiden laughs, but it's maniacal. "I suppose you're going to tell me that you're any better? How long have you known you had a sick daughter? One who has the same disease that took your other daughter's life? This is why you took her in, right? You pity her."

That's a blow to the gut I feel personally, flinching over something part of me has suspected for a while. Whether it's true or not doesn't matter; the thought lingers. And regardless of that actually being the reason, I think it is at least a driving force in why I'm here.

Cam shakes her head at him. "I've let you talk down to him for long enough. This matter doesn't concern you. It wasn't information you needed to know."

I swear he growls as he barrels down the stairs, shouldering past both our parents. He grabs his jacket and I hear the faint rattle of keys before he storms toward the door.

"Kaiden!" Cam calls out, following him.

Dad looks at me.

I don't know what to say.

He doesn't deny what Kaiden accuses him of, and I don't question it. Does it really matter at this point? Words hurt. It's a good thing I have a high pain tolerance.

Something crashes in the foyer before the door slams shut.

Dad and I make our way downstairs to see a vase shattered on the floor, with Cam staring at all the little pieces. He squeezes her arm and says he'll grab the broom. I don't know what to tell her, so I count all the shards—eight bigger pieces and twenty-six little ones. I remember her mentioning it was her great-grandma's.

Priceless.

The pain medicine from earlier has long worn off, and a headache teases the confines of my temples. I blink away the tears of frustration as the backs of my eyes pulse in sharp irritation. I know the likely culprit is stress, something I've become accustomed to here when things don't go Kaiden's way.

I don't regret telling him.

I regret believing he could handle it.

People like him will never be as strong as people like us. They get a choice in how to feel, live, and think.

We never will.

We're forced to fight.

And sometimes…we don't want to.

Twenty-Nine

STRENGTH DOESN'T COME WITHOUT a price. If there's anything I've learned over the past few years, it's that you're forced to fight when you don't have the energy and have no chance at surrendering even at your worst.

Strength doesn't have a definition. We all have it. We just might not all think we do because it's buried under layers of pain and depression and anxiety. The truth is you never know how strong you are until being strong is the only choice you have.

So I lock my door after going back upstairs and settle under the warm blankets. Only a faint lingering scent of pine and cedar remains on the empty side of the bed, so I turn my back on it and close my eyes.

I rarely lock my door.

I could fall and nobody could get in.

I could struggle getting out of bed.

That's not the real truth though.

I didn't want to stop Kaiden before. Knowing how he

acted makes me hate myself for getting attached to any form of possibility with him. Friend or not, stepbrother or not, I was starting to like him—trust him.

Go figure; it was a waste of time.

The tears dry before they fall, giving me one more ounce of strength I didn't know I could conjure with my chest hurting the same way my head does.

When I wake up in the morning, a familiar scent is kissing my skin from close behind. A nose presses against the back of my neck, with a warm breath tickling my skin and making me hyperaware of who's spooning me right now like last night was a dream.

I squirm out of his hold, but he tightens his arm around me and drags me back against his chest. "I want you to meet my father."

Thirty

BASED ON THE TIME on the dashboard, there's a silent understanding between us that we won't make it to school today. I'd already planned on skipping, hoping by Monday morning nobody remembers my little mishap from Thursday.

I'm not sure why I agreed to come with him, but before my conscience could get me to rethink things, I was bundled in layers and following him outside. Not before noticing my bedroom door was perfectly intact, making me think Kaiden's skills stretch to picking locks.

Not that it surprises me.

What does surprise me is when Kaiden pulls into the cemetery we've spent so much time in. He doesn't take the normal path that leads to the fenced-off clearing but one that takes us to a huge gathering of gravestones.

Considering there was a chain covering two of the three entrances to the cemetery, I'm fairly certain we're not supposed to be here. Snow covers the pavement, but not enough to get stuck. The walkways aren't cleared off, and most of the headstones are surrounded by snowdrifts that would make it difficult to get to.

Kaiden shuts the car off and stares out his window without a word.

I blink, glancing at the line of stones he's staring at. "Your father is buried here?"

He nods once.

Running my tongue across my bottom lip, I study the area around us. "You visit him a lot, don't you?"

He hesitates. "It's how I found the tree. I would come here all the time and yell at the asshole until I needed to take a walk. One night, I climbed the fence and found the spot. It's my favorite place to go."

"Because you're close to him?"

He doesn't deny it.

Unbuckling and opening the door, he leaves me to walk through the packed snow. It crunches under his boots. I can hear as much from where I sit watching him.

Giving him a moment, I see him kneel in front of a stone in the middle of the lineup. He brushes his bare hand against the front, dusting off the snow sticking to it. After a few moments, I finally get out of the car, adjusting my hat over my ears and walking over to him.

I notice slightly filled-in footprints from the other side of the stone, like someone else was here. Does Cam visit him too? It dawns on me when I notice the prints are identical to the fresh ones he just made. There was no new snowfall since yesterday afternoon.

"You came here last night," I whisper.

He stands, brushing off excess snow from his hands. "He

grounds me in ways nobody else can. There's no way he can judge me for anything."

"He just listens," I say for him.

He hums in agreement.

Like me with Lo, he talks to his father. I thought he ignored everything about the man, but he probably spends more time here than he does in his own bedroom.

Especially since he sleeps in mine.

Rubbing my arms, I study the engraving under his name. It's a generic *loving husband and father*, which Kaiden must know I'm staring at.

He laughs dryly. "Funny, right? Cam ordered the stone for him. They weren't even married by then. The whole thing is a joke."

I stare at him, wondering if he's being serious or not. He doesn't look bemused though. He's deflecting.

"Stop calling her that."

"That's her name," he deadpans.

"She's your mom."

No reply.

I sigh. "You saw how me and my mother are, Kaiden. We don't have a perfect relationship. We've been through a lot because of what happened to Logan and, yes, what's happening to me. Because like it or not, I *am* sick. She hasn't dealt with it well but that doesn't mean I take it out on her."

"Maybe you should."

Shrugging, I tuck my hands in my pockets and watch my breath in front of me. "I don't see the point. We can't change what's been said or done. If we spend all the time on the negative, we'll be angry for the rest of our lives. Why let it consume us?"

His head turns to me. "How could you just let it go? Your mother hurt you."

I close my eyes and inhale the burning cold air, letting it fill and sting my lungs. "I hurt her just as much. Don't you understand by now?" I whisper, opening my eyes back up. "We get one life. One chance. One opportunity to live. Why should I spend that in more pain than I already do? Anybody can hurt me, but if I choose not to let them, I can find some solace in what life has given me. It's not much, but it's something."

For a split second, I see awe in his features. It disappears in the blink of an eye, but it was there. It gives me hope that I'm breaking through, like maybe he's starting to get it.

"Why did you come here last night?" I ask before he can say anything.

His brow furrows.

I elaborate. "There must be a reason. You could have gone anywhere, right? To a friend's house or something. You chose to come here."

His eyes go back to his father's grave, contemplating his answer. I think he trains his focus on the chipped edges from weathered wear, because his eyes don't move from that area once. "You find solace in the living. I find it in the dead. Like I said, he can't judge me when I come here. It doesn't matter how much of an asshole I am. It's just me and my dad when I visit."

Is that an apology? In his own freakish way, I think it is. Not that I'll squander the moment by asking, because something tells me he'll deny it.

I fight off a smile. "And what did you and your dad talk about?"

He doesn't look at me. "You mentioned a while ago that watching people suffer from disease is tough. You weren't just talking about my dad or your sister, were you?"

Slowly, I shake my head. "For the record, Cam was wrong when she said it wasn't any of your concern. I moved into your home, your old bedroom, so I made it your business."

His tongue clucks. "Your sister died from what you have..."

I hear his unspoken question. "Any of us could die tomorrow, Kaiden. People die all the time. Does that mean I'm going to die from lupus? I don't know. Maybe. Maybe not. It's not always a fatal disease, and a lot more research is being done on it nowadays."

His eyes narrow. "Lupus? That's what you have?"

I nod.

"And there are no answers?"

"Regarding my mortality?"

He grumbles.

Trying to give him a reassuring smile doesn't seem to work because it probably ends up looking more sad than anything. "You want to know a secret? Sometimes I would think about how I'd be better off dead. I wouldn't hurt Mama anymore or be in pain and I could be with Lo. I won't lie, Kaiden. Things were really bad for a while. I was hospitalized for days, sometimes weeks at a time. I go through depressive stages when I'm at my worst because I have to accept my body is failing me. It's..." Not knowing what else to do, I shrug. "I've never told anybody that before."

He visibly swallows hard. "Do you still think that?"

Do I? I have my moments when I want to escape it all. I used to think they were moments of weakness, but I think they were just moments of humanity. We all want peace, salvation. Lo got peace. Kaiden's dad got peace. Why not me? Am I deserving of all this suffering?

"No," I answer carefully. "I think things happen for a reason. The medicine I'm on helps the inflammation, which can be the biggest problem. It's about balance. Eating right, finding ways to stay active, and remembering not to overdo it."

He puts his hand to the top of his father's grave. "Do you think he was afraid?"

No elaboration is needed. "I think when he got to a certain point, fear eluded him."

"Like he welcomed death?"

I shake my head, stepping closer to him and putting my hand on his arm. "Welcomed relief, Kaiden."

Before he can say anything else, my phone goes off in my pocket. When I pull it out, Cam's name flashes across the screen. Answering it, I step away and give Kaiden time with his father.

Her bubbly voice greets me. "You've got a spot to see a neurologist today at one o'clock. I'm leaving work early to go with you, okay? Your dad offered, but I thought it'd be easier since I already know him. Dr. Aberdeen is a good man. He'll help you."

Dad offered to leave work for me?

I glance at Kaiden as he speaks in murmurs to his father's gravestone. Clearing my throat and turning my back to him for privacy, I say, "I appreciate that, Cam."

"You're welcome, sweetie. I'll pick you up at the house, okay? I can call the school and get them to allow you to go—"

"Uh, that won't be necessary."

There's a pause. "You're not at school?"

My lips twitch. "I'm sort of at the cemetery with Kaiden. He's…he's at Adam's stone right now. I think he needed it after what happened last night. He loves him a lot."

This time when she answers, her tone is lighter than before. "He's not the only one."

Not sure what she means, I tell her I'll see her later before ending the call. Slipping my phone back into my pocket, I walk back over to Kaiden.

"Do you mind if we go? I'm a bit cold."

He gives me a single nod before guiding us over to the car. After getting in and thawing out, he turns to me. "I never bring anyone here."

Huh?

He's not the only one…

I thought maybe Cam meant she loved Adam too. It makes sense, since he's the father of her only child. But maybe…maybe she meant Kaiden loved someone else.

But she couldn't mean me.

Right?

Thirty-One

For the first time in months, I feel human. It's so foreign that I cry. Not because I'm in pain but because I don't remember what it's like not to be.

Dr. Aberdeen and my rheumatologist theorized that the medication I was on for my inflammation was causing the migraines. Between switching to a different prescription that still helps combat my symptoms on top of an additional new pill to ease any oncoming headaches, I'm a new person.

To celebrate, Kaiden surprises me by driving us to a small restaurant after school on Friday. It's much homier than Le Sal's, with a laid-back atmosphere that I love. The way he speaks to the hostess makes me wonder if he comes here a lot.

He reaches down and weaves our fingers together, sending shock waves up my arm until my heart reacts by pumping faster. When he leads us to the back without the hostess, I know he must have planned this ahead. Our table is separated from the rest, farthest from the subtle noise of early dinner conversations.

"You don't like noise," he prompts when he sees me looking around the half-empty room.

Nibbling my lip, I give him a timid smile.

Shortly after opening up to him about my disease, I saw him googling it and reading various articles on causes and symptoms. He would close out of anything if he saw me looking over at him from my homework and give me lip about what a nerd I am or how messy my hair looked at that moment.

Anything to make it look like he doesn't care when there's no doubt in my mind he does. It's in the little things he does, like putting an extra blanket over me after I fall asleep or telling Dad and Cam I can't go out to eat at certain places because their food isn't something I'm supposed to eat when I'm too shy to tell them myself. He leaves me silly pictures everywhere from my dresser to bathroom mirror—Post-its with cartoon images like kissing lips and frozen yogurt and a sun with shades on.

He doesn't pester me to take my medication like Dad or remind me to get more rest on the nights I have enough energy to stay up and get ahead on homework or read. He lets me live my life and supports whatever I choose to do with it.

The other night, we stayed up making brownies. Double chocolate. I ate way too much batter until my stomach hurt and then promptly ate way too many warm brownies as we watched a few movies. Things have been great. Fun, even.

After a waitress gets our drink order, we're left alone to look over the menu. I smile when I see the array of options, debating on one of their cheapest salads just to see what he'll say.

Surely he won't throw my plate on the floor here and demand I order a pizza.

I look at him staring at his menu, the tip of his tongue peeking out of the corner of his mouth. A light fluttering feeling fills my stomach over the image in front of me. He's reading the food list with such intensity and precision, yet he looks so boyish at the same time.

Cute isn't the right word to describe Kaiden Monroe, so why do I have the urge to call him that anyway?

He catches me staring, but I don't dodge his eyes like normal. "What?"

I shake my head. "Nothing. I…" My tongue feels heavy in my mouth, tied over his attention toward me. "I, uh, don't know what to get is all."

"Liar," he muses, sitting back. "You can get whatever you want. Their chicken stuff is pretty good. I think I had the marsala once. They're known for their fish entrees though, and I heard that salmon is good for people with autoimmune diseases so…" He clears his throat and rubs the back of his neck, avoiding my gaze by staring at the menu.

My eyes narrow. "Are you…blushing?"

His brows pinch but he won't look up.

"Oh my God." I laugh, smiling wider than I have in forever. "*The* Kaiden Monroe is blushing. I feel like I should take a picture. The school has an Instagram account, right? Maybe I should tag them in it so they'll share it to their student pride story."

He grumbles and sets down his menu, giving me a dirty look that looks more like he's pouting than anything. "I don't blush. I'm just saying that I heard it's good for you or whatever."

I play along, nodding. "I'm sure. Google does like to suggest the best salmon dishes for people fighting inflammatory diseases."

His eyes cast downward.

When the waitress comes back, I order the salmon dinner with mashed potatoes and green beans, all while smiling at Kaiden. He gets chicken Parmesan with the same sides, but I know he won't eat the green beans because he always leaves them when Cam makes them for supper. He knows I'll eat them.

After it's just us, I toy with the wrapped silverware. "I think it's sweet that you did research. Not a lot of people put in that kind of effort because they choose to believe what they want to instead of getting the facts right."

He doesn't fight me on the compliment, which surprises me. "What do you mean?"

I settle into my chair, letting go of a hefty sigh just thinking about the ridiculous stereotypes I've heard over the years. "When you have a disease that nobody can see and they find out, most of the time they won't even believe you. On the off chance they take your word for it, they say the stupidest things, like I can be cured if I sleep more or eat healthier."

Grinding my teeth, I think about a conversation I had once at my old school. My old phys ed teacher was trying to get me to participate in the unit, but I'd had a note letting me sit out on my bad flare days. It wasn't something I did often, just when standing too long put too much strain on my knees and hips. She told me if I cut out junk food and exercised more, I'd be fine.

Diet is always important to stay healthy, but healthy isn't a universal concept. Eating a carrot won't make the swelling go down, and running the mile certainly won't help me walk better the next day.

I rest my hands on my lap. "People have preconceived notions about illness. Like when they assume you can't get sick unless you're overweight or old or something. Do you know how many times people tell me I can't possibly be this sick because I'm young? Or how many times I've been accused of having an eating disorder because I'm too thin?

"It's already tiring to live the way I do because my body is attacking itself, but having everyone else attack me becomes too much. I have to deal with everyone making their own conclusions about me when they hear I have an autoimmune disease. Like being told to not get stressed, like I'll be cured for life then. And don't get me started on those who think I'm making it up. People rely too much on what they can see because everyone says that seeing is believing. It's never been that way though. It's always the other way around."

I lick my dry lips and reach for my water, taking my time to absorb the silence.

"How do you deal with it?" he asks once I set my glass down.

"Honestly?" I shrug. "I don't."

His brow quirks.

I elaborate. "Some days it's easier than others to just let what people say bounce off me, but that doesn't mean it doesn't bother me at all. I'm just good at pretending it doesn't."

There's a tick to his jaw. "You shouldn't have to do that at all."

"What *should* I do then, Kaiden?" I ask, genuinely curious. "We're human. We say mean, hurtful things. We're naive. We're cruel. When you're in my shoes, something I hope you never are, you see life differently. You stop taking every day for granted because you have absolutely no clue if you'll wake up the next morning. That may sound harsh, but it's true."

"Don't say that," he all but growls under his breath.

I raise my hands up in surrender. "You want the truth? It's not pretty, is it? I watched Lo slip away, but there's a big difference between witnessing and experiencing something. She never showed her pain or fear if she could help it. Instead, she acted like it couldn't get to her until..."

"It did," he finishes.

I nod silently.

"Are you afraid?"

Every single second, minute, and hour.

I whisper, "Wouldn't you be?"

He could pretend he's strong, act like nothing can touch him, but I see through him. He hurts. His father's death still affects him. The possibility of losing his mother, even me, terrifies him. Any of us could pretend like we're invincible and put up a front in the public eye, but behind our masks are tearstained faces.

Instead of answering, he rests his arms on the table and studies the room. "There have been a few deaths at Exeter. One of them was from cancer. Remember what Rachel told you on the first day? There was a girl who had Hodgkin's lymphoma. She'd been battling it for most of her life, but it kept coming back. It got worse her sophomore year, and she ended up passing away around homecoming. There was a huge ceremony and dedication to her."

I frown. "That's so sad."

He nods once. "Riley..." His voice gets raspy, so he clears it. "Riley was an old friend of mine. She was real, but she had a lot of problems nobody could help her with. Not even me. Shit, if I had known what she planned..." He stops, taking a deep breath. "People gave her shit when they found out about her disorder. No. They *always* messed with her. She used to be overweight, so the bullying started then. I always heard her talk about how much she wanted to lose weight so they'd leave her alone, and when she started to, she seemed happier. I didn't know that she was starving herself to do it. Not until I realized she'd skip lunch or not snack after school like she used to. When I brought it up, she'd act like it was no big deal.

"And then the rumors started about her throwing up at school. She'd been caught a few times by some girls who told everyone. At that point, she'd lost so much weight she looked like a walking corpse. She would eat and then disappear, but I never believed she was purging..."

His nostrils flare. "I should have done something about it, but nobody listened to me back then like they do now. I would tell people to stop screwing with her, but nobody cared. Then some teachers heard the rumors and contacted her parents, and it spiraled. She couldn't take the negative attention anymore."

I hold my breath when I hear the sadness weighing down his words. "Kaiden?"

Our food comes and is set in front of us, feeding the intensity of the moment. When the waitress disappears, Kaiden's eyes meet mine.

"She committed suicide."

My lips part.

I notice the slightest tremble of his hand resting on the table, so I reach over and put my hand on top of his. He stares like he doesn't know what's happening, then flips his palm and wraps his fingers around mine.

Ignoring the delicious smell of the food in front of us, I ask, "Is that why you're set on stopping people from giving me crap at school?"

"I don't want anything to happen to you."

I give him an appreciative smile.

He huffs, letting go of my hand. "Guess it doesn't matter much, does it?"

My smile disappears.

No. I guess it doesn't.

Thirty-Two

CHRISTMAS IS IN A couple of weeks. Dad and Cam ask to talk to me after dinner one night, so I stay behind while Kaiden goes upstairs to get ready for another movie night.

Sometimes I wish I could read Dad better, because his features almost never change. "What is this about? Did I do something?"

Cam's eyes widen. "Oh! No, it's nothing like that. Your father and I were just thinking about plans for the holidays. Usually we do a family dinner here. You know, a big lunch after opening presents and all that. It's tradition to have the entire family here for it."

Fighting the urge to wince over the idea of their entire family doing this every year, I stare at the place mat on the table. It's white with snowmen and reindeer on it.

Mama used to decorate the entire house like Cam does. I don't remember when she stopped.

Had Dad ever mentioned inviting me to their celebration? Whenever we'd talk around the holidays, he'd just wish me a good one and tell me he sent my present via priority mail. It was always a gift card to Amazon, which I always took the longest time to spend because I hated using anything he gave me.

Dad brings me back. "We were wondering if you had plans to go to your mother's house for the holidays."

"Not that we don't want you here," Cam jumps in, smiling at me. "In fact, we were hoping you'd spend it with us. I think Kaiden would love that. You two get along so well."

If they only knew how well.

"Uh…I haven't really talked to her about it," I admit, squirming. Grandma called me the other day after I spent some time texting Mama, asking me what we had planned here. When I told her I wasn't sure, she didn't push it.

"Do you think she'd want to come?" Cam asks excitedly. "Your grandmother too, of course. It could be good for them to see you here. You could show them your room. The book collection you've started. Maybe around town."

My eyes cut to Dad. He looks a little uncomfortable, but nowhere near as much as I feel. "I think it's a good idea," he admits.

I blink a few times. "You…what?"

He takes a deep breath. "Your mother and I haven't been on great terms for obvious reasons. We have our differences, but we also have you. If you want to spend your Christmas with them, we'll understand. However, if you'd consider staying here to spend it with us, the invite is extended to them. That way, you can see all of us on the same day."

I'm not sure what to say. Dad and Mama in the same room after all these years? Grandma never has anything bad to say about him, but I know she loves Mama. I can't say Grandma blames him for how Mama is, but I don't rule it out.

"Do you think...I mean, is that a good idea?" I ask, frowning. "You and Mama haven't spoken in a long time, right? She's not the same person you knew."

Cam rubs Dad's arm. "We spoke to your mother last night. Your father left the invitation open in case she wants to come. She's welcome here anytime, Em. I hope you know that."

I stare.

Dad straightens. "Cam is right. Your mother and I will always have a past, but you're important to both of us. She can come here and visit. I know it's quite a drive, but it might be good for all of us to be together for Christmas."

"Mama and you?"

"And you."

"Like...in the same room?"

He chuckles, which sounds so foreign coming from someone as serious as him. "Yes, Emery. In fact, she seemed interested in the idea. Your grandmother thinks it'll be good."

"Fun," Cam corrected. "She said it would be fun. She even said she looks forward to seeing Kaiden again."

I sink in my chair. They had no idea he'd gone to see me until we arrived back together a day earlier than I was supposed to return. Dad looked suspicious and Cam looked happier than ever. Neither said anything about it though.

"Yeah, Grandma liked him," I mutter.

Dad grumbles.

"So they're coming?" I ask.

"That's up to you," he replies, shoulders pulled back. "Your mother and I agreed that it would be your decision. We won't mind whatever you choose."

Did I want to spend Christmas there?

No.

It's a brutal admission but one I can't help but make. Mama and I talk more than before, but it's still strained. She only calls once every couple of weeks to tell me how support group is going or to share stories from work about the excuses that kids make to try getting out of class just to nap in the nurse's office. We text more times than not, and the replies are sporadic.

I don't want to complain.

She's trying.

Christmas together though? I should be happy for them offering, but jealousy settles into my chest over them thinking of this now. Where was our invitation before I moved? Did they think I wouldn't want to come? Did they even think about me beyond the usual gift card purchase?

Pressing my lips together, I will myself to take a calming breath and exhale through my nose. *This is a fresh start*, I remind myself. "It could be good. I miss them."

Cam's smile grows.

Dad remains stoic. "Are you sure?"

Are you?

"Yeah," I choke out, shrugging. "I think Christmas here will be fun. Different."

Not knowing what else to say, I ask to be excused. There's a warm bed and a new movie waiting for me upstairs. It beats this conversation a million times over.

They tell me good night.

When I get upstairs, Kaiden's smirk is what I'm greeted with. "Something tells me this Christmas is going to be the most interesting one we've had yet."

"Eavesdropping much?" I mumble, grabbing my pajamas and heading toward the bathroom.

His laugh is what I'm left with as I close the bathroom door.

I wake up to the caress of warm kisses down my shoulder and back from where I sleep on my stomach. Still groggy from sleep, I unwrap my arms from the pillow I'm hugging and turn onto my side.

Kaiden stares down at me from where he's propped up on his elbow. Blinking, I look over at the glow of my alarm clock, yawning when I see it's only three in the morning. My head rests on the pillow with a sleepy smile gracing my face.

"Why are you up?"

"Couldn't sleep."

"Hmm."

He grins and leans down, brushing our lips together. We haven't done anything more than kiss since break. Sometimes his hands will roam, but they never go far. The most courageous I've ever gotten was sliding my hands under his shirt to feel his muscled stomach during one of our make-out sessions.

This feels different though. There's electricity in the room as he pulls me under him and explores my mouth. Every time his tongue does something, mine mimics his.

He touches my side.

I touch his.

He slides his palm under my shirt.

I slide mine under his.

Before I know it, the kiss grows deeper. He groans when I arch up at the same time as he lowers down. His weight feels welcoming, his body heat radiating into me.

I wrap my arms around his neck as he nips my bottom lip before trailing kisses down my jaw and neck. His hands push him up so he's not crushing me, one of them trailing down my side and then sliding underneath my shirt, and he moves back up.

"Is this okay?" he whispers against the crook of my neck.

I swallow, eyes closing from the feel of his palm against my belly button. "Yes."

He kisses my neck before moving his palm up further, making me shiver as he gets closer to my breast. I stopped caring about wearing a bra to bed. Sometimes I'll catch Kaiden staring at my chest, and it makes me feel confident. Pretty. Wanted.

His thumb brushes the underside of my bare breast, causing me to suck in a breath. He takes the moment to kiss me again, his tongue flicking against mine before he cups my breast in his hand.

We both groan at the same time, my eyes rolling to the back of my head when he squeezes me and then brushes my hard nipple with the pad of his thumb. I kiss him harder, tightening my arms around him and arching my pelvis up to meet his. Our breaths get heavier as he grinds against the spot where I need the most friction, his palm moving from one breast to the other until I'm writhing under him.

"Kaiden," I whisper, burying my face in his chest when his pelvis grinds faster into me.

He lowers onto his elbows, kissing me softly in every

angle possible before pulling back and staring down at me. His palm rests below my bust, his eyes studying mine.

"What are we doing?" I ask, unsure of what's going to happen next.

He bites down on his bottom lip before pulling his hand out from under my shirt. "We can stop—"

"No!" I blurt before blushing deeply.

His shoulders shake with laughter, which makes me cover my face with my palms. "Hey, don't hide. We can do whatever you want. Or nothing at all."

I peek at him through my fingers. "I'm no good at this, Kaiden. You have way more experience than I do."

"How do you know?"

I eye him. "Don't act like you're an angelic virgin. It's embarrassing enough to admit that I'm one."

He brushes hair away from my face. "I don't want you to be embarrassed, Em. Trust me, I know plenty of girls at school who brag about how many guys they bag. It's not attractive."

I scoff. "And what? Virgins are?"

His shoulders lift. "It's hotter than knowing someone lets literally anyone between their legs. To be the one person you trust enough to get intimate with, that shit is special. Flattering, even. And I'm not saying that just so you'll let me go that far with you. I'm being honest."

I blink, gnawing on my inner cheek. "I feel like it won't be good for you."

He pecks my lips. "Mouse, you don't have to worry about that. If or when we get to that point, it'll be good for both of us."

Blushing, I wiggle under him. "What if I want that point to be now?"

I hear the shift in his breath.

My shaky hand goes to his face. "Let's be honest, Kaiden. I don't like people knowing about my health. It takes too much effort to get anyone to understand what it's like. I know you've done research, and you're careful with me. I…I know that first times hurt. I know it may hurt me more because of my condition. But the pain has been minimal lately, and I don't know how long it'll last."

His Adam's apple bobs. "What exactly are you saying? I need you to spell this out for me so we're on the same page."

Locking eyes with him, I raise up and kiss his lips. "I want you to be my first, Kaiden. There's nobody else I trust with it."

I think he stops breathing.

Waiting for his reply kills me because he could decide he doesn't want this. Or that he thinks we should wait. Or that I'm too fragile.

After what feels like an eternity, he asks, "You'll tell me to stop if it gets to be too much?"

Licking my lips, I nod.

He studies me, brushing his thumb against my cheek before nodding back. "I haven't slept with anyone since before you moved here."

My eyes widen. "But Rachel…"

Shaking his head, he kisses me again. "I just said that to mess with you. I'm an asshole, remember? I do stupid shit."

"Do you think this is stupid?" I hate how vulnerable I sound, but it's a question worth asking.

"Sleeping with my stepsister?" he replies, unblinking. "Probably. Sleeping with Emery Matterson? A fighter? Someone who's strong and resilient and doesn't give in to my bullshit? No. I don't think that's stupid at all."

His words warm my heart, but not as much as when he grabs my hand gently and interweaves our fingers together. Squeezing gently, he kisses me, trailing his lips across my cheek and to the shell of my ear.

"I think," he whispers, his breath tickling me until I shiver, "that this is beyond us. It makes sense. Probably more sense than anything else."

"Why?"

"Because we fit together."

We do?

"Don't you feel it?" he murmurs, nipping at my earlobe.

My chest fills.

My stomach flutters.

Yes, I want to say. *I've felt it for months.*

Before I knew what *it* was.

Living. Not existing.

"I need to get a condom."

Thirty-Three

NERVES GET THE BETTER of me when he's hovering over me with wandering hands. I'm hyperaware of the foil packet beside us on the mattress, and I know where it goes and what it's for. I never thought I'd ever see one or experience this though.

"Get out of your head," he tells me, pushing up to meet my eyes.

My palms rest against his waist. "I can't help it. I know what's going to happen and I keep thinking I'm going to mess it up. You know, do something stupid."

He chuckles, reaching up and brushing hair out of my face. "What do you think you're going to do?"

"I…" *I don't know.*

He kisses me, tasting me slowly before pulling away slightly. "I promise you're not going to mess this up. There's no way you can. So stop overthinking and tell me what you want."

What I want?

His hands travel down my body leisurely, resting just below my navel. His thumb brushes the elastic of my pajama pants until a heat rises between my legs and makes me squirm. "Where do you *feel* you want me, Mouse?"

My lips part, then close.

His thumb dips under the band, tracing my skin. "Am I getting close?"

I let out a tiny noise that sounds both desperate and nervous. His lips dip to the crook of my neck, kissing and sucking and licking until I arch into him. He makes an approving noise, but when his hand moves away, I protest.

"What do you want, Emery?" he asks against my skin, nipping my collarbone and then my shoulder. "Tell me with words."

Fluttering my eyelids for a moment, I grasp his soft cotton shirt and pull it up. "I want your shirt off."

He reaches behind him and yanks it off by the collar, throwing it on the floor. "Done. What else?"

My heart flips in my chest as I trace the slight ripples of his toned stomach. He shivers when I glide my palms up his body, resting them on his shoulders. His skin is soft and warm and flawless. The corded muscles in his arms pop from holding himself up over me, and I trace them too with my finger until his eyes close and his breathing hitches.

I take advantage and sit up on my elbows to initiate the kiss. He's taken by surprise but quickly returns it, our lips and tongues and breaths dancing and tangling together until I reach for my shirt and start pulling it up too. He helps, slipping it over my head until we're both bare from the waist up.

His eyes burn my chest as he stares, brushing his knuckles

against my breast until I'm shuddering. When I move his hand to cup me fully, I bow up until he's squeezing me the way I want.

"Touch me," I whisper, kissing his jaw, neck, anything to feel close to him.

He doesn't disappoint. Lowering onto his elbows, he shifts so his full attention is on my chest, kneading, kissing, and driving me mad. My nipples pebble under his touch, and when he dips down and takes one in his mouth, I cry out until I'm covering my face with my palms to keep quiet.

"Mm," he murmurs, tugging on me with his teeth before nipping the side of the same breast. "Remember to keep quiet, Mouse. Wouldn't want one of our parents to walk in."

Oh my God. "We need to lock—"

"Already did," he says, moving his mouth to the other breast and mimicking his actions until I'm panting and needing him more.

"K-Kaiden."

He looks up through his lashes. "Yes?"

I cup his face, brushing my thumb over his bottom lip. "Can I…would it be okay if I touch you?"

His eyes heat until they're puddles of dark chocolate. "You should be more specific. Where is it that you want to touch me exactly?"

Licking my lips, I gather the courage to slowly trail my hand down, down, down his body until it rests just above his shorts. They hang low on his waist. All it would take is just one little movement…

"Fuck," he murmurs, dropping his forehead on mine. "Your eyes say it all and it's killing me."

"Sorry?"

He shakes his head. "Don't be. You're hot as hell when you go after what you want."

Blushing, I tug on his shorts.

"Want me to take them off?" he purrs, pulling my bottom lip into his mouth and suckling it.

"Y-yes."

"Want to see my cock, Mouse?"

My mouth practically waters as I nod, getting him to let go of my wrist and help me push his shorts down.

Eyes widening when I see him spring out of the nylon material, I can't help but stare. I don't know what I was expecting, but it wasn't something so big or pink or veiny.

I blink. "Oh, God."

It twitches. *Twitches.*

"It moved," I whisper-hiss.

He laughs, kicking his shorts off until they land on the floor in front of the bed. "Yeah, it'll do that."

I groan, realizing that thing is going to try fitting inside me. "You're not going to fit. That is *not* going to work, Kaiden."

"Hey," he murmurs, lips wavering like he wants to keep laughing. "Trust me, Em. It'll fit. People do this every day."

"Yeah, but…" Not knowing what to say, I shake my head.

"Do you want to do this?" he asks for the billionth time.

"Yes."

"Do you want to touch me?" He takes my hand and slowly starts lowering it toward the very thing I'm still fascinated by. "Words, Mouse. Do you want to touch my dick? I know *I* want you to."

I choke on oxygen. "Yes," I rasp.

He grins. "Do you want me to touch you? To take those cute little pajama pants off until we're both bare? I know you're not wearing panties under there."

My eyes widen. "How would you know that?"

He leans in closer like we're sharing a secret. "Do you know how many times a day I stare at your ass? I'd know if you're wearing underwear or not."

My whole face heats up.

"So?" He licks his lips. "Can I?"

For a split second, I debate my answer. I'm not sure why, because I know I want this to happen—to sleep with Kaiden. To lose my virginity. To feel…normal. A normal teenage girl doing normal, careless teenage things.

I also know it's a horrible idea for so many reasons.

But I also don't care.

I whisper an audible "Yes."

And just like that, my pants are on the floor tangled with his discarded clothes.

The nerves come back in full force now because we're both completely naked. My hand is back on his stomach, his eyes are raking over me, and I'm suddenly so self-conscious that I want to pull the blanket over me.

My stomach is flat, but my thighs aren't as thin as they used to be. I'm hyperaware of their sudden roundness in contrast to the ribs that decorate my torso from the rapid weight loss I experienced before moving here. I'm no longer proportional. Not too skinny like I was, but also not fat. The in-between my body has shaped itself into is foreign territory.

Yet Kaiden doesn't seem to mind at all. His eyes cut to mine before drifting down my nakedness, taking in every square inch. "Don't hide. You're beautiful, Emery. You're beautiful and you're *mine*."

That one word, four little letters, is exactly what I need to gather the courage to make my move, wrapping my hand around his hard length. He groans loudly and bucks into me, twitching in my palm as I stare at how my fingers look around him. Not sure what to do, I squeeze him a little before moving my hand down and back up in a fluid motion.

He curses, most of the words that escape his lips making no sense. "So good. That feels so fucking good."

"Can you show me?"

His eyes are closed, his head tipped back, and I think maybe I don't need him to show me anything. I still want him to though. He's feeding me confidence by letting me experience this.

"Show me how you touch yourself," I whisper, causing him to grow harder in my hand.

"Fuck, that's hot." He wraps his hand around mine and starts jerking our palms up and down faster than I was, twisting the grip to put more pressure under the head. The sounds he makes as his hips roll make dampness settle between my thighs, and I feel a strong need to experience everything with him as long as it means I can see his face so carefree and lost and beautiful in the moment as it is now.

He moans my name, whispers it like a plea, until I notice a little bead form at the tip of him. Following my urge, my thumb slips out from under his palm and glides over the wetness gathering there until he chokes out my name and jerks so hard in my hand that his forehead drops into the crook of my neck and our hands become frantic and needy.

A moment later, I feel something wet hit my lower stomach as he repeats my name over and over again before letting go of my hand.

His breathing evens out and he lifts up, kissing me hungrily until our teeth are clattering against each other. "I need to taste you. Let me kiss you, Mouse. Let me know how sweet you are between those pretty thighs of yours."

My whole body catches on fire, and I want to tell him no because I'm embarrassed, but the thought of him doing that wakes something new in me.

"O-okay."

The smile I'm rewarded with is like I agreed to give him a million dollars, and if I wasn't so turned on, I'd giggle.

I watch him slowly lower down my body, his hands parting my legs as his lips kiss my inner thigh up, up, up.

"Oh my *God*," I whimper when his tongue swipes my slit. I watch his head disappear between my legs, his mouth and breath and tongue on the most intimate part of me. I writhe under him as he gently holds my legs open and devours me, paying special attention to the bundle of nerves that demands release.

When his tongue dips inside, my fingers go to his hair and dig into his scalp. Unintentionally, I arch up until his face is buried further, his nose brushing my clit as his tongue brings me to the brink of orgasm.

"Too much. Too much." I shake my head as I build up, Kaiden not relenting as he eats me out and makes noises that sound a lot like mine as I tug on his hair and move my body to get more friction against him.

It's an intense feeling, the way my stomach warms and tingles and my legs tighten on either side of his head. It's consuming and alluring and addicting. Like I don't want him to stop but need him to before I lose my mind.

When I come, I come harder than ever before and have to throw a pillow over my face because I'm afraid I'll be heard. My legs quake and rock against him as he rides it out with me, his mouth pressing open kisses against me until I finally ease back onto the mattress with heavy pants and heavier eyelids.

My hips ache from being held open, but the sated feeling washing over my body helps me forget the slight discomfort.

Kaiden moves the pillow away from me and wipes his mouth off before running a hand down my cheek and jaw. "I almost came again just hearing you make those sounds."

I swallow, not knowing what to say.

"I need to be inside you," he says, watching me carefully to gauge my reaction.

After a short moment, I'm nodding, realizing this is it. I'm going to lose my virginity to the boy who's made me feel thousands of different things since I moved in with him.

He's insulted me.

Picked on me.

Isolated me.

But he also gave me his room.

Cooked me omelets.

And taken me to his favorite spot.

He's given Cam a chance for me, played nice with my father, and opened up to me when he wouldn't with anyone else.

"I need this too." I put my hands on his shoulders and squeeze, realizing maybe for the first time how true that statement is.

It's odd. I never thought about this moment before—never

wondered what it would be like or who I'd share it with. I always assumed it wouldn't happen because I'd be with Logan.

He grabs the condom and tears it open, sitting up on his knees to slide it on. I'm mesmerized as I watch him cover himself with the latex, and I feel my heart go into overdrive when he lowers back down and kisses me.

I return the kiss and wrap my arms around his neck, holding him to me. He tastes different, like me I realize, but I don't think about it because all I feel is him moving to my entrance.

Using his hand to position himself, he slowly slides in, pausing, stretching me, and causing me to gasp through the pain. Further, further—the sharpness intensifies. Tears well in my eyes as I try taking calming breaths.

"H-hurts," I whimper, squeezing him harder until our chests are pressed together. I need the pressure to ease, the pain to go away.

I knew it was going to hurt, but I feel like I'm being split in two despite how wet I must be from what he did. He's so big, it doesn't matter that he's trying to be careful. Wiggling, I try relieving the sting, but it gets worse. So much worse.

"No, not like that," he comments, sounding pained in a different way. "Fuck, Em. You're so tight. You're squeezing my dick."

"S-sorry." My voice is hoarse as a tear breaks free and slides down my cheek. Is it supposed to feel like this? Like someone shoved a burning rod between my legs? Like my pelvis is on fire and demanding it to be put out?

"Don't be." He kisses me, reaching between us and rubbing between my legs in small, circular motions. "I need you to try relaxing, okay? I know it hurts. I can make it a little better."

I close my eyes and hope more tears don't spill, but even when I feel my body loosen a little to his touch, his movements don't make the pain lessen. He moves out of me, and slowly back in, going further than before. Over and over he does this. He repeats the movements, playing with my clit, kissing me, nipping my lip and chin, until I'm saying his name in a choked plea.

Not to stop him.

I want this. *Need* this.

Need to be *that girl.* Not the sick one.

The one who winds up with Kaiden.

The one who gets to experience what she never thought she could.

But I also want this to end. I want the pain to stop and the pleasure to begin like in the books. I want to be able to move my hips to meet his as if I know what I'm doing. I want to feel confident and sexy and to know he can't get enough of me.

That's not how it is though.

It hurts. I'm used to pain, but this is so different from the everyday kind. My hips ache and my pelvis hurts, and I think I may be choking Kaiden with my death grip on his neck like I'd squeeze my pillow when my hips or knees or body hurt from a flare.

"Need me to stop?" His voice is heavy, lust-ridden. He doesn't want to but he's offering, and I don't want to disappoint him or to shorten this moment when it should be perfect.

"N-no."

"Emery—"

"Please keep going," I plead, kissing him the way he kissed me. Wanting. Needing. Yearning. "I want you to get off. I want to feel you do it inside me."

I don't know where those words came from, but I mean them. Every one of them.

"*Shit.*" The words must be the right thing to say, because he picks up the pace and enters me faster, harder. I bite my lip so hard I think it may start bleeding, but I do start feeling a new sensation enter the pit of my stomach when he changes position so he's moving in me differently and grinding down on my pelvic bone.

I gasp as he puts pressure on my clit again, teasing it and rubbing it as he bucks into me over and over.

He cusses, moans, makes noises I didn't know were possible. The way he kisses me becomes frantic and desperate, and I feel every emotion he normally bottles up pour into me. My chest swells as he whispers my name, his sweaty head diving into the crook of my neck while his hips drive into me in a jerky pace.

The headboard starts to hit the wall with loud thuds, so he curses and grabs ahold of it with one hand while he grabs my hip with the other to keep me from sliding up as he thrusts into me.

Any control he had when he started is long gone, because now he's ravenous—chasing a high that he's so close to getting. The way his body begins moving deeper and harder until he slams into me one last time and moans my name into my neck has me gasping and digging my fingertips into his back. I keep my hold on his body as he empties himself, his heartbeat racing against my chest as he comes down.

The room fills with our breathing and no longer smells of just trees and cinnamon. It smells like us. Of what we've just done.

Kaiden carefully pulls out, making me wince, before dropping to the side of me. His hand finds mine on the sheets and he wraps his fingers around me as we catch our breaths.

"Are you okay?" he asks softly.

I swallow. *Yes. No. Maybe.* "Yeah."

He sits up and studies me, seeing my damp cheeks from the glow of the streetlights coming in my window. His jaw ticks. "You should have told me to stop—"

"I didn't want you to, Kaiden."

We stare at each other for a moment longer before he gets out of bed. "I'm going to grab a washcloth to clean you up. Stay there."

I take a deep breath and listen to the toilet flush and then the sink turn on. My heart is making weird sounds, racing but not, excited or anxious probably. I just had sex for the first time, so it seems normal to react differently.

I move my legs and flinch over how sore they are from staying open. Sitting up, I inspect my slightly bloodied thighs, but besides a few droplets on the gray sheets, there's nothing else.

Kaiden walks in, noticing me looking at the aftermath.

"I thought it'd be worse," I admit, heat creeping up the back of my neck. "You know, the blood and stuff."

He has two washcloths. Using the first one to clean off my stomach from the first time he came, he sets it off to the side and grabs the other to carefully wipe my thighs off before dabbing between my legs.

I suck in a breath at how tender I am, which he apologizes for. "I've never done this before," he admits, not meeting my eyes.

"Done what?"

Once he's done washing me off, he uses a towel to dry me. "Taken someone's virginity and cleaned them up after it's all done."

I'm not sure what to say, so I just reach out and brush his face. He finally glances up, his features softer than I'm used to. Sheepish. "Thank you. I-it hurt but I'm glad we did that."

He kisses me. "You should try peeing. Hear that's important so girls don't get UTIs or whatever."

Giggling, I kiss him back and then he helps me out of bed, passing me my pants and shirt. I get dressed and head to the bathroom. Pushing past the sting, I do my business and wash up before inspecting myself in the mirror.

I'm flushed and my hair is a mess, but the smile on my face is all I can really see. Kaiden did that. He changed the flattened or downturned lips I'm so well acquainted with.

When I go back in the room, Kaiden is dressed and on his usual side of the bed. "You know," he says quietly, opening his arm for me to curl up next to him, "I think it's a good thing your mom is coming here."

I choke. "You want to talk about her right now?"

He chuckles. "I just think it means she's finally willing to put in an effort. It means things are changing."

I'm quiet as I consider his words.

He's right.

Maybe things are finally changing for the better.

Thirty-Four

BEFORE THE SUN FULLY rises, nausea wakes me up with its brutal clutches on my stomach. Back and hips aching as I slide out of bed, I grab my midsection and limp to the bathroom. I barely make it in time before I'm emptying little to nothing into the toilet bowl, stomach acid burning my throat and causing me to gag worse from the cold floor.

Kaiden must have slipped out before I woke up, because there's no doubt he would have come in here demanding to know what's wrong. When I feel a little better, I hold a palm against my back, wash up, brush my teeth, and head back to the bedroom.

The sheets and comforter are still rumpled from last night's escapades, which causes me to smile despite the pulsing sensation in my back. It doesn't surprise me that I tweaked it, given what we'd done, so I grab some Motrin from my nightstand and swallow a couple of pills before pulling the blankets over me again.

I ball up and hug the pillow Kaiden uses close to me, taking in his usual scent until sleep calls for me again.

Thankfully, the nausea lets me be.

But something else plagues my consciousness.

Sadness.

Logan isn't here for me to share everything with.

Thirty-Five

CHRISTMAS BREAK FINALLY ROLLS around, and I'm glad to be out of school. Despite my new medicine working to keep headaches away, the winter flurries and stress of finals got the better of me. Thankfully, I haven't missed any more school, but my energy is depleted by the time I get home in the afternoon.

Mr. Nichols announced that book club wouldn't continue when school started again in January. There wasn't enough interest, and the school felt it wouldn't be appropriate if it were just him with two young girls. I'm not sure what they're so worried about. Nichols has never been inappropriate with any of his students, even when the girls showed him no mercy. Maybe the school is worried for *his* safety.

Dad and Cam tell me that there may be a reading club I could join at the city's library, but I know in my gut that it's better if I just keep reading in the confines of my room. At least then I won't have to argue about an author's point or the reason why books will always be better than the real world.

Fiction has a way of revealing the types of truths that reality obscures. There's nothing that books can't talk about, regardless of how readers interpret them. We can accept or deny what we want, but the facts are still immortalized on paper.

Kaiden knows I'm upset over book club ending, but he can see the paleness to my skin and the bags weighing under my eyes. He says it's probably better if I get home sooner to rest.

More time to play later, he adds. He jokes around about it, but I think there's underlying worry that he hides with humor. Joking is his coping mechanism. That way, he doesn't have to accept what's right in front of him.

The truth.

It's only been a couple of weeks since we first had sex, and since then, I've been too nervous of the pain to do it again. Sometimes we make out until we fall asleep, and other times we'll explore each other's bodies until he senses my hesitation to go further.

He never pushes.

He simply takes what I'm willing to give.

Tomorrow is Christmas Eve, which Kaiden seems to dread. He told me that Cam gets everyone up early to have cinnamon rolls and open one present of our choosing.

"Mama used to ask us what we wanted for Christmas Eve," I tell him when he asks if our family had any traditions. "Usually we could choose something small, like pajamas or books. Sometimes they'd let us have our stockings too, because they were full of candy and little trinkets."

The last Christmas holiday we spent together as a whole family, Dad had given me both the gifts I wanted even though we were only supposed to get one. I still have the Harry

Potter series on its own little shelf, along with a few action figures, wands, and collectables that Dad gifted me throughout the years since. He'd also gifted me Hufflepuff pajamas that I still have tucked away in my dresser even though they no longer fit. I wanted to throw them out when he left, but I couldn't do it.

I smile. "Lo got mad when Dad gave me more presents than her one year. She kept telling him she didn't want anything and then threw a fit when I opened my presents. Mama was upset at Dad the rest of the night, but I don't think he minded because I practically fell running up the stairs to change into my new pj's."

Logan had gotten Cinderella pajamas because she would watch that movie nonstop and talk about finding her own Prince Charming. Mama would tease Dad about how hard it'd be to see their little girls date because there was no doubt Lo would be a handful.

Smile slipping, I lick my bottom lip and glance over at him from the movie. "Anyway, our traditions would usually start on the night of Christmas Eve. After dinner, we'd open our one present and then snack on cookies while waiting for Dr. Seuss's *How the Grinch Stole Christmas* to come on. Our parents would always make us go to bed after that because Santa would be on his way."

Rolling my eyes, I let out a tiny laugh. "I think Lo tried telling me once that Santa doesn't exist. She'd been snooping through Mama's closet and found wrapped presents that had Santa's name on them."

He looks amused. "You didn't believe her? Did she show you the presents?"

I shake my head. "I think once she realized I still believed in the creepy guy, she didn't want to ruin it. Plus, I'm pretty sure our mom moved the presents once she realized Lo had been looking around."

The arm he has around me tightens for a moment before loosening. "Your sister loved you, huh?"

I rest my cheek on his chest. "Of course she did. Logan loved everybody. It didn't matter what they did to her, she looked past the bad things and saw the good. Like when Dad left. She never stayed angry at him like I did."

"When did she…?"

Biting down on my lip, I close my eyes and let out a heavy breath. "She passed a year after he officially left. He'd been gone a lot before then. Mentally. Physically. I want to believe that Logan never saw the version of our parents that I did when she got sicker. I kind of owed it to her to keep her in the dark for as long as I could."

His thumb brushes against my arm in circular motions. I sink into him and the feeling he creates. "Why?"

I reach up and thread our fingers together, letting a moment pass before I answer him. "She let me believe in Santa. She deserved to believe in our parents for as long as she needed to."

I just wish she'd gotten to for a little longer.

My shoulder hurts throughout the next day, making it hard to roll the cookie dough like Cam asks me to. After waking up draped across Kaiden, my entire side was stiff. He tried helping me up when he noticed I was struggling, but I kept telling him I was fine.

Now he's side-eyeing me from the other end of the island where Cam put him to work placing the cookies on the paper sheet to cool off. He told me to stay in bed and watch movies, but I could hear Cam frantically rushing around downstairs and wanted to help.

Dad left to go pick up Mama and Grandma right before we started, saying he'd take them to their hotel before bringing them here to have an early dinner with us. I've been nervous about it since I woke up, the worry of how Mama will act plaguing my conscience any time I'm not being distracted by cookies or meal plans or Christmas music.

Kaiden appears next to me, gently nudging me out of the way and taking over. "I can't keep watching you mess these up," he comments, shooting me a wink.

Cam gasps. "Kaiden!"

I wave it off. "He's right. I'm not doing a very good job. Maybe I can help decorate them when they're ready?"

Cam's expression brightens. "Of course, sweetie! It's Kaiden's favorite part. When he was little—"

Kaiden groans.

"—he would bounce in his seat until we got the frosting ready to color and apply. He'd spend at least ten minutes on each cookie trying to add the right amount of detail and yell at anyone who just slapped the frosting and sprinkles on them."

"Dad wouldn't even spread the damn frosting around. He just put a spoonful on top and doused the thing with whatever sprinkles were closest to him."

Cam laughs. "He did that on purpose."

I grin. "Are you still like that?"

Kaiden says "No" at the same time as Cam answers "Yes."

Glancing between them, I see how light Cam's eyes are as she watches her son. The holidays are meant to bring people together, and it seems like they have here.

Cam looks from him to me. "He's nowhere near as obsessed with perfection, but if we put him in a baking competition, he'd win first place hands down."

Kaiden's face turns pink. "*Mom.* Jesus."

Cam's eyes widen as she stares at him.

He grumbles and rolls the dough flat, not meeting her teary eyes.

I can't help but stare though, because the watery gaze she gives Kaiden is nothing like the one I'm used to seeing from Mama. Cam's is full of awe and love knowing her son finally called her something other than her first name. It's so beautiful, I feel like I shouldn't be intruding on the moment.

Jabbing my finger behind me, I make an excuse to go to my room. I suppose I could be honest and admit I need to lie down, but instead I tell them I have presents left to wrap. Considering I don't have any money, it's a stupid one to make, but neither says a word.

Once I'm in my room, I play with the beaded bracelet on my wrist before walking over to my dresser and pulling out the old pair of Harry Potter pajamas. Running my fingers across the worn, dingy material, I set them on the bed and stare.

If Kaiden can let Cam in, I can do the same for Dad. Mama too if she'll let me. The difference between them is that Dad let me in a long time ago—when he said yes to moving in, when he picked me up, when he brought me back to visit. He's tried more than Mama has. It's *her* turn to let *me* in.

After playing around with a couple of items from my

room, I stand back and smile at the outcome of my makeshift Christmas Eve present. Dad didn't ask for it, but I think that's what makes it more special.

Running my hand over the thick frame housing my flattened Hufflepuff shirt with a picture of Lo and me as kids, I swallow past the lump in my throat.

After stealing some wrapping paper from Cam, I finish taping up the end before setting the gift off to the side. Finally taking Kaiden's advice, I grab his laptop from where he keeps it on my nightstand and put on a cheesy Christmas movie before pulling the blankets around me.

Still aching, I rest on my back and feel my lids grow heavy before I succumb to sleep.

"*Emery.*"

Someone is shaking me, pulling me away from a nap that I don't want to end. I can feel the exhaustion settle into my body—limbs heavy and brain foggy and back sore. I grumble and try ignoring the intruder, but they keep persisting.

"*Wake up, baby.*"

"Go away, Kaiden," I murmur, wanting to push him away. He usually lets me sleep when I need it, so I'm not sure why he's being pushy now.

A throat clears. "Not me, Mouse."

My eyes crack open, and the first thing I see is Mama beside me. She's sitting on the edge of my bed with a weary smile on her face. Grandma and Kaiden are off to the side, Kaiden leaning against my dresser and Grandma looking amused from behind Mama.

"Does your stepbrother usually call you baby?" Grandma asks. Her curiosity is mixed with a teasing tone, which makes me blush.

Mama squeezes my shoulder. "You look a little pale, Em."

Em. I haven't heard her call me that in a long time. It almost sounds off coming from her unpainted lips.

"I'm okay," I say, sitting up. She helps me, noticing my slowness, and then hugs me to her until I'm breathing in her lavender scent.

"When did you guys get here?" I look at Grandma and smile, reaching out to squeeze her hand before pulling away from Mama.

"Only ten minutes ago," she answers.

"I'm glad you came."

She glances at Kaiden, then Grandma, and then back to me. "Can I speak to you alone for a moment?"

Wanting to ask Kaiden to stay might not be a good idea, because I don't know what she's planning on talking to me about. Based on her distant study of his casual demeanor, I think he is a big part of it.

"We'll be downstairs," Grandma says, tugging Kaiden along with her. He relents, shooting me an amused grin before Grandma closes my bedroom door behind them.

"Please be careful, Sunshine."

I blink slowly, unsure of where this is heading.

She takes my hand in hers. "That boy has heartbreak written all over his face, and the circumstances aren't exactly ideal for you two."

At first, I'm not sure what the feeling in my chest is, but it builds up and up the more I replay her words.

That's when I realize that it's anger.

"No."

Her lips part.

"No," I repeat, pulling my hand away from hers. "You

don't get to warn me away from people. I love you, Mama, but you gave up that right a long time ago."

"Em—"

"Kaiden has been in my corner from the very beginning," I inform her gingerly. "He's annoying and sometimes downright rude, but he's also a realist, probably more so than anyone else I know. He tells it how it is even if it hurts. I need him in my life."

She's speechless.

"He's my friend," I continue quietly, making sure she meets my eye. "He's my *only* friend since Logan died. When things get tough here because Dad doesn't get it or kids at school irritate me, he's there. Not you. You were the reason I even came here, and I'm not blaming you for it. We both needed this, Mama. You needed time before you could ask for it, and I needed space before I could admit it."

Mama and I were bad for each other.

But we could get better.

"You brought me to Dad. To Kaiden."

Her eyes don't glisten, but her lips falter like she wants to frown. I won't let her though, because I'm not sad. She shouldn't be either.

"I'm happy, Mama."

I mean it.

I hold her hand again. "Being here makes me happy. Now it's time for you to be happy too."

That makes her smile. "I'm trying, Sunshine."

For once, I believe her.

Thirty-Six

DAD TEARS UP WHEN he opens his gift. He stares at it for so long, I start to worry that I should have chosen something else. Maybe not even given him anything at all.

Then he hugs me. A big bear hug like I remember from when I was little. He'd wrap both me and Lo in his arms and squeeze until we giggled and latched on to him too.

I start tearing up too, which makes Cam get emotional. Mama and Grandma sit on the couch watching, Grandma smiling and Mama doing the exact opposite. Her lips are twitching downward until she's frowning, and Kaiden notices too.

Focusing back on Dad, I brush the frame in his hands. "It's my favorite pair you ever gave me. I thought…"

I shrug, not knowing what I thought.

Dad's throat bobs as he brushes my cheek with his thumb. "I love you, baby girl. Always have and always will."

So why didn't you try harder? I want to ask. Only I don't, because I remind myself that we're trying to move forward, not back.

Mama's frown deepens when I return to the spot between her and Grandma. Thankfully, the gift exchange is over and we're all full from dinner, which means Dad will take them back to their hotel soon.

Mama was relatively quiet during supper. She asked me how school was, and I told her okay. Cam mentioned book club, so I explained how it ended, and Dad brought up my report card because I made the principal's list with all As.

Nobody was surprised.

When Mama asked Kaiden about school, there was motive woven into her words. I studied her as he replied something generic, then Cam intervened and told Mama that Kaiden has been taking college classes to earn credits before graduating high school in June.

That's when Mama asked him about college.

Honestly, I never thought about Kaiden going away. Not once has he brought up attending college anywhere. He barely talks about the classes he's away for in the mornings.

I didn't even know he'd applied to any schools until Cam started talking about his early acceptance to Colgate University to play lacrosse. Apparently a bunch of scouts were at his games over the past two years, and he got offers from all over when they saw what he could do.

Massachusetts wants him.

Philadelphia.

Maryland.

Of course Mama would ask why he chose a college in New York when he could have traveled, but Kaiden never offered an explanation. She can assume whatever she wants, but his family is here—his past. Not all of us want to escape it.

Now Mama watches everyone like she's putting

something together in her head. I've stopped wanting to figure out what because it only hurts me more to guess. Grandma always changes conversation to something lighter if the topic gets too difficult or the silence grows too thick. She's always been good at that.

Shortly after presents, Grandma gathers their things to get ready for Dad to take them back to their hotel. When I go to the kitchen to grab a glass of water and take my medicine, Mama and Dad are by the back counter with their backs to me.

"…doesn't need to know that."

"How long, Joanne?" Dad whispers harshly, crossing his arms. His back and shoulders are tense as he stares at her.

I stay hidden behind the wall, biting my lip as I study Mama from around the doorway. Her head is down, her hands resting on the edge of the counter like she's a child being scolded. "I was angry, Henry. You can't blame me after what you said."

Dad throws his hands up. "She's still my daughter, for Christ's sake. Did you ever tell her about the terms *you* made me agree to?"

I swallow. What is he talking about?

"No."

"No," he repeats blandly. "She's hated me for years. I'm not an idiot. If she knew the damn truth, maybe things would be different now between us."

A hand curls around my arm, startling me. I look over my shoulder to see Kaiden, whose finger is pressed against his lips like he's shushing me. Settling into his body, I peek back over at my parents.

"One of us is telling her, Joanne. I don't give a shit which one it is, but she needs to know that I never intentionally avoided her."

Drawing back in surprise, Kaiden wraps an arm around my waist. When I gather my bearings, I try escaping his grasp to confront them. Kaiden tightens his grip and backs us up despite my silent protests.

When we get to the living room, I turn around and glare at him. "Seriously? I need to talk to them."

"No, you don't."

"Kaid—"

"Trust me," he says quietly, letting go of me when he sees I'll listen.

Sighing, I find Grandma watching us with interest. Ignoring whatever she must be thinking, I walk over and give her a hug. "I'm glad you're here. I think I'm going upstairs for the night though. Maybe watch a movie with Kaiden or something."

One of her white brows rises. "Is that what the kids are calling it these days?"

My whole face heats as Kaiden chuckles from behind me. "It's not like that."

Grandma rolls her eyes and swats my butt as I turn around. "I'm old, not naive, Emmy. I personally don't see a problem with it. I'm sure I've done far worse in my youth, and he's a looker. *You* could certainly do worse too."

Groaning, I make my way to the stairs with Kaiden following close behind. "I like your grandma."

I shove his arm. "She practically called you hot, so I'm not surprised." When we're closed in my room, I sit cross-legged on the bed and toy with my shirtsleeve. "Why wouldn't you let me talk to them? That seemed like a vital time to announce I heard everything."

He sighs and sits down next to me, flicking a piece of hair on my shoulder. "Your dad said he was going to tell you, so let him come to you."

"But tell me *what*?"

He grins. "It's the curiosity that you hate, isn't it?"

Staring at the wrinkles of the comforter, I shrug loosely. "When you live every day not knowing what's going to happen, how you're going to feel, you crave answers. If I knew for a fact I'd wake up tomorrow pain-free with tons of energy, I'd do things I can't when I'm too tired to lift the blankets off my body or walk from the bed to the bathroom. I'd get my nails done because it wouldn't hurt for the technician to touch my fingers or bend my hand the way she'd need to. I'd dye my hair a stupid color that I'd probably regret because it wouldn't fall out or burn from the sensitivity.

"It kills me not to be a normal nineteen-year-old. I was held back for missing too much school. I should start considering college like you are, but I have no idea if..." I take a deep breath, chest aching. "Who knows if college is in my future? Going to class now is hard. Finding the energy for college courses, which is way more work, would probably be too difficult."

His jaw ticks. "You don't know that for sure. If there's anyone who should go to college, it's you. You love school for whatever reason, so start researching ones you'd love to check out. I don't want to hear any of that other bullshit. If I can go, you can too."

Drawing my knees to my chest, I shake my head and meet his stern eyes. "I love that you think it's that simple,

Kaiden. It's not though. And why *are* you going to Colgate instead of one of the others that made offers to you? Why are you going at all if you don't want to? I'm sure it's not too late to change your mind if you wanted to go somewhere different. Any of them who want you for their team would probably make an exception if early admission is closed."

"We're not talking about—"

"Yes, we are," I cut him off, reaching for his hand. He doesn't move away like I expect him to but weaves our fingers together instead like it's his default mode. "I know you do just fine at school, but sports have always meant more than academics. You love lacrosse and I hear you're amazing at it. At least that's what the entire school seems to think. Cam says so too, and she's hardly one to lie, even if she is your mom."

A grin appears on his face, washing away the seriousness from a moment ago. "And the three trophies with our school's name on them don't hurt."

I smile at him. "Does Colgate have a better team than the other ones?"

He hesitates. "No."

"So why choose them?"

His shoulders draw back. "Mouse—"

"If I had the chance, I'd move," I admit, squeezing his hand. "I would see the world. I've always wanted to move to Virginia. Did you know that? Sometimes I even go to the University of Virginia's website and look at their campus pictures and study the program listings. I'll pretend I'm one of the students posing while the camera snaps pictures of the quad or library. You know I'd spend a lot of time there, reading, studying, you name it."

"Then *go* to Virginia."

If only.

"And what about you?" I prod.

He doesn't answer.

Letting go of his hand, I give him my best serious face. "Kaiden, not all of us are so lucky in life. We have to accept what we're given. At best, I could attend school online. There's less stress about missing class and failing because of poor attendance or not getting the notes from lectures. I wouldn't have to worry about walking across the huge campus on days when it hurts to stand or get trapped in a dorm room with someone who doesn't understand that I'm sick and need lots of sleep. I know what's best for me. What will work. You need to figure out what that is for you."

His lips part and then close. "I do it for my mom," he says distantly. "It was her idea to take the college classes and get credits. That way, I was ahead. She was thinking of a future for me when I was too in my head about my dad. I went along with it because…"

Because it made Cam happy.

I brush his arm with my hand. "If you could go anywhere without anything holding you back, where would it be?"

The hopeless romantic in me wants him to say *wherever you are*, but the truth is that he may not be able to go where I end up.

So I'm thankful when he quietly answers, "Maryland."

Christmas Day brings a fresh snowstorm that blankets everything in white. It takes Dad a little longer to get Mama and

Grandma here, but when they arrive, breakfast is on the table waiting, along with homemade hot chocolate.

Without asking, Dad turns the television on to *A Christmas Story*, an old tradition of our own that we've had every year. The movie plays all day on the same channel, background noise for present opening and lunch digesting. I always fall asleep to it while a small smile tugs on my face for Ralphie and his BB gun.

Mama kisses my cheek before sitting down beside me to eat, even though she kept saying she wasn't hungry. I think she feels weird being around Cam, not that Cam has shown anything other than hospitality to her. I guess I'd feel strange too seeing my ex-husband with his new family.

It was weird enough seeing my father interact with them knowing he left the very same thing behind.

But did he?

After breakfast, we make our way into the living room for presents. Kaiden and I sit beside each other on the floor, and everyone else sits on the couches and chairs. Dad passes the gifts out one by one, and after almost two hours, we're all watching the movie and arguing over *Die Hard* being considered a holiday movie.

The answer is no, but of course Dad always has to differ. Even Kaiden cracks up when he hears Dad's reasoning, which is the first time Kaiden has even smiled when Dad is involved.

Maybe Christmas miracles are a thing.

A little before midafternoon hits, Mama asks if she can talk to me. Dad glances between us, eyeing Mama like he's telling her not to chicken out of the conversation.

Biting my lip, I nod and follow her into the kitchen.

"I know you were listening," she starts, giving me a small smile. "Mother's intuition, I suppose. Although it's not always the best gut instinct to go on."

"What do you mean?"

She wets her lips and glances behind her at the open archway. The movie is restarting, and the lingering conversations are still easily heard, especially Cam's light laughter.

"When your father admitted he wasn't in love with me anymore, I was hurt." She takes a deep breath and nods slowly. "Even though I knew it was coming, it didn't make hearing him say it out loud any easier. I was so angry over him not putting in the effort even when he was there. It seemed like living with us was a chore to him, one that he preferred avoiding by staying at work later and later.

"I won't get into the details of what I thought, maybe even suspected, but our separation was a sure thing. When he asked for a divorce, I let my emotions get the better of me. I told him if he couldn't bother with his children when he still lived there, then there was no reason to bother with them when he left. Honestly, I thought it was for the best anyway. He wasn't the one who noticed Logan's symptoms or behavior changes. He wasn't there for the appointments. He always had an excuse. So I took away the opportunity for him to make it up."

It's hard to breathe as I stare at the woman sitting beside me. She's still, tight, like she knows what she did harmed so many people in the process.

"Years," I finally choke out. "You made him stay away all this time? When I cried and asked why Dad left, you never had anything to say about it. Why would you do that?"

She struggles meeting my eyes. "We do bad things when

we're upset, Emery. Our decisions are driven by emotion, and I let my hurt get the better of me."

"Did you tell him not to call more?"

She closes her eyes. "Yes."

"Did you tell him not to invite us to their holiday dinners?"

A nod.

My nostrils flare. "You knew how I felt about him, Mama. I was so angry that he didn't want us. Why would any mother think it's okay for their children to feel that kind of hatred?"

She has no good response, so she remains silent. I bet if she looked up, I'd see golden orbs staring back. But I'm done with their color.

"Do you regret it?" I ask.

"More than you know," she finally says, reaching out for my hand. "Sunshine, I live with so many regrets. They've become so hard to bear. Between your father, Logan, you—"

"Don't you dare act like you lost me!" I stand up, pushing my chair away. "You were the one who practically forced me to go. How many times did you call me Logan? Or cry yourself to sleep before dinner? I get that things were hard, but you weren't alone. Grandma lost a granddaughter, and I lost my twin! We all felt the loss. Not just you."

She drops her face into her hands, nodding because she knows I'm right. "I see that now. Group has helped me understand how wrong I was to act how I did. I'm so, so sorry, baby girl. If I could do it all over, I would."

I stare at her for a long time, unsure of how to respond. "Would it be worth it though? I think leaving the house was always what was best for me, and if by some miraculous occurrence we got a redo, I'm not sure I'd take it. Why relive Lo's death all over again? Even if we could choose how to respond differently, I never would have made it here and experienced what having a family is like."

I think of Cam's willingness to help.

Dad's silent protection.

Kaiden. Just…Kaiden.

"I miss you guys." Even knowing what Mama did, I miss the good memories and the familiarity that my hometown brings. I miss the Sunday drives and the stupid traditions. I miss being picked on by Lo's friends for not being just like my twin.

But I know deep in my chest, without a shadow of a doubt, I'd miss it here more.

I'd miss the banter.

I'd miss the movie nights.

I'd miss the late-night cuddles.

Kaiden annoys me and cares for me and gets under my skin in every way possible. We're family, sure, but we're friends too. If there was ever a time I could plan the future, I'd risk everything to make us even more.

That's not how my life works though.

Kaiden will go to Maryland.

I'll be here.

"I wouldn't redo anything, Mama."

She blinks up at me.

"Because we can't change anything."

Thirty-Seven

THE METAL BLEACHERS ARE uncomfortable to sit still on while I watch boys in running shorts and baggy muscle shirts sprint across the gym. Mr. Jefferson didn't want me coming in during practice, but Kaiden said something to him that made Coach grumble before waving me off to the side. Honestly, I wouldn't have minded going to the library and doing some reading in chairs that didn't make my tailbone hurt. I promised Kaiden I'd watch him though, and the smile he graced me with made the discomfort worth it.

After the first half hour of practice, Jefferson changed up their drills. I tried following along to the things he yelled from the sidelines but got lost almost instantly. It reminds me of the times I would sit next to Dad while he watched football. To me, it was a bunch of men in tight pants running after a ball. Dad loved it though.

When the boys were split into teams, I watched Kaiden in his element. It didn't take long to see why everyone said he was one of the best players they'd ever seen. He dominated the floor, flying past his opponents and making the most goals.

He'd told me his dad put him into school late so he could spend more time playing. Hone his craft. Get more experience. It's because of Adam that he has the opportunities he does now.

A future to build.

At almost four, I get up to go to the bathroom, slipping out while Kaiden battles it out with one of his buddies. I smile when I hear them banter, before disappearing out the side door. Most of the people on the team are friends, so watching them taunt each other makes me laugh. Kaiden may be formidable in the halls, but he's the version I'm used to seeing when he's playing.

For the past few weeks, I've been having so much back pain that I psyched myself out enough to google for answers. It wouldn't have been so bad if I hadn't noticed slight spotting after peeing with no period following. I usually refuse to use the internet to scour for answers, but worrying Dad and Cam seems pointless if I could talk myself down from the feeling in my gut that says something is off. The only thing that made sense was a possible bladder or kidney infection, so I asked Dad for vitamins and cranberry gummies and told him it was just something new I was trying.

I keep telling myself they'll help, but the blood still shows up and the pain, though tolerable half the time, is still present.

It's nothing, I promise myself.

I'm on my way back to the gym when I see Mr. Nichols walking down the hall. Smiling, I give him a small wave and hesitate at the gym door, noticing the boys in an intense match against each other like when I left.

"Emery," Nichols says in greeting. He glances in the small window. "Ah, lacrosse season. Kaiden plays, doesn't he?"

I nod, rubbing my arm. "He's my ride home, so I figured I'd watch him play since everyone says he's so good."

"What's your verdict?"

Giving him a tiny smile, I shrug. "I'm not an expert in anything sports-related, so I couldn't say for sure. He makes a lot of goals, which I assume is the whole point."

He chuckles. "Not a sports fan, huh?"

"Nope."

He watches the boys again before turning back to me. "How have things been going? It seems strange not to have book club obligations after school."

"Seems like you're still busy." I gesture toward the stack of papers he must have had copied in the teachers' lounge down the hall.

"A teacher's job never ends," he muses.

We fall to silence.

I jab my thumb to the gymnasium door, clearing my throat. "I should probably get back in there before Kaiden thinks I ditched him."

Just as I pull the door open, he says, "I don't know what you did, but he's changed considerably. I hear the other teachers talk about his behavior. You're good for him."

Blushing, I brush hair behind my ear. "I don't think it's me. Trust me, Kaiden is his own person."

He just smiles. "You don't give yourself enough credit, Emery. I don't believe in coincidences, and it sounds like he changed when you came here."

Waving it off, I try thinking of a reply that dismisses his assumption. "Maybe he just got tired of pretending to be someone he's not. I hear that happens when you're graduating."

He hums out a reply, seemingly not believing me. "Speaking of, what are your plans for next year?"

My brows go up. "Oh, uh..." I make a face, toying with the partially opened door. "I haven't really thought about it, honestly."

Lie.

"Have you considered taking a few more college credit classes? I'm offering one for creative writing this term, and I know a few other teachers are too. It could help you get some general education credits out of the way. There's room in some of the classes, and we're not too far into the semester if you still want to try getting in."

Licking my lips, I debate on what to tell him. That I'm not sure I'll go to college? That I have no clue what I want to do? I would have to explain why I don't plan things, and it's not something I like diving into. He may be my favorite teacher, the one person who has been on my side since I started, but that doesn't mean I want to tell him that my future is tomorrow, not next year. Not five years from now.

"I'll think about it," I settle on, giving him the same smile I give everyone when I want them to believe me.

Mr. Nichols seems appeased because he can't read my expression like Kaiden can. He would know I'm full of it, maybe even thinking the worst.

I wave Nichols goodbye and walk back into the gym. Kaiden glances at me from the sidelines, his hair a sweaty mess as he downs some water from his plastic bottle. Even from a distance, I notice the narrow slits of his eyes as they go from the door to my face. I just wiggle my fingers and settle back into my seat, ignoring the pain in my back and the ache in my joints.

Stretching out my legs, I watch as their practice nears its end and the boys head to the locker room. Sliding my backpack over my shoulder, I move off the bleachers and wait for Kaiden by the double doors.

Jefferson walks over to me. "Normally don't like people sitting in on these," he says gruffly, sliding his clipboard under his arm and crossing his arms on his chest. "Distracts the boys. Haven't seen Monroe play so fiercely before though, especially not in practice." My eyes widen as he studies me. "Your father married his mother, right?"

I swallow. "Yes, sir."

"I see them at almost every game," he comments. "They're both proud, especially his mother. She's always cheering the loudest in the stands. I suspect you'll be joining them from now on?"

"Uh…yes?"

I'm sure Kaiden won't let me stay home, so the choice isn't really mine. When he told me I should come to his practice, I tried telling him I had homework to do. Our argument lasted ten minutes before he distracted me with neck and shoulder kisses that led to way more touching than talking.

And here I am.

Reddening just thinking about it, I shift my backpack strap higher on my shoulder. "I know his mother is looking forward to the season starting, even though it'll be hard for her knowing it's the last one she'll see. I hear kids saying it'll be the best one yet."

He grins, grabbing his clipboard. "You keep coming, kid, and we'll wind up on top for sure."

When my whole face heats up, he chuckles and walks away. Thankfully, Kaiden comes out soon after, freshly showered and back in his jeans and Henley. As we walk to his car, I glance at him and play with my backpack.

Popping my lips, I ask, "Do people think something is going on with us?"

His brow quirks. "Why?" We get to the car but neither of us gets in. He stares at me from over the top. "Did someone say something to you?"

"Not exactly..."

"Was it Nichols?"

"What?"

His jaw ticks. "I saw you two talking outside the gym earlier. Did he say something to you?"

Is he...? I giggle. "Are you jealous? Of *Mr. Nichols*?"

He looks irritated. "Don't be stupid."

I laugh. "You so are!" I shake my head and get in the car, setting my bag down and waiting for him to join me. "Your coach just made a comment about coming to the games so you keep playing the way you did today."

His shoulders loosen. "Is that all?"

Rolling my eyes, I shrug. "It was just how he said it. It's like he assumed you played better because I was there. I don't know, it seemed weird. He knows I'm your stepsister."

"So what did Nichols want?"

"Oh my God, Kaiden. Really?"

He turns on the car and blasts the heat before pulling out of his spot. "The guy just rubs me the wrong way. He's always talking to you."

"Jealous," I singsong. "For your information, he was asking what I plan on doing next year. He thinks I should take college courses here for credit."

"You should," he agrees simply.

"We'll see."

"Stop acting like you won't be able to."

"Stop acting like you can predict the future," I fire back, staring out the window. "It isn't like I think it's a bad idea. I just don't want to commit yet."

"What *do* you want to commit to?"

The question takes me by surprise. Why would he even ask me something like that? I want to commit to getting through senior year. It's all I can think about.

I know that's not what he means though.

"Are we friends, Kaiden?" My voice is unsure, a tone I'm used to hearing. It just wasn't when it came to defining us.

The car slows to a stop. "Do you really need to ask that, Mouse?"

My lips part. "Well..." *No?* "Yeah, I guess. You said you don't do labels. It's not like I expect anything. It would just be nice to know that we're friends, because..."

You're the only one I have.

"Yeah," he says softly, as if he can read my mind. "We're friends."

I smile and ease into my seat. "Not to get mushy or whatever, but you're kind of my best friend. Annabel and I talk at school sometimes, but we've never exchanged numbers or planned to hang out."

"So I'm your best friend by default," he muses, seemingly unfazed.

I reach out and grab his free hand, which rests on the gearshift. "I've always considered Lo my best friend, even after all this time, because she was willing to love me for who I am."

He squeezes my hand. "Are you going to make me say it?"

I roll my eyes. "You don't have to tell me. It's in the way you accept me despite my problems. Even if you're annoying about hot English teachers."

He curses. "You think he's hot?"

I just grin.

He sighs. "For what it's worth, you're my best friend too, Mouse."

I smile to myself victoriously.

"Still don't like Nichols though," he grumbles before holding my hand in silence all the way home.

The weeks go on without interruption. School, practice, homework, movie nights. I get to witness the first lacrosse game of the season, where Cam does cheer the loudest and Dad whoops and hollers until I get a headache. Exeter wins the first two games and loses the third one, but that doesn't deter anyone's spirit.

On nights when I'm feeling halfway human, I ask Kaiden to show me how to touch him in every way he likes. First with my hands, then my mouth. He always returns the favor with a grin on his face and looks cocky when I have to cover my face with a pillow as I break apart.

It's been over two months since we had sex, and it isn't like I don't want to do it again. In fact, not so long ago, I thought it'd happen again until I moved wrong over Kaiden and cried out from the pain shooting down my back and hips. He'd grabbed me some pain relievers and covered us both before falling asleep.

On Valentine's Day, I find chocolate and a card in my locker. The chocolate is some fancy brand I've never heard of, and the card has a mouse on it holding a ribbon-wrapped wedge of cheese in its hands. I keep it on my nightstand at home, smiling every time I pass it.

Not long after Valentine's Day, I woke up to more hair on my pillow. Kaiden didn't freak out like Mama did, which made me feel a little better. He could tell I wasn't all right though, because he kissed my cheek and told me it wasn't a big deal. It was.

I cried while he held me, and I told him about how much I love my hair. My hair is my femininity. It's what makes me feel pretty. With every flare, I lost more and more until it got shorter each time.

The day following my meltdown in Kaiden's arms, he drove me to his mother's salon, and the same hairdresser I usually have gave me a short pixie cut from a magazine Kaiden and I looked at for styles. It's one I could play with and make messy and cute or leave to air-dry and have it sleek and sexy. I teared up when I saw the hair on the white tile, but I would have cried harder seeing it on my pillowcase.

I got to choose to let it go, even if the choice was one I was forced to make. Kaiden told me I looked beautiful. Cam hugged me and told me I was stunning. And Dad kissed my cheek and told me I looked just like Mama.

Their support made it easier, even on the days I felt like everyone stared at the way my neck and ears were exposed. No longer could I hide behind my hair like a shield when I was uncomfortable. People could gawk at me, and I'd know it—I'd feel their eyes burning into my face. I even considered asking Dad if I could get my ears pierced just to feel more girly, as if everyone stared like I was less so without long locks.

Kaiden told me I was stupid.

Then told me I was beautiful again.

Fuck them, Mouse. They don't matter.

I wanted to ask if he did, but I already knew the answer. His opinion mattered more than my own because I didn't have to stare at myself like he did. He thought I was pretty even without my long hair or pierced ears or makeup. I wasn't the kind of feminine most people considered, but it didn't change his mind about wanting to spend time with me or kiss me or watch movies with me.

Dad and I spend more time together than we used to. When he watches TV after dinner, I'll sit with him and comment on the show he watches, usually sports or news-related. Sometimes he'll let me choose, and it makes me giggle when he pretends to get into the reality show I pick. When Kaiden and Cam join us, the guys pick on one of the girls while Cam and I defend them, even if we sort of agree with the ridiculous behavior the guys point out.

Exeter has become the home I didn't know I lacked. Family dinner is always filled with easy conversation and funny banter, game days are full of team spirit, and with every passing week, I start feeling like I'm part of something more than a fractured family.

After English class, I'm halfway to my locker when I hear giggling from behind me. I feel a familiar tingle of unwanted attention on my back, so I casually look over my shoulder as I put my books away and grab my coat.

Rachel and some girls I see her hanging around with all the time are staring at me. One of them flips their hair when she catches my eyes, and Rachel grins like the Cheshire cat. It makes me nervous when she tells them something before walking over to me.

Closing my locker, I turn to face her.

She gives me a once-over. "It looks like being in a relationship is really becoming on you, Em. They say being in love adds at least twenty pounds."

I gape at her. "I'm not dating anyone."

She scoffs. "Please. I told you when you first came here that Kaiden always gets what he wants. People still talk, even when he tells them not to. His teammates are worse gossips than the cheerleaders."

Pressing my lips together, I glance at her friends. They're invested in our exchange, along with a few stragglers. Kaiden ditched after lunch to celebrate some guy's birthday from the team. He told me he'd pick me up after school.

"Kaiden and I—"

"You sit in on practices," she says, raising one perfectly sculpted eyebrow. "Nobody else is allowed to do that. He's been sitting with you at lunch with some of his teammates. They've practically adopted you."

"That's because we live together."

"Like I said—" She steps closer. "His teammates like to gossip. Every time he flirts with you, touches you, or looks at you a certain way, we'll know about it. And come on, *Mouse*. You look at him like he's your savior."

How does she know about his nickname for me? Up until a couple of months ago, he never sat with me at lunch, much less spoke to me during school hours. The first time my table was full, I was so shocked I just sat there and stared at all the guys picking on each other.

Don't look so surprised, Mouse.

That's what he told me.

I sigh. "We're friends, Rachel."

"With benefits, knowing Kaiden."

I don't grace her with a reply.

"All I'm saying," she tells me, "is that you should lay off the carbs and participate more in gym. Regardless of you confirming or denying what everyone already assumes, it's no secret you've gained weight."

The confidence Kaiden gives me every time he spares me a glance, no matter how long or short, simmers and disappears with every jab Rachel throws at me. She wants to see me defeated, just like any mean girl does. She feeds off my reaction, especially if it makes me the inferior of us.

She warned me she wouldn't play nice if I became true competition. I don't think she understands my dynamic with Kaiden though. I'm not sure he and I do either.

Rachel stares at my face, tilting her head and taking in the layered pieces of my pixie. "I mean, it could be the new hair. Unless there's another reason you're packing on pounds..."

She cannot seriously be insinuating that I'm pregnant. "Why can't you mind your own business? It doesn't matter if or why I gained weight."

Her eyes roll, but she relents. "Whatever you say, Mouse. Give Kaiden my best. He should really return my texts. I miss him."

Grinding my teeth, I walk out the front doors, leaving their loud laughter behind me.

I've noticed that my clothes fit me differently, especially my jeans. It isn't my waist that the denim hugs tighter, it's my legs. And despite trying not to let it get to me, my reflection does look different. My cheeks are fuller, the bones less defined, and my chin is slightly rounder than I'm used to.

At first, I thought I looked better. Healthier. I can still fit into my clothes, so it isn't a huge weight change, but it's an unwarranted one. My diet hasn't been too out of the ordinary If anything, my appetite is limited thanks to the pulsing pain.

If people are starting to notice at school, what does everyone at home think? Kaiden has seen me naked more and more lately, and he talks about how much he loves my body. He'll trace my slight curves and caress every inch of skin like he can't help it. Never once has he commented on me looking different.

When I slip into his waiting car, he immediately notices my mood. "What happened?"

"Your friends like to talk."

"They're idiots."

I stare at my hands that are folded in my lap. "Do you think I'm getting fat?"

"What the fuck kind of question is that?"

"One I want you to answer honestly."

His reply is immediate. "You're not fat, Mouse. Not even close. Whoever said that is an asshole that I'll happily deal with."

Part of me wants to rat out Rachel, but I don't want to battle with the repercussions. When you have little energy to begin with, you don't want to waste it on the wrong people.

"It doesn't matter," I murmur.

"You're upset. It matters."

I sigh loudly. "Things have been weird with me lately. I know I've filled out, but I didn't think anyone really noticed."

He's silent for too long, staring out the windshield with his hand twitching on the gearshift. "You don't think that you're…?"

I smack him. "Seriously? Do you not remember when I snapped at you two weeks ago because I was moody, and you bought me chocolate and tampons when you found out I was bleeding to death? Or two months ago when I couldn't get out of bed because my period triggered a flare, and you gave me your Mom's heating pad?"

He raises his hands. "Shit. Sorry."

I shake my head and stare out the window. "I'm just… angry. I didn't mean to snap, but I don't want people commenting on my weight. I used to be accused of anorexia when I lost too much from my disease. Now…"

He reaches out and takes my hand in his, the same thing I've done with him when he gets upset. Sometimes it's over his father or when he has a bad day. All it takes is one little touch.

I look at our hands. "Do you care that people think we're together? They know who we are to each other. Rumors will get nasty."

"They won't say anything."

"To you," I counter. "But what about after we graduate? I'll be known as the girl who looks like she got knocked up by her stepbrother. That's…" I scrunch my nose. "It's gross, to be honest."

He snorts. "You don't think it's gross when I lick your pussy until you're crying into your pillow."

"Kaiden!"

"To answer your question," he says shamelessly, "I don't care what people think about us. We're friends. Friends flirt. Nobody needs to know anything else."

"But they assume—"

"You're not going to get tormented when I'm gone," he promises, his tone too determined to argue with.

If we only knew how true that was…

Thirty-Eight

MARCH'S BIPOLAR WEATHER BRINGS an odd mixture of snowstorms and warm, sunny days that has more students sick than the first week of school. Since a lot of kids were out celebrating St. Patrick's Day at parties together, nearly the entire junior and senior classes were out recovering. The school closed for an extended weekend in hopes attendance would pick up first thing on Monday.

Kaiden and I spend Friday watching movies in bed. Even though he went to one of his friend's parties, he's one of the few who made it out without so much as a runny nose. If I had agreed to go like he tried getting me to, there's no doubt I'd be stuffed up and hacking out a lung with the vast majority of our peers.

As the credits roll on our third movie of the day, I stretch and settle into the pillows tucked behind me. They're toasty and conformed to my body. "Have you thought more about college?"

April is right around the corner, and I've heard Mr.

Jefferson talk to Cam about Kaiden's college opportunities. Apparently, two of the schools are holding a spot for him in case he changes his mind. He always tells them he'll think about it and then shuts down afterward.

Closing his laptop with pressed lips in a tight line, he glances at the time on my alarm clock and then finally shrugs. "Not really."

Liar. I saw him doing an online search on his laptop when he thought I fell asleep. The University of Maryland's campus was on the screen, like he was studying it closely. He searched stats on the lacrosse team and read articles on previous games.

Trailing my fingers down his arm until he captures my wrist and slips his hand into mine, I say, "I wanted to take history and creative writing for college credit this semester like Mr. Nichols suggested, but I wasn't sure if I could handle it. I probably could have done one of them, but I just..."

My energy was better being spent on other things. Focusing on me, not worrying about college credits that I may never even use.

Kaiden watches me with slightly pinched brows, like he's trying to figure out if I'm being serious or just playing. He hates when I talk down about myself because he doesn't want to see the reality behind it. I'm sick. I'm tired. I can barely keep up with the bare minimum these days.

Something is wrong.

I know it deep down.

When he sees that I've truly considered my options, he squeezes my hand in response. "Jefferson thinks I should accept UM's offer," he grumbles, resting the back of his head against the bed frame. "I think his exact words were 'Don't be an idiot, kid.'"

That makes me laugh. "He's right. I overheard Cam telling Dad that you've got a full scholarship there, the campus is beautiful, and it wouldn't be an awfully long drive to visit. It seems like she wants you to go there. She wants you to be happy."

He won't admit that he doesn't want to leave her behind, because he won't damage his pride. He's spent so long being angry at her and his father that he can't accept he'll miss them both if he moves away.

"It's not forever," I add quietly, resting my cheek on his shoulder. We sit like that for a while, holding hands, listening to each other breathing.

Forever is a scary thing.

When he squeezes my fingers again, I wince from the sharp pain shooting up my wrist and arm. Pushing past it, I sit up and look at him until he turns his head. He only has a chance to smirk like he knows what I'm thinking before I press my lips against his softly.

I don't want to think about college.

I don't want to think about my health.

I don't want to think about anything.

He's the one who parts my lips, tracing the tip of his tongue against my bottom lip before deepening the kiss. His hands go to move the laptop away before finding my waist and helping me move onto his lap. Settling with my knees on either side of him, I slowly tug up his shirt until we separate only long enough to toss it onto the floor. He mimics me, taking his time peeling mine off and then unsnapping my bra and kissing my breasts with fervor.

I rock on his lap as he takes one of my nipples into his mouth and tugs on it gently with his teeth before rolling it between his lips. Tipping my head back, I continue grinding on him until he's steel between my legs. Gripping his hair as he works my other breast the same way, I'm panting his name and building the friction I need to come undone.

"You should accept the offer," I tell him in a breathy tone. "We all know how much you want to go there."

He pulls back and chuckles, meeting my eyes with humor in his. "Are you really still talking about this?"

I kiss him, nibbling on his bottom lip, and then nod. "It's important, Kaiden. You're almost done with high school. That means you have a lot of choices to make."

He flips us over so he's hovering above me, grinning and pulling down my leggings. I arch up to get them over my butt and watch as he strips them off and throws them over his shoulder carelessly.

He kisses my stomach. "Right now, all I want to choose is how I'm going to get you off. Tell me, Mouse. Fingers, tongue, or cock?"

My breathing falters.

He waits for an answer.

I lick my lips. "I want you..." My chest rises and falls heavily as I spread my legs, embarrassed but needy. "I want to feel you again, Kaiden."

His eyes flare with heat, one eyebrow quirking inquisitively. "So you're choosing option number...?"

I groan, covering my face. "You're going to make me say it? I'm ready, Kaiden. I know it's been months and you're probably frustrated because—"

He dips down and kisses me hard, his hand traveling between us until his fingers trace the seam of my slit over my cotton panties. "I can feel how turned on you are already," he praises, licking my lips before dragging his teeth along my jaw and to my neck. As he bites down on my flesh, I buck up until he's cupping me fully between my legs. "I want to make one thing very clear, Mouse. I was never frustrated that you weren't ready to have sex again. If we're going to do it, you need to be comfortable. Are you?"

I swallow. "Yes."

He sits up, moving his hand over me so he's leisurely rubbing my clothed entrance and putting pressure on my bundle of nerves with the heel of his hand. "How are you feeling?"

"F-fine. Good. I'm good." I choke on my words as he dips a finger under my panties and strokes me.

"Yeah? Define good."

I moan out his name as he circles my clit before moving downward and entering me with one of his fingers. "Stop teasing me."

"Are you going to tell me how you want me to get you off?" he presses, making me want to smack him in the face with a pillow.

Digging my fingernails into his upper arms, I bite back, "Are *you* going to tell *me* that you're accepting UM's offer?"

He laughs and applies more pressure on my nerve endings before adding another finger to work me. "Give me one good reason why I should."

I put my hand on his to force him to move quicker as I ride out the feeling, meeting his movements with my hips every time.

"Because your family wants you to."

"Mm. Going to need another reason."

I cup his face with my free hand, brushing his bottom

lip with my thumb and making his features softer. "Because *I* want you to. I love you, Kaiden. I'm not saying that I'm *in* love with you"—a long moan escapes my lips when he hooks his fingers in me and picks up the pace until my belly tingles—"but I do love you as a friend and someone I trust. Wh-which means that you should go to Maryland and play lacrosse and make us proud."

Just as I'm about to come, he stops moving altogether. "Are you saying you love me, Mouse?"

I move my hips, trying to chase the feeling that was building before. "P-please keep going."

"Do you?" he whispers, not obeying.

His lips are so close to brushing mine that I feel his warm breath and smell the buttery popcorn from our snack earlier. "Of course I do, Kaiden. I mean it. You're my friend. You've always had my back here, even when I kind of loathed you for the weird ways you showed that you cared."

He moves his fingers just right a few more times, hard and fast, before I'm crying out his name. Quieting the sound with a brutal kiss, he lets me ride his palm through my orgasm, my hips jerking and quaking and aching in all the best ways. When my body settles back onto the bed, his kisses become softer, longer, and deeper.

Drawing back, he rests his forehead against mine and nudges my nose. "I love you too, Mouse."

I swallow past the harshness of breath that he's allowed me to feel. "I want you to go to UM because one of us has to live."

He's silent.

Too silent.

Thinking.

Contemplating.

One of us has to live.

My heart seizes in my chest as I wrap my arms around his neck. "I'll take option number three now, please."

Whatever he's thinking is replaced with a wicked grin before he pecks my lips and moves away to remove his pants and boxers all in one shot. He's done thinking too.

My cheeks heat when I see him in his full glory, proud and confident. When he climbs on the bed, he peels off my panties and grabs a condom from my nightstand that I didn't even know was there.

Shooting me a wink, he rips open the package and rolls it over himself. "Can't be too prepared, right?"

I roll my eyes at his smirk, sitting up on my elbows and kissing him before anything else can be said.

He takes his time, kissing every piece of skin he can. By the time he positions himself at my entrance, I'm begging him for more.

More touches, more kisses, more time.

This is different from before. It still hurts a little but nowhere near as bad. He's slow, careful, and he tries not to grab my hips like I know he wants to. He enters me from new angles that make him go deeper, causing me to gasp and scratch and whimper for anything he'll give me.

When he tells me to climb on top of him, I hesitate until he kisses the worry away. His fingers go through what little hair remains on my head as he tells me he wants this, that I'm gorgeous, that I'm his best friend. Everything. He makes me feel everything—pretty, confident, normal.

He helps me guide him inside me, then set a pace. I have no idea how good it'll feel from this position, but I can't help but quicken my movements when he hits me in just the right way until my head tips back and a familiar, warm feeling fills my stomach.

It isn't until he thrusts up at the same time as I move down that I'm yelling his name and breaking apart. He supports me when I turn to Jell-O, flipping us back around until he's slamming into me over and over so hard the headboard hits the wall.

The sound of the bed creaking and metal frame smacking drywall has me writhing again as he starts twitching inside me. When he thrusts one more time, I come with him, holding him to me so tightly he couldn't pull away if he tried.

We're both sweaty and out of breath as we lie there. "So?" I whisper, finally letting him pull out and roll onto his side. "Will you go to UM?"

His amusement comes off in waves, but deep down, there's something buried. "I'll talk to Jefferson about UM on Monday."

I smile sadly and fall asleep.

Thirty-Nine

APRIL AND MAY BRING more sunshine than showers, which I'm thankful for. The warmth breathes life into everything and everyone, which adds to the anticipation of June's graduation. The seniors are talking about their trip to Orlando, the staff is chatting about summer vacation, and all I can think about is not dealing with Rachel anymore.

I know I should believe Kaiden if he says nobody will bother me when school starts, but I can't anticipate that. Usually I could brush off comments because they don't matter compared to everything else, but the malicious taunts I've dealt with whenever Kaiden isn't by my side have been brutal.

All thanks to Rachel.

I know it's jealousy. I also know there's a chance it'll all be better once she graduates. Then again, all it takes is one person to start a riot before others join in. Her friends have.

Instead of cute pictures of mice drawn on sticky notes, I find doodles of rats and whales on my locker and assigned desks. The first few made me roll my eyes as I balled them up and threw them away before Kaiden found them.

Then came the whispers.

The pregnancy rumors.

The stares.

Brother fucker is my new nickname.

Someone called me a dyke once when I walked down the hall, and my fingers instantly went to my hair and played with the short strands.

At first, I expected the talk to die down on its own. When it didn't, I thought Kaiden would kill it, because there's no way he hasn't heard people say anything about me. Unfortunately for me, the same reason people don't talk back to him is why they don't bring up gossip on touchy subjects.

They're scared of him.

I can't blame anyone. He may be more approachable, at least in my eyes, but that doesn't take away his painted-on scowl from seven thirty to three. They see him as untouchable in the halls and invincible on the field. It's a deadly combination for someone like me.

But I'm not helpless.

Not even when Rachel approached me asking if I could be part of the school's annual fashion show…as a plus-size model. Apparently there's a club here that earns credit at the community college for people interested in designing, and they pair up with local stores to get material for the event. It's a cool idea.

That's why I smile and tell her I'd love to but already have plans with Kaiden. Being petty has never been who I am, but it seems appropriate for the situation. Giving Rachel the gratification of wearing me down by calling me fat or something else doesn't sit well with me.

I'm stronger than that.

I always have been.

On practice days, I'll split my time between watching Kaiden and reading in the library. Once, I saw Mr. Nichols and helped him organize his classroom to make room on the bookshelves for new reading material. He offered me copies of books that were no longer part of the curriculum, so I went home with five worn paperbacks that I read within two weeks.

Kaiden likes calling me a teacher's pet, but I think it's his way of not showing the jealousy that I still giggle over whenever he finds me in Nichols's room.

Annabel and I talk on and off every week, but we never try hanging out. She gets nervous when Kaiden approaches us if we're speaking after class or walking down the hall together. At first I thought she had a crush on him, which made my vision filter with green. Her dodgy eyes and distant expression tell me it's something else. She's uncomfortable.

We may have never become besties, but I thought we were on some spectrum of friendship. She sat with me once at lunch but left early when Kaiden and his friends joined. She'll tell me about a book she's reading and make recommendations on what I may like but then walk with her eyes down if someone sees us. There's never been anything more and I never thought to ask why.

Sometimes acceptance is easier.

It doesn't make it less lonely though.

Kaiden says that most of the girls at Exeter aren't friend material anyway, but I don't think that's true. His perceptions of people are different from mine. I try seeing the good in them. He says he sees them for what they are.

The bullies.

The fakes.

His protection is fading because people see him as something different. A graduate. A softie. After all, he's taken me of all people under his wing. Someone unlike them.

When Kaiden tells Cam and Dad his plans to go to the University of Maryland, Cam wraps him in a hug and starts crying. Dad shifts like I do, almost as if watching it feels like we're invading a special moment. Or maybe he wonders why I haven't made more of an effort to apply for late admission to colleges I'm interested in.

He knows the reason. He's not dumb.

Cam insists that we should all go out to celebrate, so we go to a new restaurant that opened in town a few weeks ago. Its yellow walls and wooden counter and stools give it a homey feel, but the light fixtures above the clothed tables make it seem fancier. It's a mixture of comfort and class, like my two lives merged into one single place with people who have given me a chance I didn't think I deserved outside my isolation.

Dad convinces Kaiden to sit by Cam instead of by me, which throws off our usual seating arrangement. When Dad pulls out my chair, I give him a small smile before sitting down and watching him do the same beside me.

Our relationship has changed so much since Christmas. Mama gave us room to build a relationship that she prevented us from having all those years ago, and Dad and I have done a lot of talking since the holidays. About Logan. About Mama. About life.

We've moved on from the bitterness wedged over a ten-year time period. Neither one of us wants to dwell on the past, because there's no point in trying to change the unchangeable. Our understanding is mutual; we just have different justifications backing the reasons.

Reluctantly, he reads books that I suggest even though Cam says he prefers newspapers and *Reader's Digest*. I go easy on him and never force the romance books I love so much into his hands, but fantasy novels on wizards and fairies and dragons. He pretends he doesn't love them, but there's a gleam in his eyes when he tells me he finished. It's the same gleam I get.

"I should take you dorm shopping!" Cam chirps once we put our orders in with the waiter. I stifle a laugh when Kaiden shoots the man a deadly glare after he glanced at my chest while writing my eggplant Parmesan down on his notepad.

Dad sips his water. "I think it's a little early to think about that."

Kaiden nods in agreement. "Move-in wouldn't be until the end of August. It's not even June."

Cam frowns. "Time will fly by though. If we get things now, there won't be as much picked through when it gets closer." She claps her hands and looks at me. "Why don't you come with us, Em? It'll be so much fun! Maybe you can get an idea of what you want for your dorm when you go to college."

My lips part and a polite rejection is about to escape them when Kaiden says, "She'd love to. Right, Em?"

"Uh…"

Dad smiles, giving my arm a pat. "Sounds like it could be fun. You should go."

Glancing at the three of them, I realize I can't say no. Kaiden is smirking, and Cam seems hopeful. Nobody has asked me about college besides Kaiden. So I tell her I'd love to go and watch as Kaiden hides a victorious grin behind his glass of lemonade.

When we get home, it's late, but we all watch a movie before going to bed. I'm pulling on my shirt in the bathroom when sudden dizziness has me swaying. I hold on to the edge of the vanity and blink a few times until it passes. Taking a deep breath, I hear my bedroom door open and close quietly, a sign that Kaiden is here for the night.

Finishing my business, I hesitate when I glance at the foamy pee in the toilet bowl. There's a slight pink tint to it that has my heart beating just a little faster.

It's the vitamins, I tell myself.

It's dinner.

It's dehydration.

Over and over, I play the game, making excuses until they cycle back through. It's a game I've played for months.

Flushing, I walk over to the sink and wash my hands, ignoring the bite of pain in my fingers and wrists. Giving myself a once-over in the mirror, I note my pink nose and cheeks that are quickly forming a rash.

It's my period triggering it.

It's the weather changing.

It's end-of-the-school-year stress.

When I open the door and flick off the light, I'm greeted with a shirtless Kaiden lounging on the bed. He's already got the laptop open and resting on the usual spot between where we lie.

He looks up from the screen and frowns, which must mean I look rougher than I think I do for him to notice so quickly. "You okay?"

I nod and crawl into bed, lifting the covers over my legs and wiggling my bare toes into the soft sheets. "Just tired. I'm glad it's the weekend. I kind of want to try getting some homework done and then catch up on sleep."

He grins, his eyes heating with memories of the past few nights. "Someone keeping you awake, Mouse?"

The past two nights, he's woken me up by slowly stripping and kissing me until I'm naked and wet. I came twice, first by his mouth, then by his cock. He always laughs when he makes me say it because I turn bright red.

If you can't say it, you can't have it.

He works me up too much to shove him off the bed, so I always reluctantly surrender. The outcome is always pleasant for both of us, so he never has a cocky grin on his face for long. Until he makes a comment about my face when I come, which always makes me blush harder than when he makes me use certain terms for his anatomy.

"You're pale," he notes when I don't answer him right away.

I swallow. "Like I said, I'm tired."

His lips twitch. "Don't bullshit me. I know what you look like when you're in pain."

I don't reply.

He shifts so his body is turned toward me and studies me closely. "When you're tired, your eyes glaze over. Sometimes you'll have bags under them. When you're in pain, you're tense, trying too hard to focus on anything else. Your shoulders are pulled back and you do everything not to move more than you need to." He points toward my hands, which are tucked on my lap. "You make a fist like it'll help combat things, then loosen them when you realize you're only doing more damage. Want me to continue?"

"Kaiden—"

"That," he says. "Your voice is lower, tired in a way that's not just from exhaustion. I hate when I hear you talk like that, smiling at everyone who has no fucking clue."

I stare down at my hands.

"I hate this for you, Em."

I hate it for me more.

"Can we just watch the movie?"

"Do you need me to get you Motrin?"

I debated on taking some with my other meds when we got home from dinner but opted not to. Sometimes it's nice to pretend not to be dependent on the additional painkiller. I'm already taking close to twenty pills a day—three heavy-dose steroids three times a day, my birth control, iron supplements, migraine medicine that's upped to four pills total now, vitamin D tablets for my deficiency, ginger hair supplements to strengthen my roots, and the more than occasional pain reliever. Motrin for breakfast, Excedrin for lunch, Tylenol for dinner.

Kaiden sighs and gets out of bed, disappearing from my room. When he appears a few minutes later, he's got a glass of water in one hand and two red pills in the other.

"Thanks," I murmur, knowing there's no point in arguing with him over it.

He ignores the waiting movie. "When was the last time you saw your doctor?"

I was supposed to have a follow-up over four months ago, but she had to cancel for some family emergency. She was out for two months, and nobody ever called to reschedule. I know I should have reached out, especially because one of my prescriptions is close to being empty with no refills, but I couldn't make myself pick up the phone.

Because you know…

Swallowing, I answer, "Before Christmas."

He swears. "You need to be seen."

"I'm—"

"You're not fine," he snaps. "I wish to hell that you were, Emery. I'm upset that you're sitting here pretending that what you're feeling is no big deal to appease me. I'm not your parents though. I'm not your mother, and thank fuck I'm not your father. It's okay to admit to me that you're not doing well."

My eyes tear up as I try calming my breathing. "Why would I do that? Look at you right now, Kaiden. I don't like seeing other people miserable just because I am."

He chucks my chin lightly. "Don't you get it, Mouse? That's what family does. They worry. If someone loves you, they're going to experience the same misery because they can't do anything for you."

"But Mama..."

"She's been doing better, right?"

She calls me almost every day to tell me about group. I texted her earlier after missing her call because I was still at dinner, and she mentioned getting a job offer at the local hospital. It isn't in the peds clinic like she used to work, but she seemed excited. It's more money and benefits, and from what Grandma told me a while ago, there's even a man who she talks about who works as a physician on the same floor.

"Mama is doing great," I answer, feeling the tension ease slightly from my body.

Getting a new job is huge for her, but if she starts dating, then I'll feel even better. I saw her invest all her free time in Logan and, shortly thereafter, me. There was nothing left to give anyone else. I suspected she had been seeing someone before Lo got worse. Her mood changed, and I don't think it was just because of her sick daughter. She stopped doing her hair and makeup like she wasn't trying to impress anyone anymore.

Grandma says she wears lipstick again.

It makes me smile.

"I want to make people's lives as uncomplicated as possible. I already accept that mine can't be so easy, which is why it has to be different for everyone else."

"That's ridiculous," he scoffs. "Em, your pain is always going to be ours. That doesn't have to be a bad thing."

Confused, I give him a doubtful stare. "I don't see how it can be a good thing."

"It makes it real."

"What?"

He pauses. "Love. Life."

I blink.

"I told you before that I loved you."

I remember.

"You don't have to go shopping tomorrow," he says, going to the laptop and clicking out of the movie.

"I told Cam I would."

"She'll understand."

Sighing, I watch him surf the selections before choosing a Disney movie. "What are you doing? I thought you hate Disney."

"I do," he grumbles. "But that doesn't mean you do. Plus, these are better to watch when you're not feeling well."

I told him a long time ago that I used to put on *Pocahontas* when I was sick. Seeing it on the screen makes my eyes water worse than before as Kaiden opens his arms for me to curl up in his side.

Using his chest as a pillow, I refuse to acknowledge the pain from the hip I'm resting on. It shoots up my body and causes a tear to slip down my cheek, but all I can do is hold Kaiden tighter as the movie plays.

Right before I fall asleep, I whisper, "I love you, Kaiden."

I love you and I'm sorry.

I love you and I wish things were different.

He brushes my hair back and kisses the crown of my head. "You're feeling warm, Mouse. Try getting some sleep."

I wake up feeling my stomach churn so violently that I vomit all over the blankets. The abrupt illness and sour taste of dinner, mouthwash, and stomach acid have me too distracted to be embarrassed. Kaiden swears and nearly falls when his foot gets caught as he tries getting out of bed.

Groaning and clutching my stomach with one hand and my back with the other, I feel a second wave of nausea coming on strong. Tears stream down my face as I lurch over the bed, this time into the waste bucket Kaiden puts in front of me just in time.

"Jesus, Em," he murmurs, staring wide-eyed at me. He cradles my head, but his touch doesn't ease me.

I empty my stomach and cry. If Kaiden wasn't holding the bucket, I would have dropped it. My arms feel like lead at my sides.

"S-something's wr-wrong," I whimper when I'm finally able to breathe. All I want is water to rinse my mouth, but my body is completely drained of everything.

"Shit. Okay." He looks around. "Do you think you're going to get sick again?"

I shake my head, letting the tears hit my thighs. The room smells horrible, and I need to change before I do puke from the fumes alone.

He quickly gets rid of the bucket in the bathroom, the

toilet flushing and the shower turning on soon after. My eyes slowly drift to the clock.

Two twenty-seven.

I groan again and feel the need to close my eyes, my body swaying to the side that I know is covered in something I don't want to lie down in.

"Whoa," he says, catching me. "I need to get you cleaned up. Can you walk to the bathroom?"

I'm barely able to nod but stand with his help and shakily walk to the bathroom with him. My right leg drags behind, leaving Kaiden taking the brunt of my weight. He supports me as he peels off my pajama pants and tries getting my shirt over my head. I attempt to help him, but my arms aren't moving easily on their own.

"My r-right a-arm," I cry, realizing that my entire right side is numb and unmoving.

He keeps cursing as he practically picks me up and carries me to the tub. He steps in fully dressed, instantly getting soaked. The water isn't too cold or too hot as he grabs the loofah and starts rinsing me off. My back sinks into his front, one of his arms wrapped tight around my waist as he lets the water run through my hair.

He's talking to himself, but I can't make out his muttering. I should be embarrassed that I'm completely naked and smell, but I can't muster the energy to care.

That's when I know.

"Wrong," I repeat. "S-somethi..."

"I know, Mouse," he rasps, reaching over to the faucet and turning it off. We're both dripping wet as he carefully grabs a towel and starts drying me. I'm not sure how he manages it since I'm no longer standing on my own.

He ignores drying himself off as he carries me out of the tub and sets me down on the closed toilet lid. Once he sees I'm not going to tip over, he quickly strips off his drenched shirt and pajamas pants until he's just in his boxer briefs.

"Hold on," he says, rushing out of my bedroom. I hear him rustling the blankets and sheets, probably taking them off the bed.

Closing my eyes, I rest my head against the wall, slumping down. The bathroom is cold, and the towel he wrapped around me does little to warm me up.

Kaiden starts shouting for Dad and Cam. I flinch over the desperation in his tone but do nothing about it but sit there.

Helpless.

Did Lo ever feel this way?

So defeated? So…

Warm hands are on my arms, then soft material slides over my head, shoulders, and torso. He's careful to slide my arms through the holes, then kneels and slides sweatpants over my feet one at a time.

"Not…used…to…this…" My tongue is heavy in my mouth.

Having you dress me, I want to elaborate.

I can't though.

Once I'm dressed, I hear Dad's booming voice from my bedroom. Cam gasps loudly, probably seeing the state of disaster that my room is in. Kaiden tells them we're in the bathroom, and suddenly everything gets chaotic.

"What happened?" Dad demands, replacing Kaiden's position in front of me. He puts his hands on my face and forehead, looking frantic. "She's burning up. Emery? Baby…"

"I tried rinsing off the puke," Kaiden tells him, his fingers dragging through his wet hair. His voice is hoarse as he stares, Cam next to him with her hand on his shoulder.

"She needs to go to the hospital," Dad says, carefully putting one arm behind my back and the other underneath my knees. He huffs when he picks me up, holding me to his chest, and walks us through my bedroom.

Cam and Kaiden are close behind as he walks downstairs. Kaiden has the car keys to Cam's vehicle in one hand and my jacket in the other. When we get outside, the night air brushes against me and feels oddly welcoming to my overheated body.

"D-Dad," I croak, not knowing what to say.

"We're going to get you help," he promises, opening the back door.

Kaiden offers to sit in the back with me, but Dad practically barks at him to drive. I only then realize that Kaiden is in gray sweatpants and a black hoodie with no shoes or socks on.

He and Cam take the front while Dad holds me in the back seat. It's probably a funny image, a man his size squeezed back here. He brushes his hand across my cheek as he stares at me intently, his eyes glassy until…they're emerald.

"Da—" I try again, but the word slurs.

"Shh. Try resting."

My lids grow heavy. "Tire…"

"Rest" is the last thing I hear.

Forty

MY EARS THROB WITH the noise of high-pitched beeping coming from somewhere close by. It echoes in my skull, causing me to wince and whimper until something tightens around my arm.

Where…?

"Henry!" a different high-pitched voice calls out. It's a mixture of desperation and relief and…fear?

My eyes crack open to darkness. The large rectangular light above me is off, which I'm grateful for based on the pulsing pain in my temples. A sharpness in the backs of my eyes has them watering as I try moving.

"Sit still," Cam insists. She doesn't have to push me down because my body never lifted. There's no willpower, no energy, to even fight off the unfamiliarity of my surroundings.

The words are there, circling my mind. I can taste them on my lips, but nothing comes out. I try opening my mouth…and nothing. Instead, I focus on Cam, on the room, on anything that could tell me where I am and what's happening.

Her light hair and kind eyes greet me with the slightest comfort, though not enough to feel like I've made it out of the woods. I may not know what's happening, but after a long moment, I'm familiar with the feel of a firm mattress and scratchy sheets. The thin white one covering me is no better. The material is rough, not soft, and hurts the skin that isn't covered by the hideous paper-thin blue gown.

Glancing down at myself, I see wires upon wires hooked to me everywhere. There are two different needles in my arms, a monitor attached to my finger, and black cuffs on one of my arms and legs. Something is coursing through my veins, a potent drug that eases a majority of the pain I'm almost certain I should be feeling. It leaves me warm and tingly, eased but not eased enough so I'm unaware.

My heart goes haywire with anxiety, trying to piece everything together. How long have I been asleep? How long have I been here?

Dad rushes in and pales when he sees me, his expensive cellphone almost falling from his hands. That's when I know something is happening because he lives on that. "Baby." His voice is thick with worry as he replaces Cam by my bedside. "The doctors are going to come in here and explain everything to you that they told me, okay?"

"D-Da…?" His face is more wrinkled, more aged, than I've ever seen. I did that to him. My slurred words and unknown state broke him.

I look around the room slowly, blinking past the tears that I know are because of more than just the headache blossoming. "Wh-where…is…K-Kaiden?"

Swallowing past the lump in my throat, I try internalizing why my tongue feels so heavy. It's weighing in my mouth, drowning every syllable that tries escaping my thin lips.

Cam peeks her head around Dad's shoulder and gives me a small smile. "He's waiting in the lounge outside. The ICU doesn't allow more than two people in here."

My eyes widen. "I'm in the…ICU?"

I've never been here before. All the times I've been admitted, it's always been in the inpatient center, where I had to share a room with angry old people who complained about the food or the television not having anything good to pick from.

Dad kneels beside me, his throat bobbing and eyes a shade of green I'm not accustomed to seeing. "Emery, you're very, very sick. At some point during the night, you had a stroke. It's honestly a miracle you didn't choke on your vomit when you got sick, because the function on your right side is minimal. And that's…" He struggles with his words. "That's not all, baby girl."

My eyes go to the hand he's holding.

My left hand.

I stare at my right arm for too long, which has a needle in the vein on the side of my wrist that I can't feel. "S-stroke?"

He nods.

I've heard about strokes. Old people had them whenever a call came over the police scanner at Mama's house. *John Doe, age sixty-three. Stroke. Jane Doe, age seventy-one. Stroke.*

Not nineteen-year-olds. Not me.

Cam's eyes water, and hers don't turn any other color. Not in the darkness. Not from the tears. They're the same as always. "Your mother has been called, sweetie. She and your grandmother are already on their way."

I swipe my dry lips with my tongue. It feels lighter, but the weight in my chest hasn't eased as much. "K-Kaiden? He must...be worried. Plea—"

A doctor walks in, opening and closing the squealing door behind him. I know Kaiden. He must be pacing the waiting room, his hair a mess, and cursing at anyone who asks if he needs anything. Is he still barefoot? Did someone get him shoes? Hospital booties? A cup of coffee?

"Ms. Matterson," the doctor says in greeting. He squeezes Dad's shoulders like he must have done hundreds of times since our arrival.

"Emery," I whisper, taking a deep breath of relief when the word forms correctly.

His hair is still dark, not graying like most doctors I've crossed paths with. His face is wrinkle-free and kind, like he hasn't witnessed true tragedy yet. Does that give me hope? Or will I be the one to break him?

"Emery," he corrects, washing his hands and drying them off at the sink in the corner. "I'm Dr. Thorne. I was assigned to you when you arrived at this wing. After reading over your medical file and seeing the image tests, EKG, and lab work they did on you tonight, I contacted your rheumatologist for some additional information. I'll need some further answers from you on how you've been feeling to get a better picture. Can you tell me about some of the symptoms you've been experiencing? Is there anything out of the ordinary you've noticed over the past few months? Every detail will help."

Dad's breathing is unsteady, and I wonder if he's going to cry. I've never seen him do that before, and I'm not sure I ever want to. Tearing up and letting them spill are two different things. It's like an acceptance that things have changed. When you tear up, you're simply unsure. When you cry, you know.

I don't want to know.

I don't want Dad to know.

For some reason, I struggle looking at the young doctor. Instead, my eyes go from Dad to Cam to the door. I think about Kaiden and pretend he's right here. He should be. He's family.

My ears pick up on the drum of my heart, which pounds in a rocky beat. It doesn't sound normal at all. It's been like that for too long, and I reasoned with its abnormality with excuse after excuse, as if it made a difference. It overpowers the noise coming from the various machines hooked to me. *Thump thump. Thump thump. Thump thump. Thump. Thump.*

"Emery?" Dr. Thorne repeats.

"H-head…aches."

He nods, glancing at the computer screen I didn't know was on. "It looks like you came to the emergency room over the winter because of a migraine that turned into a fainting spell?"

I don't answer.

Dad says, "Yes. She got sick at school and fainted but insisted it was from the migraine."

Pressing my lips together, I finally meet the doctor's eyes. "I saw a…neuro…logist right after who helped me get medication."

"Does it help?"

"Yes." *No. I don't know anymore.*

"You no longer get headaches?"

No answer. My lips tingle.

His eyes scan the screen once more before he proceeds with his questions. "Have you noticed any changes in weight?"

I know for a fact any fluctuation is right in front of him, documented from my many visits and check-ins. "Gain. I'm n-not sure h-how much."

"Bruising? Bleeding? Dizziness?"

Exhaustion sweeps through me. "Dr. Thorne, I'm t-tired. I–I'm sorry, but I want to know what's going… I've never felt… I never had…"

I'm used to being here.

I'm used to the interrogations.

The assumptions.

The medical jargon.

But not in the intensive care unit.

"Please," I whisper brokenly.

Dad squeezes my hand, and I ignore the bite of pain that greets his strong grasp.

The doctor moves the computer away from him, giving me a firm-lipped expression. I know it too well, the distance he puts between us while he figures out how to deliver the news.

"We're running additional tests," he begins, not looking at anyone but me. I appreciate the effort he puts in that no other doctor does. I'd get worked up when doctors talked to Mama like I couldn't possibly understand what they're saying, much less be affected by the diagnosis as though I'm not the patient. "The scans that were done on you tonight showed many alarming things. Your brain tissue shows signs of extensive inflammation, as does the area around your heart. And your kidneys…"

I hold my breath.

My heart drums.

The clock on the wall ticks.

His voice is so soft it's like velvet against my skin. "Emery, your kidneys barely showed up on the images done."

Blinking, I shake my head.

His eyes are softer than his voice, but his body is straight and tense and professional. "The levels of your creatine and BUN tests also drew red flags. As soon as the radiologist read your images, the lab was contacted to do an additional glomerular filtration rate, or GFR, test that gives us an idea of your kidney function."

My bottom lip trembles, but I refuse to cry. I know what he's saying before he even says it. After I heard Mama talk to Grandma about Lo, I figured out how to do an online search to read about what she died from.

Kidney failure.

"The good news is there are treatment options," he proceeds to tell me, though his optimism is further than I can see. "Depending on what the labs show, we can figure out the best course of action for you. Your rheumatologist will be involved to speak to you about the medications you're currently on..."

On and on he goes.

He tells me that the headaches are most likely related to my kidney problems and asks about any issues urinating.

Bloody urine? Dark? Trouble peeing?

When my lips part to answer, nothing comes out. My brain is too wrapped up in the months I've spent seeing pinkened pee. The slight twinge of blood on the toilet paper. The foam. The back pain.

How long have I known but wouldn't admit it? How long could I have said something instead of pretending nothing was wrong?

You could have stopped it.

Slowed it.

Something.

Thorne must know that I've noticed changes, because he simply nods before telling me about further steps.

Dad and Cam listen so intently to everything Thorne says, nodding along and sometimes interjecting with questions.

What is a nephrologist?

Will she need surgery?

How long do you think she'll be here?

The questions and answers are fired so rapidly, I'm not sure I absorb them all. I think about everything that's happened in the past twenty-four hours.

I think about Dad.

Cam.

Kaiden.

How many doctors in my past told me I was fine? That I was too young to experience the pain I felt? How many times would I fall asleep at night crying because I couldn't move? How many doctors are going to be responsible for the outcome that's dangling in front of us?

I swallow once Dr. Thorne excuses himself, slipping out the door and leaving us to digest everything.

"I want to s-see Kaiden," I tell Dad and Cam. It shouldn't be the first thing out of my mouth, but the words can't be stopped. I want Kaiden.

"Em," Cam says softly. "Sweetie, I know he wants to see you too—"

"Please?" My voice cracks as I stare at her with watery eyes until her frown blurs. "I just want to see…him. That's all…it's all I'm asking for right now."

She looks at Dad before nodding.

Dad watches her leave before turning to me, his hand still on mine. He watches the way his rougher, darker skin contrasts with my brittle paleness. His hand is twice the size of mine, the warmth of his palm soaking into me.

For the longest time, I don't think he's going to say anything. He doesn't ask me how I'm feeling, because that seems pointless. He doesn't question me over what I'm thinking, because he knows I'll hold back.

In a hushed tone, he says, "There's a card of a mouse on your nightstand. I saw it when he called us in..." He swallows and takes a deep breath. "He called you Mouse once."

Not knowing what else to do, I nod.

When the door opens again, it's Kaiden looking wide-eyed right at me. He looks paler than I've ever seen, maybe even paler than I am right now if it's possible. His hair is a mess like I expected, sticking straight up in different directions like he's been running his fingers through it nonstop.

Dad glances between us. "I guess I'll leave you two alone then."

He called you Mouse once.

In a blink of an eye, Kaiden is beside me, towering over me, staring down like I'm going to disappear. Am I? Will I?

I lick my lips again.

"I was fucking worried," he growled, scanning over the wires surrounding me. His eyes dart to the monitor that's showing my irregular heartbeat before turning back to me. "I was about to risk getting arrested just to see you. Do you know how damn hard it was standing out there while they had you in here?"

"I—"

"The nurses are assholes," he informs me coolly, sneering at the door. "They kept telling me someone would be out to give me answers, and nobody ever did. Not once did those doors open, Emery."

Emery. Not Mouse.

"I'm s-sorry," I whisper, pressing my lips together. What else is there to say?

"Mom said…" His nostrils flare. "Mom said that you're not doing well. Tell it to me straight. What the fuck is going on?"

That's the million-dollar question, isn't it? Right now, my blood is being tested to see how screwed I am. Thorne may have had optimism that we could slow the progression and damage based on the results, but there's calmness to my stomach that shouldn't be there, and it's not the medicine making me feel that way.

"Em." He brushes hair behind my ear and watches me closely, his bottom lip trembling in the slightest way.

"Are you going…to go to M-Maryland still?"

He gapes at me. "What the hell does that have to do with anything? We're not talking about college right now."

"Are you?"

He blinks.

"Kaiden…" I take a deep breath and feel my own defenses completely shattering. "I need y-you to go to UM, okay? It'll make me h-happy."

His throat bobs and his anger becomes tenfold as he studies my face.

"Cam will be h-happy too," I continue, wrapping my fingers around his. The way he looks at me is in pure disbelief. "I'll v-visit when I can. When you have g-games, I'll… come see you play and cheer you on."

His expression morphs into something unreadable. There's pain lingering in his pinched lips, that much I can see. Kaiden Monroe has never been stupid. He knows I offer him that little bit of hope to ease the reality that's about to hit us whether we're ready or not.

Swallowing past the lump in my throat, I give him a tiny smile. "Don't t-tell Cam I told you this because she w-wants it to be a surprise, but she already b-bought a bunch of… UM sweatshirts and m-memorabilia. I'm p-pretty sure I even saw one of those foam fingers."

His lips twitch upward, then flatten. The tiny shift of his anger for even a millisecond means he's trying. He's willing to let go of his anger.

Trying to focus on what I want to say, I give myself a moment before managing a small, sad smile. "And…I think she bought something for all of us to wear, maybe…even customized the backs with your n-name." We both know she'd do that. I'm sure once she finds out his jersey number, that'll go on the back of any shirt she wears to games too.

He flips our hands so his is squeezing mine. "Your skin is so pale."

That must say something considering we're cloaked in darkness. Only the glow of the computer's screen saver lights up the corner of the room. The narrow window on the door barely allows any of the hallway light to creep in.

I brush my thumb against the top of his hand, noticing the smooth skin and tiny brown freckles. "I hear college food is way b-better than the stuff they serve in high school. There are options that don't involve…mystery meat."

He chuckles, but it doesn't sound the same as any other time he's laughed.

"Kaiden?" I murmur, my thumb stopping in the middle of its movement.

"Yeah?"

"Th-thank you." He blinks up at me. "Thank you for...being my friend. My best friend. Anyone could have stepped up and... tried knowing me, and th-they didn't. It was always just you."

He purses his lips. "Like you said, they were just blindly doing what I said."

I shake my head. "Annabel talked to me despite you w-wanting everyone to leave me alone. Sometimes girls would try g-getting gossip out of me about you. They were all willing to take and not give. Not even Annabel."

For a while, he doesn't answer. "I was selfish. I didn't want you making friends with anyone else."

I just smile.

I know is my silent reply.

"But you," I add, "were a-always there."

He allows himself to smirk. "Especially when you didn't want me to be."

That's when I needed you most.

The door clicks open, and Dr. Thorne is followed in by Dad and Cam. His face says it all. It's serious. Firm. I stay withdrawn, staring at the dark-haired man standing in front of me. He looks sympathetic, his eyes drowning in untold apologies and answers that weren't there before.

He had hope then.

"Ms. Matterson," he begins, "I'm sorry to have to tell you this..."

I hear his words but don't absorb them. Instead, I try to calm down Kaiden, whose body is shaking violently next to me.

Dad is ashen.

Cam is crying.

Where is Mama?

Kidney failure.

End-stage.

Thorne tries to explain that the disease has eaten away at the vital organs, killing off my kidney function. The headaches are from a mixture of inflammation attacking tissue from the disease and the toxins not being filtered correctly from my impacted kidneys. The weight gain is from water retention building in my legs and face.

Lo hadn't looked like she'd gained weight in the end. She was fragile, like one touch could shatter her. Her eyes were sunken in the back of her head and her skin was an off-white that resembled a pale yellow. They said her liver had been impacted by then too.

When Thorne clears his throat, he looks between everyone in the room. "There is a complication with moving forward with treatment options that you all need to be made aware of." His eyes focus on me. "Dialysis would be the next step, because your body is no longer able to filter clean blood through your system. However, it has come to our attention that your heart is being impacted by the strain of your disease. The amount of inflammation around the valves is putting an immense amount of pressure on them, which means your heart is working much harder to function properly. That's what caused the stroke and heightened your blood pressure, which you're still experiencing.

"Dialysis tends to impact the heart for patients who are on it long term. If patients willingly go on dialysis knowing they have heart conditions, the chance of cardiac arrest resulting in death is very likely."

Someone gasps.

Someone chokes out a sob.

And I just…stare.

It all makes sense.

My lack of friends. My unwillingness to settle down, to find a promising career path, to dream. I never wanted to date—to make time for people in my life. I make thousands of excuses that hold me back from truly living, and the final puzzle piece reveals the reason why.

I'm not meant to.

The realization slams into me, slices through me, opens me up. But I welcome it—the truth.

Maybe the reason I could never feel satisfied with life is because I'm not meant to live a full one. I'm not meant to meet my future husband or have children. The fewer people who care about me, the fewer people I hurt when it all ends.

"What are you saying?" Kaiden growls at him, somehow getting closer to me as if his protection can change things. "If her kidneys are failing and dialysis is the only way to stop her from…dying, then she has to go on it!"

Cam steps forward. "Sweetie—"

"She could fucking *die*!" he yells, probably waking anybody in the rooms around us from the bone-chilling tone.

"Son," Dr. Thorne says slowly, "this is not an easy decision either way. You're correct. Dialysis is necessary to keep filtering the blood before toxins take over, making her worse, but the risk of death from her heart condition while on it could also be an outcome."

Three sets of eyes turn to me.

I just sit there, propped against pillows on a hard mattress.

The machines still beep around me, the monitors giving away how I'm feeling as my heart rate accelerates.

They watch me silently.

I stare at nothing across the room.

An empty wall.

An open space.

Nothing important or exciting.

Dr. Thorne steps closer. "Emery, the best course of action I can think to take is speaking to your rheumatologist as soon as possible and considering medication adjustment. If we could lessen the inflammation and keep it at bay, your chances of doing better on dialysis are far greater than choosing to do emergency dialysis starting tonight."

My lips part slightly as I blink.

Once.

Twice.

A third time.

"Where's Mama?" I rasp, slowly turning my head to Dad. His cheeks are damp, and his expression is bathed in panic.

"She should be here any minute," he answers, his voice sounding foreign to me.

I nod.

"Emery," he says, walking over to me. I notice the way he eyes Kaiden until he replaces my overprotective best friend. "Baby girl, there is a lot to consider here. When your mother comes, I think the three of us need to sit down and talk it through."

Talk what through? That's what I want to ask him now, in front of our waiting audience. Does he want to talk about which choice will make me die faster? Or make me suffer longer? Does he want to hash out Mama's opinion and watch her cry when I tell them I disagree?

My eyes are dry.

Why are my eyes dry?

Taking a deep breath, I turn to the doctor and ignore the way everyone's eyes burn into my face. "How long?"

His jaw moves side to side. "It depends."

"Mouse," Kaiden whispers brokenly.

"If I don't…" I swallow, my nostrils twitching and throat closing. "If I don't do dialysis, how…long?"

Kaiden growls.

Dad's jaw drops.

Dr. Thorne takes a deep breath. "You are at end-stage renal failure. To be honest, it's not long. But everybody is different."

I close my eyes. "So even if we try adjusting my medication first, there's a chance…?"

"Yes."

The room grows eerily silent.

When my eyes open, they instantly find Dad's. "There's nothing to d-discuss then."

"Emery—"

"Jesus. *Fuck!*" Kaiden slams his hand against the wall as he storms out with Cam chasing after him, her palm muffling the sobs escaping her lips.

Thorne walks over to me, standing just before Dad. "We can make you as comfortable as possible if that's what you decide, Emery. If you want to talk to your family further about this, make sure you press the button once a choice has been made, and I'll come back in. Okay?"

I'm not sure if I nod or answer, but he leaves Dad and me alone. Once the door is closed behind him, Dad shoots up.

"You are *not* dying."

"I am."

"Emery—"

"Dad!" My teeth grind. "You heard him. My heart isn't g-going to take well to the treatment. I know you don't want to h-hear this, but you need to. I'm going to die. Lo knew it right before she passed away, and I know it…too."

The calmness washing over me.

The lack of tears.

"It's about how," I continue, trying to make myself sound stronger than I am. "I don't want to keep suffering, Dad. The hassle of trying to readjust my medicine for the billionth time is pointless. The meds should have r-reduced the inflammation to begin with. And…and it wouldn't matter if we tried w-waiting it out, and you know it."

He palms his face, shaking his head and attempting to even his breathing. "I just got you back, Em."

I simply nod.

"I just…" Tears overwhelm him.

Feelings.

Reality.

Acceptance.

"We got a year, Daddy."

"It's not *enough*."

There's a knock on the door.

"Sunshine?"

Mama.

Forty-One

THERE'S A RAINBOW ARCHED over the small patch of trees outside the hospital. I don't get to see all the bright colors because my view is obstructed from the wheelchair I sit in by the large window. I'm nowhere near eye level from where the glass sits, and the brick building hides part of the calling card I know Lo left for me.

Mama sat with me and cried for hours last night while Dad watched from the cot someone brought in. It looks more uncomfortable than my bed, which I tell Thorne they need to consider changing. It's bad enough patients have to deal with additional discomfort, but families shouldn't have to.

He told me he'd bring it up to someone.

I doubt he will.

Kaiden was missing in action until eight this morning. I'd fallen back asleep but never stayed in unconsciousness long. Between nurses coming in and out, Dad whispering to Mama, and Mama hissing arguments like I couldn't hear, I couldn't get settled.

There was an elephant in the room taking up the open space that wasn't occupied by expensive machines and my upset parents.

I'm unsettled because I know this is it.

I can't sleep because I'm afraid of never waking up. Just like Lo. Her body was so still when Mama came in to check on her. I'd woken up to Mama's loud cries as she kneeled beside Lo, holding her stiff, unmoving hand.

Her eyes had been closed.

Peaceful.

Sleeping eternally.

When Kaiden showed back up, he was wearing jeans, a tee, and his letterman jacket. His feet were shoved into a pair of his favorite blue sneakers that were some fancy brand made by an ex-basketball player, which was a step in the right direction from the bare feet he sported the night before. He and Cam brought Dad a change of clothes, so he could finally get out of the pajamas he's worn since we arrived.

Kaiden's knuckles were red. Swollen.

I spent that time pretending to sleep and listening to Mama and Dad argue about my well-being. They were trying to figure out what to do next, how to move forward. It was only when I finally opened my eyes that they painted smiles on their faces and acted like they weren't trying to figure out how to convince me to try fighting.

Internally, I scoff.

I've been fighting for years. I fought for Mama's attention. For her affection. To fit in. I fought against my ill feelings toward Dad. The way I resented Lo for leaving me.

I fight myself every single day.

I fight to pretend I'm fine.

To admit I'm not.

To survive.

So I tell them both they can't change my mind. What's done is done. All the times I've been denied by professionals. Criticized by peers. Questioned by relatives. I'm not fighting anyone anymore.

It's too late. Don't you get it?

Mama had to walk out. Her body shook so bad I thought she'd faint. Dad stayed in my room and just watched me in silence. He wants to say something, to argue, to make a point.

He's learned by now that there is none.

He's gotten to know me.

He's figured me out.

Like when I tell Cam that asparagus sounds good for dinner, but then he sneakily slips it off my plate onto his when she's not looking because he knows I don't like it.

Or when I scrunch my face at something he chooses to watch on TV at night and he switches it to something everyone would like.

He asks about Kaiden.

We're friends. Best friends.

Because it's true.

Kaiden Monroe made everything bearable. School. Home. He turned out to be the person I could trust enough to share my firsts. In my eyes, he was my only true ally. I lived thinking I wouldn't experience what it felt like to be cherished because my body was too depleted by my health. Kaiden gave me everything I couldn't think of asking for before moving to Exeter.

Dad didn't seem to buy it.

But he didn't question it either.

Because he called me Mouse once.

Now Kaiden is pushing me along the hall with Dad and

Cam trailing behind. Mama and Grandma went to get food in the cafeteria, giving us time together as I stared at the rainbow and its pretty pastel colors.

The dull ache in my body is tolerable because of the medicine they pumped through me first thing this morning. There's feeling in my right side that seems promising in the grand scheme of things. I can process my words and talk without too much hassle. Despite the nurses giving me sympathetic smiles and Dr. Thorne asking me how I am every hour, I'm okay.

Okay as I can be.

Calm. Relaxed. Realistic.

Much to the dismay of my parents, I convinced Kaiden to get me the rest of my schoolwork in order to finish senior year. After quiet arguments in between nurse and doctor check-ins, Dad relented and called the school, asking if I could take my remaining exams in the hospital. The school, even the poor disorganized Principal Richman, knew they had no place to deny me a simple favor.

How many other people wanted to spend their time in a hospital bed filling in bubble sheets and calculating statistics? I only knew about one statistic that mattered, and I'd accepted it. The answers I scrawled across my paper, while seemingly unimportant, allowed me the mundane normalcy I needed even now. Even considering…

Everyone helped me when fogginess made me forget how to put together my words. Dad would put in numbers in his phone's calculator app so I could write down the answer on my math exam. Mama would read aloud a poem so many times I'm sure the elderly lady next door could recite it by heart. Grandma would try helping me figure out a chemistry question based on the diagram, and Kaiden drew pictures on the notepad provided by Thorne. He said there's no art final, but he wanted to cheer me up. So every ten minutes, I'd get a new image on my lap, distracting me from my homework. A mouse. A pill bottle with a penis drawn where the prescription would be—that one I hid from my parents, though Grandma saw it and snickered.

But my favorite was the one tucked into the hoodie Cam had brought me during one of her few trips home for different clothes. It was Kaiden and me leaning against a tree with a grave between us. A grave labeled with Lo's name.

He didn't say a word. I didn't either. I just reached into my pocket and touched the wrinkled paper when I needed a moment to collect myself.

My eyelids want to droop and close from lack of sleep at this point, but I don't tell Kaiden that, so we keep going down the hall. Besides some random ramblings, he's been quiet almost the entire time. Once in a while, he'll make comments on the old photographs on the walls, making fun of the old portraits of patrons and founders. He teased me when I finished all my finals, calling me a nerd. A *graduating senior* nerd. Since then, he's barely spoken a peep.

There's a set of vending machines by the elevators at the end of the hall. Kaiden stops the chair right in front of one and pulls out his wallet. I watch carefully as he inserts a dollar and presses a couple of buttons before a Reese's falls out.

"Split it with me?" he asks, knowing I won't say no. He wheels me over to the closest lounge, where Dad and Cam give us space. They linger just up the hall, glancing between the window and us.

I give a small wave to Dad.

He tries to smile.

When Kaiden unwraps the candy and passes me one of

the peanut butter cups, I play with it until chocolate melts onto my fingers. "I used to get an Almond Joy all the time at the hospital back home. There were five vending machines lined up in a long hallway that led to the building across the street from underground. Lo and I used to pretend we were on an adventure. Dad would take us down there and feed us sugar before going back up to see Mama and leaving."

He watches me bite the chocolate-ridged sides of the cup off first, leaving only the middle left. "I know. I heard him telling Mom that once. You'd get angry when the machine would give you a Mounds because you hated them."

My lips part. "He…?" I shake my head, peeling the top layer of chocolate off. "I don't like just plain coconut. The almonds make it taste way better. Did he really say that?"

He nods, rubbing his lips together. "I didn't hear about you often from him, but I don't think it was because he didn't think of you. It probably hurt him knowing he agreed to stay away when your mother asked him to. Anything I heard was something he told Cam. The Almond Joys, the days you went to work with your mom at the hospital…" For a moment, he stares at his untouched candy in contemplation. "I had been to your house before October break."

His voice is no more than a whisper that I think I mishear. "You…what?"

He sits up straighter and meets my eyes hesitantly, shyly. "Not long after your dad moved in, I was trying to figure out how to get him out. It seemed like he was running from something, but he'd barely talk about his old life. He moved hours away, I knew that much, and used to be married. Mom mentioned that he had kids, a girl around my age, but that was the extent of the information they offered me.

"I got some information on the town you lived in and searched for his old address. Honestly wasn't too hard to do, which should probably alarm people. Anyway, I skipped school one day and drove there. I'm not sure what I planned on doing or saying if anyone was home. It seemed safe considering it was the middle of the week. But..."

My breathing hitches just knowing he was there, fitting himself into my life long before we ever officially met.

"I saw your grandmother through the front window first. She was holding a bowl of something and talking to someone, and when I moved to the other side of the house, I saw you on the couch with a blanket over you. The one with the blue birds on the edges."

"Grandma made that," I whisper.

He takes a deep breath. "Anyway, I saw you there smiling at her like you didn't care that you dad was gone. You seemed happy. I walked around the town for a little bit before coming back to your house and couldn't knock on the door or ask anyone about you guys. So I walked around the side until I found you under the sycamore tree talking to someone. I didn't realize it was your sister's grave until I came back during break last year."

I let every word he speaks seep into me as I play with my peanut butter cup. The chocolate is all over my fingers, so I pop what's left in my mouth and lick off my fingertips.

"Your grandmother caught me," he admits, sinking back into his chair.

My eyes widen.

He has a small smile on his face. "When I was trying to sneak back to my car parked down the road, she stopped me and asked what I was doing there. I lied and said I was lost and wandering around, but she saw through me. She noticed you out by your sister's grave and then looked at me like she was connecting the dots."

Grandma never said anything to me about a random boy showing up, and not once during break had she outed him. "Did she say something to you last year?"

His smile turns into a grin. "She told me that I was full of shit, but she already sensed that about me. The first morning she made breakfast, she asked why I'd bothered coming."

I wait for him to continue, wondering why he showed up the first time and wasted time saving me before I realized I needed it the second time around.

He shrugs, staring at the floor. "I'm not sure I have an answer, even now. Sometimes you just know when you're needed, even if nobody says they need you. That's why I came there for break. I had plenty of shit I could have done, but I wanted to be there with you."

We sit in silence for a long while, finishing off the candy bar. He throws the wrappers away in the garbage can in the corner of the lounge before gesturing toward our waiting family.

I hear Mama and Grandma talking, which means they must have finished breakfast already. Both of them give me smiles when they see Kaiden wheel me over to them.

Grandma winks at him.

Mama reaches out to hold my hand.

Dad and Cam squeeze Kaiden's arm.

I look at Mama, then glance at everyone else. "Can we have some time alone? I just want…" *I just want Mama.* "I'd like to be with Mama for a while."

Everyone nods except Kaiden, who hasn't let go of the wheelchair. Cam puts her hand on his shoulder and gives him an encouraging nod.

He lets go and kneels in front of me. "I expect you to be at every game, Mouse." His voice cracking has my heart doing the same, a big split right down the middle. "Best friends support each other. They're there for each other."

The smile I grace him with is genuine. "I promise I'll be at every single one."

He wets his lips and nods once before standing, stepping back into Cam's hold. Mama smiles down at me, Grandma brushes my hair behind my ear, and Dad offers me a single head bob like Kaiden.

It seems so final. Yet not final at all.

A beginning.

Kaiden will go to college.

Dad and Cam may have a child.

Mama could be happy. Date. Get remarried. Have more children.

There's nothing that would hold them back. No excuse or emergency would stop them from living their lives, and the thought calms me completely until my body sinks lazily into the chair that Mama pushes.

Mama wheels me back to my room, greeting the nurses who say hello and ask if we need anything.

Mama. That's all I need.

Once the nurses are done checking my vitals and it's just Mama and me, she tells me about the friends she's making. The understanding she's accepting about how it all went wrong…and in many ways right.

"I'm sorry, Emery," she whispers, stroking my hand with her thumb.

Sorry for shutting down.

Sorry for abandoning me.

Sorry for not realizing it sooner…

"It's okay," I tell her honestly.

Mama brought me to Dad. To Cam. To Kaiden. Her understanding that she couldn't take care of me the way I needed brought back my father and more family that I had no clue I needed. She gave me a best friend when I lost the only one I ever knew and an innocent love that I would have never felt otherwise.

I love Kaiden.

Like a friend. My *best* friend.

Like family.

I move over and slowly pat the empty spot beside me. "You gave me so much, Mama. We can't change what's happened and I don't want to. Everything happens for a reason, right?"

She swallows. "Yeah, Sunshine. It does."

Mama curls up in bed beside me, wrapping her arms around my body, careful not to tug on the wires and tubes. Her face is wet, matching my own damp cheeks. Her head rests on the same pillow mine does.

Sometimes words aren't enough.

Sometimes nothing has to be said at all.

Mama opens her lips…and starts singing.

You are my sunshine, my only sunshine,

You make me happy, when skies are gray.

You'll never know, dear, how much I love you…

Her words become suffocated by fragmented shards of emotion that slice the open air between us as the machines make pitiful noises.

Please don't take my sunshine away.

Epilogue

Kaiden

FIVE FUCKING DAYS. SHE lasted five days after being admitted before her mother's wails chimed louder than the flatlining machines. It was long enough for her to submit finals from her hospital room and complete her senior year.

All she wanted was to finish senior year.

To graduate.

And she did.

Security had to escort me out when I put my fist through the wall, and Mom didn't talk to me until I calmed down outside.

Emery wore a fucking UM sweatshirt before she fell asleep on that too-tiny bed, and sure enough, there was a makeshift patch with my name on the back. Her eyes never opened back up though.

She never officially said goodbye.

I promise I'll be at every single game.

She lied.

One Year Later

Rain nearly cancels our biggest game of the year, which half the upperclassmen bitched about, considering it was their last one before graduating from the University of Maryland. We worked our asses off in practice and won almost every game against the other college teams. I could see their disgruntlement.

Then it happens.

The fucking sunshine.

The dispersing clouds.

The rainbow.

Once upon a time, I'd been told by a girl full of hope that her twin sister looked down at her from the sky. I thought it was bullshit. As much bullshit as the damn song she loved listening to that I can't stand hearing when it comes on.

But there it is.

The weather report told us we were done for since we woke up. Ninety-nine percent chance of thunderstorms and rain showers. High winds.

We were fucked.

We were *supposed* to be fucked.

Someone slaps my back. "Is that a miracle or what?"

Murphy is a dipshit who spends more time high than sober, but he is still one of my closest friends. He leaves me be when I get moody but then distracts me with pot and girls when I sulk for too long.

He also kicks ass on the field.

I stare up at the sun. "Yeah. A miracle."

I think about the two matching headstones underneath the sycamore tree in Bakersfield while staring up at the sun beaming down on my teammates.

"Let's kick some ass!" Murphy shouts, getting equally enthusiastic yells from everyone around us.

Two Years Later

There's a knock at my apartment door that peels my eyes off the football game on the screen. Setting my beer down, I smack a half-drunk Murphy and shuffle over to see if our other friend Spencer decided to show up.

I don't expect to see a tiny little redhead on the other side of the door.

"You're not Spencer."

Her eyes widen. It's dark, but the porch light makes the color staring up at me an eerie tone of crystal blue.

"Uh…no. I'm Piper." She shifts something in her hands to jab behind her. "I live next door with my friend. Anyway, this was delivered to our place. It has your address on it."

She shoves the box toward me, and my face scrunches when I see my name on the flap. Mom must have sent another care package and wanted to surprise me.

"Thanks," I murmur, putting it under my arm and grabbing the door to close it. "Well…"

Nodding, she steps back and tugs on the oversize UM sweatshirt she's wearing. It's the same one Emery wore when she…

I clear my throat. "Bye."

Her lips part when I close the door, not thinking about much except what's inside the parcel. Setting it on the coffee table and taking another swig of my beer, I rip off the tape and open the flaps.

Murphy mumbles before passing back out, half draped

on the couch and half hanging off. Rolling my eyes, I pick up a glass jar full of…paper?

"What the…?"

At closer glance, I recognize some of the colorful Post-its inside. When I unscrew the top and pull one out, my jaw grinds.

They're the Post-its I left for Em.

Stupid pictures of cartoon objects and animals with sayings only she'd get. Insults. Taunts. Nicknames.

She saved them all?

Pulling a few more out, I notice some that aren't mine. The drawings aren't very good, and half of them are smudged like she kept running her hand across the ink.

I can still tell what they are.

A lacrosse stick.

The UM emblem.

Sunshine.

One of them has words.

If you don't go to UM, I'll haunt you.

A choked laugh escapes me, and Murphy jerks up, falling off the couch. He lands with a loud thud on the floor before groaning. I snort and nudge his leg with my foot.

"You good down there?"

He mumbles something unintelligible.

I nod, going back to the pieces of paper.

The very first mouse I drew for her is resting in front of me. Brushing my fingers against the aged paper, I manage to smile before clearing my throat and putting all of them back into the jar.

There's a note from Mom.

Henry found these in Emery's room. He said you'd want them.

Palming my face, I take the jar to my room and place it on my dresser. The Valentine's card I got for her is resting there too, something I grabbed before I moved.

Sitting on the edge of the bed, I stare at the new addition to my space before grabbing my phone and typing out a text to Mom. She responds almost instantaneously.

Mom: Love you too, baby boy. And your little sister says hi.

BONUS SCENE

MY FRACTURED THOUGHTS ARE washed away by Mama's voice before her thin figure appears in the mirror behind me. "Emery?"

Her eyes widen as she takes me in where I hold large chunks of fallen hair in my hand by the sink. It's happening again, and I can see the pain living in the golden-brown hues glazing with a fresh set of tears I see too often. I get my eyes from Dad, a pretty hazel green, although it's been so long since seeing him that it's hard to remember how similar we look.

"I wanted to know if you were hungry," she inquires, voice cracking in the process. She averts her eyes, looking at my beach-themed bathroom décor—the blue shower curtain, seashell bathmat, and matching towels hanging on the rack. She pays attention to anything but me.

I want to say *Look at me, Mama. I'm still your little girl. You still have me.*

"Please don't be sad," I tell her, turning around. "I'm okay. Promise."

She presses her lips tightly together, blinking away tears because we both know I'm not. Logan wasn't. Unlike my twin, I was never as great an actress. Rather than smiling in comfort, she's honest for once. More honest than me. "No, Sunshine. You're not."

Her eyes are transfixed on the fallen hair, the streaks of blond sad as I roll them between my fingers. Her gaze trails up to my head, where I'm sure a thin patch now rests. I feel a draft there, and her horrified look only confirms my suspicions.

Taking a deep breath, I grab a pair of scissors from the medicine cabinet. It's full of prescriptions, most that I can't even pronounce. Mama keeps a weekly organizer full of them, so I remember to take them each day.

Turning back to her, I reveal the scissors in my hand. "I don't want to watch it fall out anymore," I admit quietly. "I can't cut it on my own."

Her hurt transforms into something completely different—a pain that is far deeper than any I can ever experience from my disease. It spreads in her eyes like a fire consuming her. And like always, I have to acknowledge that I'm the one who set it.

I think, *Just remember that I love you, Mama.*

"Baby," she whispers brokenly, quickly closing the gap between us. Her fingers reach out and lightly caress my hair. "Please don't make me do that. Your hair… You and Logan had such beautiful hair. Always so long, so thick. Don't cut it."

Cringing, I nod. "I have bald spots that can't be hidden. It needs to go."

"We can always look into a wig," she prompts, taking the scissors from my hand and setting them onto the edge of the countertop.

But I don't want a wig or to pretend I'm fine.

I want to make my own decisions—ones that won't make Mama cry anymore. I don't want to hide in the room that's still full of Lo's presence—untouched yet full of life.

Finally, I look at Mama. She stares at the floor with a distant expression cloaking her face. I reach out and hold her hand, and for a moment, I think I may cry with her. There's a blur of tears glazing my eyes, but no tears escape.

Mama meets my eyes, and chokes out, "Your eyes are emerald."

When Mama cries, her eyes turn gold.

Our song is playing.

Closing my eyes, I turn to my side in bed and listen to the slow rendition of the upbeat melody about sunshine and gray skies playing. A frail smile tugs on my lips, stretching the corners into a smile that I wish Logan could see right now. Especially when Mama starts singing along.

Her voice is low and distant as pots and pans rattle together. Maybe she's baking again. We used to bake together all the time, but she hasn't done that since…

Swallowing, I open my eyes and stare at the closed door.

The bedroom feels too big and too small all at once now. Suffocating, even though half the room is full of unused furniture. My sister's presence is everywhere in here beyond the hidden pictures I've slid under the bed. She's in the walls, where we shared hours and hours of laughter over the silliest things.

Mama would have to come in and shush us, but eventually

join in because she couldn't help herself. I miss *that* version of the woman who raised us. The one who would stay up late braiding our wet, blond hair while listening to music together. We'd all sing along to whatever played on the little radio, mostly out of pitch, but none of us cared.

Ever since Lo passed away, I barely hear Mama sing at all.

So today is…it's special. Bittersweet.

Even more so when I hear her abruptly stop right before the music does long before the song actually ends. That's when I hear the familiar sound of a choked sob instead.

Sitting up, I draw my knees to my chest and debate on what to do. Grandma told me to give Mama time. *Everyone grieves differently, Emmy.* I don't think time is what she needs though, and I have a feeling Grandma knows that as much as I do.

I wait it out, staring at the empty side of the room that I swear sometimes still smells like the girl I see every time I look at my reflection. It's impossible though. It's been years. Years of mourning. Years of grieving. Years of missing her. It'll never end, but it'll get better.

I have to believe that.

Better.

Better gives me hope.

Better isn't always easy though, and definitely not always pretty.

So, I decide to check on Mama.

She's hunched over the sink, gripping the edges with white knuckles when I approach the kitchen. If she bothered to glance over her shoulder I know I'd see those sad, glassy golden orbs staring back at me. I wonder if they break Grandma's heart like they do mine since Mama is her only child. I overheard her telling one of her friends that she couldn't imagine losing Mama the way Mama lost Lo.

"Mama?"

Her voice is hoarse when she straightens and says, "Not now, Logan."

I blink.

Then blink again.

Mama's shoulders tighten.

She doesn't correct herself.

I don't have the energy too either.

Not again.

"Is there anything I can—"

"*Not now*," she repeats. No name. It's safer that way, I suppose. She takes a deep breath before dropping her head and standing to full height. "I'm sorry, sweetie. I didn't sleep well."

She never sleeps well, but I don't point that out.

"It's okay" is my default answer. It's not. I know it isn't, but I can't tell her differently.

Look at me, I silently beg her.

Her eyes don't lift.

Look at me, Mama.

I wait. And wait. And wait some more.

She turns around, making sure she doesn't see me at all.

"Your grandmother mentioned shopping" is what she tells me, as if she isn't crying over the person we both lost. As if nothing is wrong. "Why don't you see if you can go with her?"

It's her way of saying she wants the house to herself. To be alone.

Isn't she lonely like I am?

Anger bubbles under my skin.

Then guilt for feeling angry.

I'm halfway out of the kitchen, each backward step weighed down with exhaustion and defeat, when I ask her the question I've been dreading since I found the courage to bring it up weeks ago. "Have you thought about it?"

When she doesn't answer, I swallow the hope that started blossoming when I heard the song playing.

"Mama," I whisper, tightening my hold on the hem of my shirt.

Logan's old shirt, with a smiling sun in the middle.

Nothing.

I want to tell her to look at me, but I know why she doesn't.

I know who she sees.

Not me.

Never me.

So I finally say it. "I think it's time I go live with Dad."

This time, she lifts her head and stares.

But it's through me, not at me.

She doesn't tell me to stay.

She doesn't tell me to go either.

So that's when I know what I have to do.

AUTHOR'S NOTE

I know what you must be thinking. Screw you, Barbara. Am I right?

I'm sorry for the emotions you're probably feeling right now. For the record, I loved Emery too. In fact, I *am* Emery. That's why I needed to write this book in all its raw, real glory. I knew how it'd end. It's a fear of mine that I've battled since I realized something was wrong with me years ago.

When you have a chronic condition, you spend a lot of your life being doubted by others. Not all diseases can be seen. In fact, a lot of them aren't. That's why invisible diseases can be so deadly—because nobody knows they're there until it's too late.

Not only do you have to suffer silently from pain and other symptoms, but you have to watch what your misery does to everyone around you. Loved ones. Friends. You name it.

Underneath the Sycamore Tree started as a short story called "Mama's Eyes" that I wrote for my creative writing class in undergrad. It was a story I wrote from the heart about how the relationship between a mother and daughter changes when the daughter becomes chronically ill. It's a story I reflected on for many weeks before submitting it and maybe years before choosing to take everyone's advice and expand it into a full-length novel.

This book was both one of the easiest and hardest ones to write. When a story comes from the heart, it's going to gut you and cleanse you all at once. It's therapeutic but also painful in ways that are hard to explain. You're reliving moments you wish to forget.

Like the first chunk of hair found on a pillow, the first of many prescriptions, missed classes, seeing your family look at you like you're slipping away, and the fear—the fear of not knowing what's going to happen because doctors don't seem to believe you even though you struggle getting out of bed, you're skin and bones, and your hair is falling out. After a while, you begin believing them when they say you're crazy.

This book is the representation of something very rarely found in literature. Often, we're scared of reading stories that remind us of real life. I get it. We all want to escape reality, right? Reality always finds us, though, when we finish the last page.

I wanted to write a story that was so raw it stripped the soul. Every now and again, I think we need a reality check. Fiction can speak millions of truths that we're not always willing to hear in the real world.

So this is mine.

This is my pain.

This is my fear.

This is my worst nightmare.

Please keep in mind that this *is* fiction. Getting a lupus (or any illness) diagnosis does not mean you're fated to die. It means you're fated to fight, and that's something you need to accept from the start in order to make the most out of the life you're given. It's not easy, but I promise you'll get through it a day at a time.

No other book I write will be like this, and I promise you'll get a more traditional happily ever after from here on out. Even if you might not love me right now, know that I love all of you.

Keep fighting,
B

ACKNOWLEDGMENTS

A lot of people helped me polish this book, but I want to shout out someone specific. This is for my mother, who went to every appointment and raised hell when I didn't have the energy to. I know it was hard, but I appreciate everything you did for me. Thank you for not being like Emery's mother.

ABOUT THE AUTHOR

B. Celeste was born and raised in upstate New York where she still resides with her four-legged feline sidekick Oliver "Ollie" Queen. Her love for writing began with poetry, which she learned to write after watching her father write poetry for her mother, before she found interest in short stories, novellas, and novels.

After getting two degrees in English and creative writing, B has written more than twelve full-length novels, has been invited to many signings around the world, and hopes to begin traveling to see readers worldwide.